IF I CAN'T HAVE YOU

G.M. LAWRENCE

INKUBATOR
BOOKS

Published by Inkubator Books
www.inkubatorbooks.com

ISBN (eBook): 978-1-83756-307-4
ISBN (Paperback): 978-1-83756-308-1
ISBN (Hardback): 978-1-83756-309-8

1

Blood.

Not only the coppery tang of it in her mouth, but the scent of it, flooded her senses. The feel of it too, as it dried and scabbed over the deepest wounds, pulling at her feverish skin.

Lying on the hospital bed, she was surrounded by it, the white cotton sheet that covered the plastic mattress beneath dappled with blood. Little reminders – dots and smears – of the beating she'd just suffered.

But it wasn't only blood that served as a reminder, there was pain too. Fist-shaped pain that racked her body, where knuckles had rained down repeatedly, bruising her skin, his desire to hurt, to damage, a need to be satisfied whatever the cost. Punishment for a crime she was unaware she'd committed. But then, the punishment didn't have to fit the crime, in his eyes; it only depended on how he felt. She discovered quickly that it had little to do with her. A particularly difficult day in the office or an argument with a colleague was enough to bring him home in a mood that meant discipline needed to be dispensed. And he was always so diligent, so thorough in his discipline.

She had been preparing their supper when he walked in and disliked the summer meal of cold meats, salad and new potatoes that was presented to him. But it wasn't the meal that mattered. It could have been anything – a poorly cleaned room, the wrong type of coffee, or his clothes not folded to his satisfaction. Simple things that she had no way of anticipating and actions that brought about great pain.

He decided when and what parts of her body would get the harshest beating, as if her body was not her own, but his. But of course it *was* his. He'd owned Freya from the day they first met. Another decision he made without her knowledge or input, that she would be his come hell or high water. Because ownership came with responsibility, and he took that very seriously.

She was all too familiar with the dull aching pain signals each of the bruises sent to her brain, her skin hot and tight, and the grazes that stung her skin. Her head pounded, and her hair ached where it had been pulled, her scalp sore. She knew how long each injury would take to heal and what she needed to do to aid them – the dosage of painkillers required, and the compresses to be applied, if they ever worked, which she was never quite sure they did, though it was soothing to apply them nevertheless whilst she waited.

Freya let the nurses buzz around her with easy efficiency, answering 'yes' to the offer of painkillers and 'no' to their enquiries of any dizziness or nausea. One nurse took her blood pressure and then pierced a vein to draw some blood.

After they were done, and she'd taken the morphine given to her in a needleless plastic syringe, plunging the sweet sticky liquid into her mouth, a doctor came in and looked over her. Shining a torch in her eyes, he asked gently probing questions about what had happened and if there was anyone she'd like them to call, which was hospital speak for *what do you want us to do about your physically abusive partner because we can call the police for you right now, even though experience tells us that that's the last thing you want.*

She appreciated the effort, but he was right, she did not want the police involved, so apart from answering their questions, it was easier to withdraw, to remove herself from the moment. It protected her well-being and mind, the latter unable to cope with anything else, a learned behaviour that came with each punishment. There was no point expending any more energy than required; she'd used too much trying to survive the beating; she had no need to weaken herself any more.

She was just glad she was alone this time, no Liam hanging around in the waiting area, anxious to see her, ready to dictate what the story would be this time. Stories that Freya could never comprehend a medical professional ever believing, even though she recited them word for word. She'd learned the hard way what further punishment Liam could inflict when she didn't. Not that it mattered; he'd become very creative with the way he varied which hospital he'd take her to. To keep them from seeing the pattern of violence. Clever man. Taking his responsibility seriously.

This time, though, he'd disappeared afterwards, so she did something she rarely did, she'd braved a taxi, ignoring the driver's horrified looks of concern, and got herself to the hospital. The choice of hospital didn't matter now either because the crushing pain behind her eye caused a sensation she'd never felt before, the swelling too. With his beatings becoming more intense, she worried she might lose her sight, so the need to be seen by a doctor outweighed the fact that they would know who she was and what had happened.

The casualty department was reasonably quiet, being a weekday afternoon, and the tang of clinical disinfectant hung in the air. She enjoyed the sense of being hidden behind the blue curtain of her cubicle, it offered her a level of privacy she'd had so little of, and let the sounds of the department surround her while she rested her head against the pillow – the hum of the harsh ceiling lights above, the beeping machines, and the chatter from the nurses to their patients. A nurse brought her some water to drink and advised that because of her eye injury, she would need a scan, and they were likely to admit Freya for the night, for observation.

She had no desire to stay; hospitals were never her favourite place. Although the sanctuary of peace at the hospital was appreciated, it was never quite enough to keep her safe from the man who'd be collecting her in twenty-four hours from now. But, she told herself, playing devil's advocate, at least it would be twenty-four hours, and that was something.

She waited to be transferred to a ward or wherever they had room to put her. Even a corridor was more appealing than going home. At least in hospital, she was safe. For now.

2

Freya woke to a nurse standing over her. Smiling, and with her natural hair pulled up into a puffy bun on the top of her head, the nurse rested her hand on Freya's shoulder and shushed her quietly when she jumped at the contact, her large, brown compassionate eyes reassuring Freya that everything was all right.

Part of a new shift, the nurse checked her blood pressure and temperature before moving on to the next patient when she was done writing up her notes.

The morning routine started early. The night had been fretful with other patients in pain or crying out for assistance. Not Freya though, silence was her friend.

One of the healthcare assistants came in pushing a trolley of hot drinks. The silver-haired woman in a purple tabard placed a mug of tea on her bedside table, which Freya drank greedily, feeling dehydrated, and winced when it stung the cut on her lip. She stared at the dappled clouds that were making way for the morning sun. The birth of a new day. Such hopefulness still resided in Freya somewhere, and she liked to cling onto it whenever she got the chance.

It wasn't long after breakfast that the doctor did his rounds. Today she met with a doctor who was young but had a poise that confirmed his experience, or at least his confidence. He flashed Freya a pleasant smile when he collected her file and disappeared to speak to the nurses. Again, a procedure Freya was familiar with, but she still watched him interact with the ladies, chatting easily, a couple of the nurses engaging in banter of some sort. She couldn't quite make out what it was.

'How are you feeling today, Freya?' he enquired kindly when he returned to her bedside.

'Well, the painkillers are working, and I managed to sleep.' She had, in fact, slept soundly when she did finally succumb, the diazepam that she'd requested working well. It was a drug she had recently become a little too reliant on, and the knowledge that she was alone and safe allowed her to switch off completely.

'And would you perhaps like to discuss what happened with me or any of the staff here? One of the nurses, perhaps?'

A nurse ventured over, a young woman wearing a student uniform and fresh out of nursing college, ready to make her mark on the world, dedicated and smiling pleasantly.

'There really is nothing to tell,' Freya replied. 'Like I said yesterday, I fell badly and knocked my head, that's all.'

'Well, this incident has resulted in your eye socket being fractured,' he said. 'It's going to take some looking after, I'm afraid. Plenty of ice packs, treating the area gently. Are you able to guarantee that?'

'Of course.'

He paused for a moment before he spoke again. 'Because there can't be any more impacts in that area, Freya, is what I'm trying to say. It's crucial that you take care of yourself. You need to treat the area with gentle care for it to heal well. You even need to sneeze gently, blow your nose gently. No more incidents like falling down the stairs, do you understand?'

'So I'll be more careful when I hoover.'

He looked at her despondently, not even trying to pretend he believed her, and she stared at the floor, not trying to make the story work. But she was determined that this particular beating would not be the one she opened up about. Not today. The doctor in A & E had also been gentle with her questioning but had stopped when Freya showed signs of fatigue brought on from the pain and trauma. This morning, she was not getting such a pass.

'Freya, I'm concerned about your safety and well-being. This is more serious than the other times when you've—' He stopped himself from saying any more, but Freya knew what he meant – when she'd come to this hospital before, messed up from other beatings. He was being kind, trying to skirt around the issue, but she knew that he had to ensure she understood what she needed to do to let her injuries heal effectively.

'Yes,' she murmured, her hands clasped together in her lap. 'I understand. This one is worse than the others. I get it.' She knew he was referencing the bruises on her neck, because she'd watched his gaze move to the bruising there a couple of times.

Forced strangulation was nothing new to Freya. She had experienced it a few times at Liam's hands. It was something

he took great pleasure in, watching her fade into uncon-
sciousness, and he would always be sitting near her when
she woke, watching. For two reasons, probably – the first to
gloat and the second to be sure she was actually still alive.

The doctor smiled, a kind, concerned smile. 'None of this
is your fault. No one deserves to be treated like this. We can
help. We can put you in touch with organisations you can
talk to. People who can support you. We have some leaflets
that we can give you.' He pointed to her neck. 'This alone is a
recognised criminal offence that comes with a prison
sentence.'

He spoke as if she didn't understand the gravity of the
situation, or that she hadn't been given this information
before. To him, it probably seemed so easy to just admit that
things had gone south in her relationship and make the
decision to walk away, that it was as simple as taking a leaflet
and speaking to an organisation, and then she'd be safe. But
the reality was that it was nothing of the sort. These people,
although well intentioned, had no idea the power her
husband wielded over her. It was simply out of the question
to step outside the lines of Liam's rules if she wanted to
survive.

She leant forwards, looked him straight in the eye.
'There's nothing you can do for me,' she insisted. 'I appreciate your concern, I really do, but I'll cope. I have to.'

He pursed his lips and let out a tiny sigh that he probably hoped she wouldn't hear. 'I understand, but I want you
to know that whatever you tell us here is in complete confidence and always will be. We're here to help you.'

'But nothing is ever really confidential, is it? There are
ways around everything. Especially when you'll document
the signs, even if it is just a statistic, right down to this

conversation.' She knew the process, that the hospital had to report this case whether she wanted them to or not, as part of their procedure. 'Tell me you haven't already made a body map of me with a description of my injuries.'

He looked uncomfortable, confirming what she already knew to be true.

'Look, I know you're trying to help, and I'm grateful, but I've been playing this game for a long time now. I would love to discuss what happened openly with you, just as much as I would love to walk out of here and know that this will be the last beating I'm going to get, but I know it's not as simple as that. Referring me to an organisation that can help is not the end; it's not even the beginning. It'll just make things worse. He will find a way to put a stop to it; he always does.'

'I understand, but the police are there to serve you. They can intervene. Get you to safety and under the care of these organisations that have helped hundreds of women before you. It will take one phone call.'

She snorted an angry laugh. 'You don't know my husband.'

He sighed again. 'Well, do you have ways to keep yourself safe at home?'

'Nothing specific, whatever works to placate him.'

'And will there be anyone else you can rely on, someone who will be waiting for you at home?'

'Why do you need to know that?'

'At the very least we have a duty of care to ensure you are safe when you leave here.'

'I will be safe. Completely safe.'

The doctor looked at the nurse, who in turn looked straight back at him.

'Honestly, you have nothing to worry about,' Freya

snapped, 'but if you'd prefer, I'll contact my sister, and you can speak to her if that makes you feel any better. She's in London, but I can ask her to visit.'

He turned the pages of her file. 'Ah, yes. Rosie Ford. Is that correct?'

'Yes, that's correct. If I speak to her to make arrangements for her to visit me, will you discharge me?'

'That would certainly help.' He shut the file and tucked it in the holder at the end of her bed. 'You're an adult, and we're not going to stop you from doing what you have to do, but if you want my advice, you should only stay with people you trust. I assume your sister is someone you trust, yes?'

With one nod of her head, Freya set off a litany of fireworks in front of her eyes. 'With my life.'

———

FREYA HAD JUST SETTLED herself on the chair by her bed after visiting the bathroom to dress herself, when Liam hurried into the ward and towards her, ignoring the nurses at their desk. A look of devastation etched on his features when he caught sight of her. 'Oh my God,' he said through panting breaths. 'What the hell happened?'

The nurses glanced at each other, and then the one who'd done her previous observations on Freya walked over, fixing her glare on him. 'Are you Liam?' she asked cordially, but without any of the warmth she usually displayed.

'Yes, that's me,' he said with a charming smile. 'What did you do this time?' he asked, reaching out to touch Freya's hair.

Freya tilted her head away, not wanting any contact with

him. He ignored her efforts to avoid him and went ahead and touched her anyway.

The nurse continued to glare at him. 'Took a tumble, apparently.'

'Ah, that's the thing with this one,' he said, without missing a beat. 'Always falling down. Clumsy little thing, aren't you, my love?'

'Hm, that's interesting,' the nurse continued, unfazed by Liam's charm. 'I just wondered where the bruising on her neck came from.'

Slowly, Liam turned his head towards the nurse, his eyes bright with anger, the mask and the pretence gone, and Freya felt the rush of anxiety swirl in her mind of knowing whom he'd take it out on if this antagonism continued.

'My husband is here to see me,' she burst out, 'not to be interrogated.'

Anger changed to arrogance as Freya took hold of his hand. 'Yes,' he said, sneering at the nurse. 'My wife needs me.'

Feeling guilty that she'd so bluntly put the nurse in her place, she softened. The poor girl was only trying to help. 'Please, can you give us some time alone?'

The nurse nodded, her lips pursed as she turned and walked away, leaving them be.

Liam's expression was triumphant, proud even, his smile broad, his gaze intense. She'd done well. He'd been defended, and the nurse had been put in her place. He'd be pleased with her for that. At least she hoped he would.

When the nurse disappeared, he sat on the bed and scanned the room and the other patients. Probably deciding whom he needed to watch and who would be oblivious.

She waited in silence until he was ready to talk. When it

almost became unbearable, he turned his attention to her and finally spoke. 'Well, my love, they have worked wonders here. You don't look half as bad as you did yesterday.'

Yesterday, she thought. *When you beat me black and blue all because you'd had a bad day at work and didn't fancy the dinner I'd prepared.*

She nodded.

'The medical team are doing a good job. Well, if the nurses lost the attitude and concentrated on emptying bedpans and mopping up vomit or whatever these women do,' he said with a shrug. 'And what have they been asking?' He ran his fingers down her arm until his hand closed over her wrist, a forewarning. 'Or rather, what have you been babbling to them about?'

'Nothing. I told them I had a fall, like the nurse said, but I've told them nothing about the bruises on my neck.' Her heart began to beat a little faster as he increased the pressure in his grip, his fingers squeezing against her skin. It hurt and ached where he made contact with bruises. She gasped. 'I promise. Nothing.' She wouldn't tell him they hadn't believed her, or that they never did when she was in this situation. He didn't need to know these details. He just needed to know he was off the hook, and that she wouldn't implicate him.

He slowly released his grip and smiled, moving his hand to brush some wisps of hair from her face. 'That's good, Freya,' he murmured. 'Very good. Now, I want you to request to be discharged tomorrow. I'll let you have one more night here, but I will be back this time tomorrow to collect you.' He checked his watch. 'Make sure you're ready.'

She nodded, and he leaned forward to kiss her forehead. 'Good.' He stood and straightened himself out. 'Don't get into any more trouble, and make sure the paperwork for the discharge is done in good time. I won't have time to wait.'

'I will,' she said, worrying about how exactly she'd manage to do it. 'I'll be ready.'

'That's better,' he said. 'I hope this attitude remains once we get home. You know I hate when we have these squabbles.'

'I know,' she assured him. 'I don't like them either.'

'Well, then. We're both going to get along very well. Maybe we can celebrate with a special dinner. What do you say to that?'

She tried a smile, but the split in her lip stung and prevented any further movement.

The moment was broken by the appearance of a police officer walking through the ward, heading straight for them. The nursing staff watched, hints of hopefulness in their gaze as he continued on to Freya's bed.

'What the fuck do they want?' Liam hissed as he grabbed her arm and tightened his grip.

A wave of dizziness engulfed her. Her heart beat out of control, her wounds throbbed, and her head pounded. The sound of blood rushing in her ears was all she could hear. Police were never a good thing. Liam despised them almost as much as medical staff.

She glanced down, a practised drill from any other time the police had appeared. Liam stared as the policeman looked their way and walked towards them.

'Sergeant?' Liam asked, his tone deceptively calm. Only Freya knew that this particular tone disguised irritation too, and that worried her because Liam might change his mind about a nice dinner and them getting along again.

Nurses drifted away from their stations and subtly watched.

She should say something or at least make eye contact with the man standing in front of her. A man in authority who could stop whatever could happen to her next. She could try to signal that she was not safe. But she would not do anything of the sort. Her husband would likely finish what he started two days ago. Surely the bruises on her face would indicate that something wasn't right here, or Liam's firm grip on her arm. But she knew the rules, and her situation was no more improved by this man's presence than if she were to run into a police station full of a hundred officers.

'Sorry, sir,' the policeman replied. 'Got a call from the office. There's an update on the investigation, and the chief wants everyone back at the station. He asked me to come and collect you.'

Of course the police made no difference to her circumstances, no matter what the doctors told her, or could guarantee her safety if she ever left him. There was no point involving them because Liam *was* the police and had been since she'd met him.

Previously at the Met, he had transferred down to Southampton for the promotion to inspector, dragging them both away from London. Now, he was so firmly ingrained in the service that he could intercept any call for help she made or any attempt at justice for his actions. He'd have access to every resource they have to find her, and that was why it was a risk she could never take.

Liam rolled his eyes and blew out an irritated breath through his teeth. He never liked to be bothered when away from the office and liked to be bothered in his private life even less. Far too much explaining to do when colleagues came snooping around, as he called it.

'Do I have to do everything at that place?' he muttered. 'When will the chief be able to wipe his own arse? Can't you see I'm busy right now?'

She turned her face subtly away from both men, wanting to hide the marks, the evidence. But she didn't turn it enough when the policeman glanced at her and let his gaze linger there for a moment before looking directly at Liam. Another one who likely knew the score but would remain mute on the subject. It wasn't his business to pry into his boss's life. There would be rumours of course. It must have been obvious what Liam got up to at home with his little lady. People would surmise, talk, but Liam was the kind of boss you didn't confront, so it mattered very little what they thought of him.

'Problem, Sergeant?'

'No, not at all, sir,' the policeman replied quickly.

'Does it bother you to see my wife's injuries?'

'No, sir.'

'No? But now you want to know how she came to be so hurt, don't you?' Liam ignored the man's awkward attempt to speak. 'Would you like me to share the details of her accident?' His tone became scarily condescending. Belittling. 'Would you like to demean her like that? Here, in front of everyone.'

'Of course not, sir,' the sergeant said, shuffling uncomfortably.

'And why is that?'

'Because it's none of my business.'

Liam nodded, a snide smile on his face, with apparent enjoyment at the awkwardness the conversation had descended into. 'Yes, that's right. None of your business. Let's keep it that way, eh?'

'Of course, sir.'

There was nothing she could do but remain still and keep her eyes cast downwards.

He checked his watch again. Time to leave. He turned his gaze to her. 'I'll be seeing you tomorrow, my love.'

He stood and walked away, smiling at the nurses at their station, ignoring their stares of disapproval. He was very good at doing that. He only took what he wanted from a situation. It was how he got to where he was today.

The officer hurried behind, looking as uncomfortable as everyone felt.

3

After pushing hard for a discharge time of two o'clock, to allow for paperwork and the usual slow turn of wheels in a hospital of this size, by midday Freya was packed up, dressed, and sat on the chair by her bed, ready for Liam to arrive. Her heart pummelled in her chest, anxious all morning trying to hurry the staff along in order to get her papers signed.

Visiting time brought family and friends to the ward, and amongst the people arriving, Freya immediately noticed her sister in the crowd, rushing in behind. She'd travelled from London especially, and the tears that stung Freya's eyes made her squint as the sensation of tiny needles pricked her eyelids. Tears now snaked down her cheeks, and she let out an involuntary gasp at the surprising sight of her beloved sister. Always close, they'd counted on each other since they were toddlers – Rosie taking the role of big sister very seriously.

Shorter than Freya at a petite five feet three, but with the same slender frame and curly hair, Rosie bustled into the ward, her phone clasped in one hand as she went to the nurses' station. She turned her head and spotted Freya right away and pointed her hand towards Freya as she smiled to the nurse and hurried over.

'Oh my God,' Rosie muttered as she drew closer. 'What the hell happened this time?'

'Please let's not do this just yet,' Freya said as she reached out to hug Rosie.

They embraced, and Freya felt the restraint in her sister, never wanting to hurt her any more than she'd already been hurt. Rosie moved gently away, but Freya hugged her close, still wanting the security the hug provided.

'No, not yet' she murmured. 'Give me a minute.' For a moment, just one peaceful moment, Freya was able to forget all the pain and anguish and just reside in the warmth of her sister's arms, allowing herself to be soothed, calmed, to release the defensiveness she'd had to wear around herself like a coat since she'd arrived at the hospital.

Rosie gently smoothed her hand over Freya's hair. 'Of course. You're all right. Just relax.'

Freya rested in her sister's arms for a few moments more and then pulled herself away. As she did, she swiped her cheeks of tears and smiled. 'Thanks, sis. You always were such a good hugger.'

Rosie returned the smile. 'That's what I'm here for.' She sat back and shuffled to a more comfortable position on the edge of the bed. 'So it looks like he really went to work on you this time,' she said gently. 'Looks more serious than colliding with a door.'

'Ah, Rosie, it was probably the worst. Well, if you exclude my dislocated shoulder and that time my broken rib nearly pierced my lung.'

'It certainly looks the worst,' she replied as her gaze fell on the bruises around Freya's face and neck.

Instinctively, Freya put her hands against the marks on her neck, feeling the ache from the contact. 'This is what brought him round. Back from his rage, I think he thought he'd killed me. And that's when he left. Just disappeared. He must have panicked.'

'Jesus,' Rosie whispered. 'Have you shared this with the doctors?'

'No. Of course not. Not officially, anyway. Do you think I am a glutton for punishment? Can you imagine what he'd do if I ever reported him?'

Rosie nodded.

'I could do it. I could file a report. They certainly want me to,' she said, glancing at the nursing team. 'The process would begin, and the team here would share their notes. I know it's important, crucial evidence of what he's done, and necessary, but it's also documentation, and documentation can be found if someone chooses to look hard enough. And he will do whatever it takes to find out what I did while left here on my own. You know his position. He'll find out and use it against me, so the very thing that's designed to help will be my downfall because he will intercept it before it has the opportunity to fall into the hands of people who might be able to support me.'

Rosie made no effort to hide the frustration she felt. 'Freya, you can't live like this.'

'I can. I have no choice.' She looked away, feeling the pain of emotion rise in her throat, demanding to be felt.

'You know that the medical staff here won't believe your version of the truth anyway.'

'I don't care, Rosie.' There was simply no escaping him,

ever. And she knew very well that he would carry out his threat to kill her if she ever tried. 'Do you remember the last time I was in hospital, when I had slipped a Women's Aid leaflet the nurses gave me in my bag, hoping to discard it before he collected me? Well, I forgot about it, and he found it. I can't tell you how I managed to survive the beating that followed, but I did, even though I was unable to leave the house for more than two weeks. How am I supposed to protect myself when there are so many cracks in the system? They can't do anything until I allow it, and that's the one thing I have control over. Can't you see? This way, I can control how much more punishment I'm given.'

Rosie reached out and held Freya's hand. 'I know, I know. I'm sorry. I can't imagine how hard this is for you, but I want you to know that I'm here.'

Freya nodded. 'I know you are, and I'm grateful. Anyway, now – his post-violence love – is the best time. He'll be careful. Attentive. He'll let me heal, and he'll apologise until I can't bear the sound of it.'

Rosie fixed her gaze on Freya. 'Have you spoken to Mum and Dad?'

'No.'

'You need to speak to them.'

'I'll tell them what I always do – that I can't visit for a while, as I'm not feeling well. When the bruises have faded and everything goes back to normal, I'll visit. They'll never know.'

'They need to know.'

'No, they don't. Can you imagine how hurt they'd be that—'

'That you live with a monster,' Rosie snapped.

'That someone could be as flawed as he is, and that I

never told them what he's done out of shame and embarrassment. It would break them. You know how they put him on a pedestal. They truly believe he can do no wrong. How can I break their illusion and not feel responsible for the hurt they'll feel after all this time of being clueless to what was really going on?'

Liam had a close relationship with her mum. Whether it was genuine or not was a question she couldn't answer, but he seemed to want both her parents' approval somehow, and a validation that he never bothered with from his own parents. His poor parents were controlled in the same way that he controlled her – with manipulation and anger. The relationship suffered as a result, and they were distant from each other. Freya often wondered if they knew what he was doing to her, but she could never speak to them about it on the rare occasions they did meet under Liam's watchful eye.

'They'll feel much more hurt when they get the call telling them that you've been killed by him.'

'Rosie, please. I can't do it. Not yet. I need time.'

Rosie placed her hand on Freya's. 'How much time do you think you have?'

A nurse, a new one to the shift, approached with a smile. 'I just need to do a set of observations,' she said as she pulled the curtain around the bed. 'You can wait outside until I'm done, if you like,' she said to Rosie. 'You might want to use the time to speak to one of the nurses about Freya's discharge.'

Freya looked at Rosie pleadingly. 'I just need you to confirm that you can be around when I'm discharged. You know, so that I'm not alone.'

'They won't discharge you without that?'

Freya shook her head and stared at Rosie, hoping her

expression could replace the words she could not verbalise. Freya mouthed the word 'please' while the nurse beside her pulled out the notes in her file.

Rosie sighed and went over to the nurses' station. When she returned, she kissed Freya gently on the cheek. 'All sorted.' She sat and waited for the nurse to finish, smiling calmly the entire time.

When the nurse pushed back the curtain and disappeared, Rosie leant forwards in the chair. 'I've told them that while Liam will collect you, I'll be around to make sure you're okay. But I'm not happy about lying to them.'

'Thank you.' Freya sighed as the weight that had been sitting on her chest lifted a little. 'It will help.'

'But I want you to think about what you're going to do,' Rosie instructed. 'I can't lose my only sister, and I can't see her fading in front of me like this anymore.'

'I know. I'll figure it out somehow.'

Rosie checked her watch. 'I've got to get back to the station if I'm going to make my train.' She looked at Freya. 'I'll call you later to make sure everything is okay, and then we can talk.'

Freya nodded, although there would be no talking later with Liam around, but she didn't have the energy to explain that to her.

Rosie laid an arm around Freya's shoulder gently, not wanting to cause any pain, before grabbing her things and leaving.

LIAM ARRIVED at exactly two o'clock and, again, strode through the ward as if he were the chief medical officer rather than a visitor. Casual smug glances were given to the staff – an *I control this situation, not you* attitude written all over his face.

Dark butterflies danced in Freya's stomach at the thought of leaving here and being alone with him. She wanted to be at home, surround herself with all the comforts she'd put there, but sharing it with him made everything tense.

'Good afternoon, beautiful,' he murmured as he leaned down to place a firm kiss on her cheek.

The bruise twanged as painful daggers bit into her bones. She flinched. 'Hi.'

He reached for the small bag she'd brought with her, and pulled her up from the chair by her elbow. 'Are you ready?'

'Yes,' she said with a gasp as her body objected to his quick and insensitive instruction to move.

In her hand were some painkillers dispensed from the pharmacy and some information given on how to take care of her wounds and what to look out for if she feels unwell. The many leaflets the nurse had given her regarding help and refuge from the perpetrators of domestic violence had been left in the drawer of the locker by the bed, out of Liam's view. Never would he believe that he was an abuser. Never. The arrogance of the man was such that he truly believed that whatever went wrong was someone else's fault, usually hers. If he beat her badly enough for her to remain in bed or on the sofa for a week just to get the headache to pass, it was because of something she had done wrong, never his temper or his lack of control. Always her.

At first, she had tried to fight back. She'd spent many hours passively trying to change him or convince him that what he was doing was wrong, but the punishments only got worse whenever she did. She had tried to time these conversations for when he was in a good or gentle mood, but it never worked. It always brought the arguments and then the fists.

'Let's get you home,' he said as he led her through the ward.

She made eye contact with the nurse who'd been looking after her as she walked by and could see the look of pity. It both saddened and infuriated Freya. She didn't need pity. What she needed was a miracle.

She knew their relationship was over. She knew he'd never change. She also knew that she'd never escape him unless she did something soon. The fight she'd had in her as a young woman had been beaten out of her in the five years they had been together, yes, but it was not dead. It still resided in her somewhere. Sometimes it would show up – perhaps in her dreams at night. In these, she'd fight him and win and feel the joy of the freedom that followed, only to wake in her reality to the sound of him sleeping soundly beside her. Sometimes it would show up as a small voice in her head, which would appear without warning, usually just before a punishment began.

So she was still there, but time was running out for her, and the will to leave ebbed with every bruise and cut to her skin. She just needed a little more coaxing to create a plan that would see her away from him for long enough to start again.

THE CAR JOURNEY WAS QUIET, his mood dictating what they would discuss. But he didn't want to talk about what he'd done, or what she expected as a means for forgiveness. He was not in the mood to discuss anything, apparently. He wasn't the usual post-violence loving or forgiveness-seeking Liam she had come to expect either, and because of that, a little tingle of unease fluttered in her stomach.

He drove down the road that led to their house with a red front door and large bay windows. The 1930s detached property had been left to him by his grandmother. He had decorated it to his taste, but even so, it was pleasant and comfortable, if a little masculine with leather and chrome the predominant design choices. It was an impressive place, with its own drive for three cars, even though they only had one. She was not allowed to have any such independence that a car would offer her.

'OKAY, honey, I need to go, but I won't be long. Why don't you go and relax in a nice bath or something. Your painkillers are in the bag, and I've stocked up the fridge. All your favourites for you to enjoy.' He unlocked the door and helped her inside, as any other loving partner would do, only this was a meaningless charade. Freya wasn't sure if this scared her more than when he used his fists.

'Thank you,' she murmured. 'I'll do just that.'

He planted a gentle kiss on her cheek and pulled the door closed, leaving her standing in the hallway of her home, a plastic bag with a scant number of possessions in her hand and a sense of despair that bloomed inside her heart.

The house was cool. She turned and checked the thermostat on the wall in the hallway. Turned off. Fair enough. It was early summer, so she could argue that they wouldn't

need heating, but with the system needing an upgrade –
something they'd never got round to doing – there would be
no chance of hot water for a much-desired bath. Despite
what he'd said on the doorstep, he had no intention of
making her homecoming a comfortable one. She walked
through the dining room and into the kitchen and opened
the large double-fronted fridge. It shouldn't have been a
surprise to see that it was empty, that he'd lied, but still, it
was a kick to her stomach that she'd fallen for it.

She closed the door and went to the living room,
expecting to see the room upturned and ornaments
smashed on the parquet floor that edged the large Persian
rug. A reminder of the night he'd lost control. Again. Everything had happened so fast, there was never any time to
prepare. He always launched at her before she had time to
react, throwing a good few punches before speaking. This
time, however, she was surprised to see he'd cleared up
instead of leaving it for her to do. It confused her. This had
always been her task whenever they'd got into a fight, and
sometimes he'd supervise her to ensure she did a thorough
job. He'd needed no motivation and had done a thorough
job too on this occasion. Even the blood that had spilled
from her mouth, the result of the hard backhand to her face
that had started her nightmare, had been wiped clean from
the hearth.

The echoes of her screams whispered through the room
as she surveyed it, layered with his roars of anger and the
sound of skin pounding skin. Her gaze fell on a little shard of
glass that had gone unnoticed in his meticulous cleansing of
the place, tucked in the groove where the hearth met the
floor.

In a strange trance, she knelt on the rug and picked up

the jagged crystal-like jewel and held it in her fingers to hold it up against the daylight that shone through the window. She stared at it and saw the tiniest smear of red merged with the glass. Blood. Her blood. The remains of her in this room. If she weren't here, that would be all that was left of her. Proof of life, a small smear of blood that had been overlooked. It dawned on her that this was what her life had become. An insignificant smear on a jagged remnant that had tucked itself out of sight.

Her fingers began to sting and burn, and she realised she'd been holding the shard in a tight grip, too hard, making her fingers bleed. She jumped to her feet and strode to the kitchen, dumping the glass in the sink, and turned the tap to wash the blood away. She'd disappeared into her thoughts again. For how long, she wasn't aware, but it had been long enough for the tiny wound on her finger to get deep enough to need a plaster, and the need to check if she'd bled anywhere that would need cleaning up.

That was when the voice in her head started again. The one with a fighter's spirit, loud and demanding. It repeated what she already knew – that this would never stop. He would never stop. Even his desire for forgiveness had waned. Now, a new thought descended, that one day he would eventually take it too far, that she wouldn't wake in hospital with doctors and nurses around her, because she would never wake up again. The feeling in her gut told her this was a possibility with each beating being worse than the last. It would build up to a time when another small smear of blood, missed in a clean-up operation, would become the last and only mark of her existence.

The voice in her head spoke loudly, instructing her to get

out, to run, run as fast as she could from the man who was supposed to love her but, instead, liked to hurt her.

BEFORE SHE KNEW what she was doing, she rushed up the stairs towards her bedroom. Her body worked independently of her brain as she grabbed the green velvet upholstered stool beneath her dressing table and then hurried over to the fitted cupboards that snaked around the bed, another thing inherited with the house, and pulled open the door to her wardrobe.

She stood on the stool, steadying herself to keep her balance, and pulled out the piles of neatly folded jumpers laid out on the shelf above the hanging rail of clothes. She reached in towards the very back of the wardrobe space and the small hidden corner that had a discreet square board covering a small hole in the wall.

There lived a black holdall. Her escape bag. Her chance to begin again without Liam and his cruel punishments. Somewhere she'd be free from violence and fear. A moment she'd planned for, lying awake at night preparing for when sleep wouldn't come or the pain was too bad to allow her to rest. A bag with as many clothes as she could squirrel away unnoticed – three T-shirts and sweaters, three pairs of jeans, three sets of underwear, a few cosmetics and a small supply of toiletries to see her through the initial escape.

She also had as much cash as she could hide away, stuffed into pockets, notes and coins – whatever spare she had. Money given to her for groceries that she'd halved by sacrificing Liam's favourite expensive brands for cheaper basic brands instead. He never ventured into the kitchen or cooked, so was always blissfully unaware of what she'd been doing. That, and the fact that she'd carefully saved the expensive packaging to cover up the basic brands sitting in her cupboards. She'd also ensured that any money her parents had given for birthdays and Christmases was also included, which meant it hadn't taken as long as she'd thought it might to build this nest egg for her future. There was a little over a thousand pounds here, and it was enough for now, enough to get on a train and far away from her violent husband. She'd figure out what to do once she was free, but for now, she just needed to leave.

There was very little time – why, she wasn't sure. Was it the fact that Liam could return at any moment, catch her in her little escapade, and unleash his fury? Probably, but that was unlikely now that he'd been summoned by his boss. She considered that if she didn't do this now, if she didn't cross that threshold to her home this very moment, she'd never do it. She'd never leave this place again except perhaps in a box with a one-way ticket to the cemetery. She hurriedly checked her wardrobe and added some more clothes to the stash in the bag.

The main challenge now, the one thing she couldn't have prepared for until she'd decided to leave him, was to find her ID – her passport and birth certificate.

Giddy with fear and the adrenaline that surged through her veins, she went from room to room, knowing that time was against her. She didn't know what he'd done to the house to monitor her, and it dawned on her that he could be watching through a hidden camera at this very moment and was already making his excuses to leave the office and return home.

With a whimper, she rushed into the spare room, his

office, and searched the wooden desk with four drawers running down the side that sat underneath the window, each drawer locked and secure. Of course they were. There was no way he'd let her snoop around his things.

She let out a cry as the need to leave the house intensified, setting off a chain reaction of panic. She ran downstairs and grabbed a knife from the cutlery drawer and rushed back to his office. Jamming it into the top drawer, she fought and jabbed at the lock, chipping away little chunks of wood as she did until the mechanism clunked and the drawer clicked open, giving up its treasures.

Somewhere in her mind the sound of a ticking clock reverberated as she opened the drawer and saw paperwork neatly filed in little plastic wallets and labelled accordingly. She ransacked each plastic pocket, searching through old statements, bills and guarantees until she reached the last pocket, headed 'Personal'. She tore it open and found his passport with his birth certificate tucked safely inside. She knew hers would be here too, and with shaking fingers, she rifled through more papers as sweat trickled down her back and dampened the fabric of her top under her arms.

As if someone, or something – an unseen guardian angel or spirit – was helping her, the corner of her birth certificate poked out from underneath the papers. She grabbed it, dragging her passport with it, and clutched them close to her chest as tears pricked her eyes. 'I found them,' she whispered repeatedly.

The first time she'd seen either since she'd moved in with Liam all those years ago, he'd taken it upon himself to ensure their documentation was handled by him and only him, something he told her she wasn't capable of doing. Something of hers, that was meant to be in her possession, something that proved there was an existence separate to Liam, and now she had it back. Another part of her she'd got back.

Rushing to her room, she grabbed the bag and stuffed her passport and birth certificate into it. She rushed to her bedside table and grabbed the packs of medications inside – her birth control and diazepam – both almost full supplies, only recently opened, and stuffed them into her bag. With a quick glance around, one final goodbye, she rushed down the stairs and towards the front door.

Convinced he would burst through the door as she neared it, that the next thing she'd see was his shadow looming through the frosted glass, she struggled to fill her lungs with air. But he didn't, so she turned the handle and pulled open the door, squinting in the afternoon light. Outside was calm, no dramas, no cars screeching to a halt outside, no Liam running down the street with a face reddened with fury. Nothing. It was too easy, far too easy. Surely he'd see her now. Surely he would pull up and confront her.

She pulled the door shut, and with no keys to let herself back in, there would be no return. She'd started a sequence of events that was out of her control.

There was only one path now, and that was to freedom.

4

E yes wide and dry-mouthed, Freya hurried into the street and strode away, her bag over her shoulder, her body trembling, and her mind racing ahead. Keep calm, she told herself. Just get beyond that red car and then take it from there.

When she reached the red car, she looked for the next, a black one, a couple of cars ahead. Feeling painfully exposed, out in the wilderness, an animal escaping the hunt, she followed this pattern until she was at the end of her road. Maybe Liam would find her, he might still turn up, but she had to try. She needed to be more than a punchbag to a man with some serious anger issues. The tiny glass shard with the smear of blood demanded it, demanded that her life be more than that.

As she rushed down the street, her mind hazily instructed her to head for the train station. She needed to lose herself, and the best place to do that – for as long as possible anyway, before he found her; he'd always find her – was to go to her sister's place in London.

She kept to quiet residential streets, and every car that passed, she scrutinised, on high alert, in case it was him. That he'd figured her out, but the half-walk, half-run jog meant she'd made good progress.

The thirty-minute walk was tiresome. Her legs and back ached, and frustration at how far she still had to go filled her. She just needed to be there, at the station and on the train, ready to leave her old life behind.

The sight of the recognisable long, box-shaped building with lines of windows that ran the length of each of the four stories gave her the energy to continue. She passed the ugly concrete buildings and flats and headed straight for the double doors of the entrance to Southampton Central, mingling with other travellers doing the same. Some commuters struggled with luggage in varying sizes, while others, like Freya, had a holdall or backpack hoisted over their shoulder.

Checking the screens and finding it too hard to concentrate, her mind fuzzy with too much adrenaline after having come this far, she headed for the ticket booth instead. Sunlight beamed in through the doors, giving her the hope to continue. She waited in the queue, watching as people glanced her way as they walked past, surely knowing what she'd done, that her actions were written all over her face. With her heart beating, she walked forwards, next to be served, and immediately fluffed the question she needed to ask.

She paused and took a breath before her second attempt. 'When is the next train to Waterloo, please?'

'Half an hour,' the large man in the booth said, his eyes quickly surveying her face. 'Five thirty-five.'

In her hurry she'd forgotten how she looked, her

battered features and messy hair. No matter, she'd never see him again. 'I'd like a single, please,' she said, lowering her glance from his gaze mainly but also to grab some notes from her bag.

'No return?' he asked.

'No, just one-way.' She had begun to tremble and checked over her shoulder, sure Liam would be there, fury twisting his features at what she'd done and where she intended to go.

The man in the booth pushed the ticket underneath the glass hatch. 'That'll be forty-five pounds.'

She pulled out two twenties and a ten and waited for her change, then went to sit in the waiting area. Her bruises ached, and her eye throbbed in time with her heart. She looked around at the coffee machine and food options, but couldn't contemplate eating or drinking anything, her stomach in knots. Her leg jigged up and down, something she couldn't stop, as her heart raced in her chest. She had thirty minutes to wait. Could she do it? Would he be home already, wondering where the hell she was? She closed her eyes, dreading his anger.

The low growl and roll of the approaching train pulled Freya from her seat. She darted between other passengers who were also making their way to the platform and hurried through the glass doors, keen to board. Keen to be away. Once all the waiting passengers on board had alighted, she stepped into the carriage and walked along until she found her seat.

It was busy, peak commuter time, so it wasn't long before a woman sat next to her. She was young, just out of work by the look of her dress, and made no attempt at conversation, instead choosing to lose herself in her phone. That was fine with Freya, even though she didn't have the luxury of doing the same. Liam had never allowed her a phone; it would have given her too much independence. He couldn't monitor every aspect of her life if she had one, so it became a point-blank refusal if she ever brought it up.

Freya rested her head against the window and gave herself a moment to mourn the loss of the life she was leaving behind, more specifically, the life she thought she'd have with Liam but never did.

———

WATERLOO WAS hot and heaving with people who were difficult to navigate, crossing her path and leaving her feeling dizzy and overwhelmed. Swathes of people scattered towards the exits or the escalators down to the underground, and the place echoed with voices and footsteps and the occasional announcement over the Tannoy. She moved with the crowd, lost and a little afraid of what she would do next. The air was filled with a strange industrial must. Not diesel or smoke, just machinery, pollution and people. The evening sun filled the station.

Alone and unable to catch her breath, she headed for the nearest bench to sit down and try to fill her lungs, fearing she would pass out. It was too much; she had done too much and now sat frightened in the middle of a busy train station in London, wondering what the hell she'd done. Fighting the urge to cry and wincing at the stabbing pain that bloomed in her eye, tender from the swell of tears, she worked hard to still her trembling chin and calm her breathing. She placed her hand gently against her eye to gently tend to it and tried to compose herself as she watched people striding past her, some glancing her way, but most in their own little world, looking at phones or animatedly speaking in them.

On an inhale, she whispered she would be okay, and with the outbreath she told herself to remain calm. She could do this; she'd not come this far to give up now. She'd outwitted her violent husband and so far, had survived, just. She could do this. There was no harm to be had from commuters simply going about their day.

She held her bag close to her side and calmly told herself that to get to her destination, she just needed to remember her sister's address. Slowly, her mind behaved and began to relax. She began with the area of London: Wimbledon. Next, the street: Quintin Avenue, and then house number. That she wasn't so sure of, but she would recognise it once she was there, remembering it had a large green door. She sighed. It had worked.

Ready to move on, she stood and walked over to the information desk. She would need to catch another train. One final hurdle until she could be safe. She stuttered out her words to the poor lady at the information desk, and after making herself understood, she found out that she'd need to go to platform five to board the train that would get her to Wimbledon in less than twenty minutes.

It was on time, so she headed straight for the platform, not wanting anything to prevent her from taking it. With steel-like focus, she checked each gate until she found platform five. She boarded the train and walked along the carriage to find a seat. Now that she was here, she felt herself calm a little. She'd done it. She just had to make this journey, and then she would be at her sister's and finally safe. Just twenty more minutes.

'OH MY GOD,' Rosie gasped as she opened the door. 'Freya!'

Freya knew that she looked a sight, puffy faced from crying, bruised and surely looked as unkempt as she felt – the journey leaving her feeling in need of a freshen-up – but she held her hand over her mouth to stifle the sob that had escaped at the sight of her sister. Unable to contain whatever was left to come out, Freya burst into tears.

Rosie rushed for her and held her in her arms. 'Shh, shh, it's okay,' she soothed repeatedly as she gently rocked her sister. 'Come on, let's get you inside.'

She shut the door and took the bag from Freya's shoulder, gently prising her fingers from the grip she had on it. Her worldly possessions were in that bag, and she had trouble letting it go.

'It's all right. We can take it with us,' Rosie said kindly. 'Come through to the kitchen, and I'll make you a cup of tea. You look like you need it.'

Freya sniffed. 'I need so much more than that.'

'I know, but it's the only place to start.' Rosie smiled.

Freya smiled back, the first genuine smile in many months. 'Thank you.'

Rosie helped Freya into a chair at their kitchen table and filled the kettle. Grabbing some mugs, Rosie tossed in a couple of teabags. 'What happened, Freya? Did he beat you again? Is that why you decided to make this journey? Has he hurt you again?'

Freya slumped in the kitchen chair at the table, so exhausted that even the effort of keeping her head up became too much. She placed her elbow on the table and rested her cheek in the palm of her hand. 'No, he left me in the house, making sure it was as cold an uninviting as possible. No violence. But I just couldn't do it anymore, Rosie. I couldn't face the possibility of another argument. The glass... on the floor. I just saw it and thought this can't go on.'

Rosie frowned.

'I can't explain it yet, but I will. I'm just too tired.'

Rosie carried the two mugs to the table. 'Of course you are. There's no way you should have taken such a trip straight out of hospital. And I take it Liam doesn't know you're here?'

Freya shook her head.

Rosie sighed. 'Okay, we don't need to worry about that now. We can deal with that later. You need to rest. Here, have this, and then I'm going to run you a nice warm bath. Do you have a change of clothes in your bag?'

Freya nodded.

'Good. Well then, you can slip into something else, and we'll get those clothes washed. You can take our bed, and I'll make up a bed in the living room.'

'No way, I'm not chucking you and Ben out of your room,' Freya said. 'I'll be fine on the sofa.'

'We'll see, but after we've eaten, you can decide if you want to talk or just sleep. You look done in.'

Freya lifted the mug to her lips and drank the soothing tea. Rosie always made it just right. Not too strong but not weak either, and always one sugar, just to taste. It was the most perfect cup of tea her parched mouth had ever tasted. 'Thank you.'

'I'm so glad you came to me,' Rosie said, placing her hand over Freya's. 'You've made the right decision to leave him.'

Just then the front door slammed, and footsteps sounded

in the hallway, jolting Freya and the mug of tea. Some of it spilled onto the table and her clothing, and she leapt up from her seat to wipe it away. 'I'm sorry. I'm sorry,' she blurted out as she rushed to the counter to grab a kitchen towel. 'I'll clean it right away. I'm so clumsy.'

Rosie stood and went to her just as Ben appeared from the hall. 'It's okay,' she said gently as she placed her hand on Freya's arm. 'It's just a bit of spilt tea. It doesn't matter. You're safe here, and no one is going to hurt you. What's more important is that you're okay. Did it burn you?'

Freya looked down at herself and the wet stain on her top. She hadn't even felt it. It was hot, and when she pulled her top up to reveal her stomach, she saw a hazy pattern of pink where hot liquid had scorched her skin, but hadn't burned her badly. 'I'm fine,' she whispered, realising she'd never had the opportunity to stop and check that she was okay first when things like this had happened before. 'It doesn't hurt.'

Tears glistened in Rosie's eyes as she took the towel from her sister's grasp and lowered her top, gently placing her hand underneath the stain so that she could blot the fabric dry without brushing against the burn on Freya's skin.

'Freya,' Ben said as he came into the kitchen. He would have seen what had just happened, but he chose not to say anything about it. 'It's so lovely to see you.' He drew her into an embrace, an emotional connection that drew out more tears from Freya's eyes. Rosie wrapped her arms around them both. 'So you left him, eh? That must have been one of the hardest things you've ever done, and I'm so proud of you for doing it. You are safe now. I'll make sure of it,' he said quietly. 'If Liam has the nerve to come here, I'll make sure the bastard knows what we think of him. No more games. No more lies.'

'Thank you, both of you,' Freya said as she let her sister and brother-in-law comfort her, finally feeling safe in their embrace.

ROSIE UNPACKED Freya's stuff from her bag under Freya's watchful eye and shuffled her into the bathroom, where she'd run the bubbliest bath Freya had ever seen. Rosie hung a pair of Freya's cotton pyjamas on the back of the door and added one of her fluffy robes with it. Next, she placed a white towel on the radiator for when Freya was finished.

'I want you to take your time,' Rosie said. 'Relax. I will rustle up something to eat in a bit.' She hugged Freya and then left her alone, closing the door behind her.

Carefully, Freya removed her clothes and left them in a neat pile on the tiled floor. She stepped into the bath, and as she did, she caught sight of herself in the large mirror above the sink. Her mouth agape, she stared at her reflection, seeing for the first time the damage he'd inflicted. She looked as bad as she felt. Her face was indeed very bruised, particularly her left eye, and elongated bruises ran around her neck. She'd become very adept at carefully choosing the moment when she'd inspect her bruises. It was usually when she was at home, alone, where she could assess the damage for herself and decide what she'd need to do to help the injuries to heal. But her escape up to Rosie had prevented that until now. Each wound was very noticeable, and she wondered what people must have thought while she travelled up here on the train. Her arms and legs were dotted with large, ugly bruises, and when she twisted her torso to look at her back, dappled bruises were there, too. He had really gone to work on her. It was just another reminder that leaving him now was the best decision she had ever made, and one that would hopefully allow her to live.

She lowered herself into the bath and gasped as her bruises prickled when they hit the hot water. She swirled the water around herself while the sound of a muted conversation filtered up to her, Rosie and Ben very likely figuring out what to do next as far as she was concerned. Even so, the sound was reassuring. Freya no longer felt alone.

She relaxed deeper under the water until her body was completely submerged. The water against her skin made all the events of the day melt away into the bubbles. She tipped her hair back until it billowed out under the water too, but this was painful. Her scalp was raw from when he'd torn out clumps of her hair, and the wounds objected to the hot water and scented oils from the bubble bath. She grabbed the sides of the bath and sat up, gently wiping away the water that trickled down her face.

She hugged her knees close to her chest while she waited for the pain to subside to a subtle throb and for her inner self to calm. Her body, her face particularly, had reminded her there was still plenty of healing to be done, and she needed to treat it with care.

When she was done and her skin had begun to wrinkle, she stepped out of the bath and wrapped the soft towel around herself, using a corner to soak up the water from her hair. This was heaven and more than she could have hoped for. For now, she was safe, but that knowledge didn't stop her from imagining him at home right now, his rage a steel-like calm when he realised what she'd done. He would have been surprised to find the house empty, and that surprise would have transformed into anger when he did a little more searching – found the drawers in his study open and ransacked – her documents missing. He had probably already begun to deal with it, speaking with contacts and calling in favours for information. He'd very likely come here too, an obvious link to family, but not tonight. Tonight, she was sure she would be free of any confrontation, and she made herself trust what Ben had said, that he wouldn't let Liam in even if he tried.

Wrapped in the robe, she wandered through to the kitchen, where delicious cooking smells greeted her.

Both Rosie and Ben turned as she walked in.

'My goodness, you look better,' Rosie said with a smile.

'I feel brand new.'

'Drink?' Rosie asked, pointing to a bottle on the table. 'We've opened some wine, but you can have whatever you'd like. Tea, coffee, water. We have some juice in the fridge, I think.'

'I'd love a small glass of wine, if that's okay. Goodness knows my nerves need it. But only a tiny one because of the painkillers.'

'Of course,' Ben said as he pulled out a glass from the cupboard, picked up the bottle and poured. 'Here.'

She took it from him, thanking him as she sat at the table, which was all laid up for dinner. Plates already set next to grey-blue gingham serviettes that lay under the cutlery, the colour perfectly matching the painted legs and base of the table, and a cute ceramic salt and pepper set neatly placed in the middle. 'Whatever you're cooking smells divine.'

'Glad you like it,' Rosie said cheerily. 'We're having Thai

chicken curry tonight with rice. Sauce out of a jar, but who cares.'

'Who cares, indeed. Sounds heavenly to me.'

'The main thing is that we eat at this point,' Ben said as he dished up the food. 'My stomach thinks my throat's been cut. You must be starving, Freya.'

'Yes, when did you last eat?' Rosie asked as she carried the plates to the table and set one down in front of Freya.

The fragrant steam filled Freya's nose, and her mouth watered. 'I can't remember,' she said truthfully. 'I think I grabbed a snack at the station in Southampton, but I'm not sure. My mind is still hazy.' She picked up her knife and fork and waited for them both to sit and tuck into the food. She could only start eating once they'd started. A stipulation from Liam that she had to wait until he'd begun.

'You don't need to worry about that,' Rosie said, noticing. 'Enjoy the food; there are no rules here. I don't care if you eat it with your fingers, toes or lick it from the plate. I just want you to enjoy it and be full.'

Freya had to stop and placed her cutlery down. 'Thank you. You don't know what it means to be here with you. My head is all over the place, but I finally feel safe. Safer than I've felt in a long time.'

Rosie reached out to her. 'And I'm so glad you're here. I will do everything I can to make sure you get a new start at life, if that's what you want. We'll deal with Liam another day, but for now, know that you are safe here, with us.'

Freya had never felt so loved.

5

Rosie's sofa made a very comfortable bed, so too the warm soft duvet that she'd made up for Freya. But she couldn't settle. Her bones ached, and the bruises around her eye throbbed. She got up and went to the kitchen to search out the painkillers she'd left in there earlier in the evening. She hadn't been more than a minute when Rosie appeared from the doorway.

'Can't sleep?' she asked.

'No,' Freya murmured. 'Mind in chaos and a little too much pain tonight. Sorry, did I disturb you?'

'No, not really, although I am worried about you.'

Freya smiled. 'There's nothing to worry about. I got away. I don't know what tomorrow holds for me, but, for now, I'm out of his clutches and live to see another day.' She saw the anguished pain on her sister's face and realised how flippant she sounded. 'I'm sorry, Rosie, I shouldn't be so blunt. Are you okay? This is a lot to deal with, I know.'

'I'm okay. I also know that your bluntness is bravado,' Rosie replied.

The words hit Freya hard. 'No.'

'A front for the pain and vulnerability you won't let out.'

Freya held on to the kitchen counter for stability as her head spun.

'You forget I know you,' Rosie continued. 'More than anyone else in this world.' She walked towards Freya. 'You're like a coiled spring, so tightly wound. It's another reason you can't sleep.'

Freya let out an involuntary gasp. 'I have to keep it together.'

'Not anymore. You're safe here. I can't imagine what you've had to live through, but you don't have to fight anymore. You can let it go.'

A sob replaced the gasp, and tears pooled in Freya's eyes. 'I... I can't.'

Rosie wrapped her arms around Freya. 'Yes, you can.'

'Please, no, no...' Freya begged as Rosie held her close until the rush of emotion burst through Freya. All she could do was hold on to her sister as every suppressed thought, instinct, fear and anguish exploded from her, forcing her mouth open to release a long and loud scream.

It was only the sight of Ben rushing into the room that brought Freya back to the present. His messy bed hair and shorts were proof that he'd probably launched himself from the bed at the sound of her scream, thinking the worst.

'It's all right,' Rosie said calmly to Ben. 'We're just letting it all out.'

Freya was now reduced to a trembling, tear-soaked waif who still clung to her sister as little sobs peppered the silence.

Ben ran his hand through his hair. 'Jesus, for a moment there, I thought that bastard had got in somehow.'

'No, no,' Rosie said. 'If anything, she just let him go.'

Ben smiled. 'Well, that's a really good thing.' He gently touched Freya's arm. 'You okay?'

Freya nodded. 'I think so.' It was only a whisper, but it was all she could give. She moved out of Rosie's hold. 'That was mean,' she said as she sniffed.

'Well, maybe a little sneaky, but long overdue. You needed to let it out. I was waiting for a time that you could do it. Sooner rather than later, too, as you'd not begin to really heal until you'd done that. Acknowledgement is the key to self-healing.'

'When did you become a wellness guru?' Ben chuckled.

'Didn't you know?' Rosie said as she grabbed the kettle, filled it with water, placed it back onto its base and flipped the switch. 'It's a vocation. I've always been like this.'

Ben raised his brow. 'What about when I needed comfort when Everton's relegation was hanging in the balance last year?'

Rosie gave him a serious side-eye. 'Not the same thing.'

Ben placed his hand on his chest. 'Not for you, but for me.'

Rosie went to Ben and planted a small kiss on his cheek. 'Aw, poor boy. Did it hurt you that they almost went out of the Premiership?'

Ben nodded.

'Come here,' Rosie replied. 'Let me hug away the pain.' She pulled away and ruffled his hair. 'And remember, they survived and remained in the Premier League, so now life is good, yes?'

He nodded, and she pulled him into another embrace and then tickled him. 'What we all need now is a hot drink,'

Rosie said, pulling away from Ben. 'I'm guessing tea, but I can make coffee if you'd prefer.'

Freya sniffed and wiped away the tears, grateful for this moment of lightness after the torrent of emotion she'd just experienced. She wished she'd had with Liam what Rosie and Ben had – a warm, loving relationship.

'Coffee for me,' Ben said, checking his watch. 'I may as well pep myself up for the day, as it's four thirty. No point going back to bed now.'

'I'm sorry I disrupted your sleep.'

'No, you didn't,' Ben said with a smile to reassure her. 'With what you've been through, I expected much worse and much sooner, to be honest.'

'I held it in,' she replied. 'I had to.'

'Of course you did. I don't know how you coped.'

DESPITE DECIDING they'd all begin their day and agreeing a rota for the bathroom, somehow they'd all gravitated back to their beds. Freya lay on the sofa as Rosie's and Ben's muffled voices and occasional laughter drifted from their bedroom, eventually fading to nothing but the soft sound of movement, indicating intimacy between the pair, and the point at which Freya stopped listening. Instead, she focused on the next step of her plan. She would need a place of her own if she was to really move on, but how she went about that, she couldn't fathom, and it felt impossible to manage right then. Where would she live, how would she fund it, and how would she deal with Liam if, or more likely when, he'd find her and drag her home?

She sat up and stared out the bay-fronted window of

Rosie's living room. She definitely needed a plan for this part of her future because it was inevitable she'd encounter him again. It was just a matter of time. There was no way in hell he'd be at home, happy to let this go, let her go.

Sometime when she'd been lost in her thoughts, she'd fallen asleep, because the next time she became aware of her surroundings, she was under the duvet on the sofa. The flat was quiet, and she knew as she snuggled under the covers that she was probably alone. When she looked at the coffee table, she saw a note from Rosie, confirming this fact. She leant forward to pick it up. The note told her that Rosie and Ben had gone to work, and to help herself to whatever she wanted. She pulled the duvet over herself, but the grumble of her stomach forced her to confront her hunger. She rose from the sofa and went to the kitchen. Pulling out a bowl, she filled it with cereal and milk and switched on the TV. The morning news programme filled the silence, and she ate contentedly.

After showering and getting dressed, she cleared away the bedding and began to clean the flat. She might not have much money, but she could make herself useful by tidying up and helping out. She'd go through the freezer and see what she could pull together for the evening meal so Rosie and Ben would have nothing to do when they came home from work.

The kitchen felt alive with activity when the front door opened, startling Freya. It took a moment for her brain to tell her body that there was no threat. It wasn't Liam, she was not at home, but she still went to the hallway to meet whoever had come home.

'Hi,' Rosie said as she hung up her jacket. 'Good day? How are you feeling?'

'I feel good,' Freya said with a smile. 'I've cleaned up a bit, not that it needed it, and made dinner. It's a concoction from your cupboards, so chicken with a tomato and pepper sauce over rice. Is that okay?'

'Sounds bloody lovely,' Rosie said as she made her way to the kitchen. 'And it means I don't have to cook, so it's perfect. How long have I got?' she asked as she glanced over the pots and their contents bubbling on the cooker top.

'About twenty minutes.'

'Lovely. I'll go and change and then come and help.'

'Great.'

Rosie disappeared just as the front door went again. This time, Ben shouted out his 'hello', and both Rosie and Freya replied in unison, to which Freya let out a little laugh.

Freya opened the back doors that led out into the small yard at the back. She'd found some wine and a carton of juice in the fridge and a bag of salted peanuts in the cupboard, which she laid out on the garden table, together with some glasses. Rosie and Ben joined her in the garden.

'You can stay as long as you like,' Rosie said light-heartedly. 'This is amazing. We should do this more.'

Ben agreed as he poured wine for himself and Rosie and a glass of juice for Freya, at her request.

'How was the world of interior design today?' Freya asked Rosie as she grabbed a handful of nuts.

'It's good. Another commission has just come in. A luxurious penthouse in Canary Wharf, so that'll keep the wolf from the door.'

'Said like she's the only one earning in this house,' Ben exclaimed.

'Oh, I'm sorry,' Freya replied, smiling. 'How was your day

in the world of structural engineering? Stop any buildings from falling down?'

'Damn right,' he said as he sat back in his chair with his glass of wine. 'Saved the day many times.'

'Well, then, that's all that matters,' Freya said humorously.

The juice was refreshing and a perfect accompaniment for the hazy summer evening, bees buzzing through the flower heads and the sounds of neighbours out and enjoying their evening too. In no time at all, Freya relaxed, knowing that she could fully do so here, with her sister.

'I suppose I should start thinking about getting a job and earning some money.'

'You have plenty of time for that,' Rosie replied as she popped another couple of peanuts into her mouth. 'In the meantime, have you thought about a phone? It would really help you to feel connected to the world again.'

'Yes, I agree, but I didn't want to venture out on my own today. Maybe tomorrow.'

Rosie glanced at Ben, who took the silent order and jumped up from his seat and disappeared, quickly reappearing with a box, which he handed to Freya.

'Now you don't have to,' he said. 'Here, it's just a pay-as-you-go, but it'll mean you can contact us whenever you need to and also be contactable should anything happen. It might make you feel a little more comfortable.'

Freya was touched. 'Thank you,' she said as she looked over the box. 'That is so thoughtful of you both.'

'I know it's been a while since you've had a phone,' Rosie said, 'but you'll be fine. We just need to get you some data, and then you'll have access to everything on there. Internet, social media, the lot.'

Freya pulled the phone out of the box and ran her fingers over the shiny glass and plastic.

'Here, let me,' Ben said as he picked out the SIM card from the box. 'The good thing about that twat not letting you have a phone is that he can't trace you with it.'

'We'll put our numbers in and make sure you know what to do,' Rosie said.

'It can't be that hard,' Freya said. 'It's been five years, not fifty-five.'

'Good point,' Rosie replied. 'Sorry.'

Freya smiled. 'It's okay. I understand what it must look like, but I wasn't locked in a cage, not able to communicate with the outside world. I was allowed a tablet even if it was to remain in the house.'

Rosie looked uncomfortable. 'Yes, exactly. It came with rules. There are no rules here.'

'Thank you, I appreciate it,' Freya said with a sigh.

'What's up?' Rosie asked.

'I've been thinking about what I'm going to do now. I need to get my life together.'

'It's only been a day,' Ben reminded her, 'and you're welcome here as long as you want. There's no rush.'

'That's really kind, and I'm very grateful, but I need to find a place.'

Rosie reached out and placed her hand over Freya's. 'Take a minute. You've just been through an awful lot. Why don't you wait a couple of weeks, and then we can take it from there.'

Freya looked down. 'But what if he finds me and takes me home? I don't think I'll make it through another of his punishments.'

A look of concern covered Rosie's features, and one of suppressed anger covered Ben's.

'You don't have to worry about that. We can sort Liam. I'm sure there's something we can do legally to make sure he doesn't come near you, get an injunction. We can look into that and maybe some sort of legal separation until you're ready for divorce.'

'You make it sound so easy,' Freya said. 'He won't like, or accept, any of this.'

'But you left anyway. You knew you had to in order to survive, and I'm so proud of you. You can do this last little bit, get him out of your life forever.'

'I felt that way earlier, but now, I feel it's all hopeless. He'll find me here. I can't imagine what he's planning right this moment.'

'So what?' Ben said. 'Let him come here. I bet he's not such a big man in front of me.'

Freya smiled. Ben was tall and naturally well-built and could easily take on Liam. Freya understood the appeal of such a man, strong arms to surround her and make her feel safe.

'The fact that he hasn't come straight here worries me too. What if he shows up at Mum and Dad's instead?'

'I've already spoken to them,' Rosie said, 'and no, they haven't heard from him.'

'You've spoken to them about this,' Freya exclaimed.

'No, no, nothing like that, don't worry. I told them that you two have had an argument and that you're staying with us for a day or so. Mum wanted more detail and to come for a visit, but I kept her away for now. She'll stay put. You can decide when you want to discuss it with them when you're ready. They wanted to speak to you, but I said you were out shopping, to give you a little more time. They understood and sent their love.'

'Thanks, Rosie, that's great. At least they have something to go on if Liam shows up at theirs.'

'Exactly.'

'Why don't you let yourself heal, take it easy here, and then we can look at places to live once you're in a better mindset. There really is no hurry; we're happy to have you.'

———

THE BLUE-FRONTED estate agent's had multiple hanging banners in the windows with houses and flats available for rent or purchase. It had been a couple of weeks since Freya had landed on her sister's doormat, and her bruises had healed well enough to be covered by make-up – another thing provided by Rosie – which meant Freya now felt comfortable enough to venture outside without looking like a crash-test dummy.

Rosie pushed open the door and held it for Freya to follow. She smiled when she saw the hesitation in Freya's eyes and waited until she was ready to move.

'Good morning, ladies,' the man, short but smartly dressed in a suit, said when he looked up from his laptop screen. 'How can I help?'

'We've come for more detail on the flat at Langham Court,' Rosie began.

Rosie had come home with information on a flat that had just come up for rent at the large art-deco mansion block about fifteen minutes' walk from Rosie's – a friend of her colleague's worked at the estate agent on the high street and had the details. Rosie suggested they go and look at it, at least. Freya was keen, getting a place of her own was what she'd wanted, but she only had eight hundred pounds left of her stash, and she was sure that amount would not cover the price of a flat in London.

'Ah, yes, the little studio unit?' he said pleasantly.

'That's the one.'

'Have a seat,' he said as he gestured to the two seats on the other side of his desk and pulled out his own to sit, 'and I'll pull up the details.'

Rosie and Freya sat as he typed on his laptop and then turned the screen to face them. 'This one is cute. Small but perfectly practical. Of course, the added benefit of living in an art-deco mansion block such as this one makes the pill easier to swallow.'

Freya glanced at the screen, taking in the photos of the building and flat. It was indeed impressive – a red-brick building with period rectangular glazed Crittall windows and large white balconies stretching across the front of the building with attractive curved corners. Large brass letters sat above a wood-panelled set of glazed double doors.

The entrance lobby was an airy space with more wood panelling, cosy seating and palms in planters dotted around. A large staircase wound around the shaft of an old lift, caged in brass filigree with a white door. From what she could see on the screen, the flat was very compact, but it was painted white throughout and looked newly decorated and fresh and clean. She didn't hate it; in fact, the bubble of excitement in her stomach indicated that she was more excited about this than she expected to be.

Rosie turned to Freya, as did the agent.

'The place is available for viewing this morning if you have time,' he said. 'It's a ten-minute walk from here.'

Freya opened her mouth to speak just as a call came in on the phone on the desk. He excused himself to answer it.

'Would you like to go and visit it?' Rosie asked quietly as the agent talked, distracted.

Freya considered it. 'It looks perfect for me, but are you sure I can afford it?'

'The cost is eight seventy-five per month, which we'll get down to eight hundred. It's certainly not the four-bedroomed house you had in Southampton, but it'll be yours.'

'And believe me, that would be amazing, but I only have eight hundred, and they'll want a deposit.'

'Look, I don't want you to think we're offering charity, but I've talked to Ben, and we can help you with the deposit and a couple of months of rent if you need it. When you're ready, you can think about getting some work, which will be good for you too.'

'You shouldn't have to do that.'

'It's our pleasure,' Rosie replied, placing her hand over Freya's. 'I'm so glad you came to us and that you're away from that monster.'

'Shh,' Freya said, glancing over to the agent, the phone balanced between his ear and shoulder while he scrolled through the laptop.

'Don't worry, he can't hear me. Anything we can do to help you get back on your feet is money well spent. Do you want to go and see it? We can sort out the negotiation if you want to go ahead.'

Freya nodded. 'I like it. It's small and simple, but it'll be mine.'

A part of her still couldn't comprehend what she was doing. Only a couple of weeks ago she was in hospital, ready to be collected and taken back to a life of pain and drudgery, only to be here now with her sister, about to view a new property. There had been no in between for her. No break-up process, no moving out, just an impulse decision that changed her life forever. And of course, there was the threat that Liam would find her, turn up one day, having used all the available resources that working for the police would allow, however unscrupulous, and would be furious that as far as he was concerned, she'd decided to disappear off the face of the earth.

'Okay,' the agent said as he replaced the receiver on the cradle. 'What do we think? Yes? No?'

'We'd like to go,' Rosie said. 'If that's still okay?'

'Yes, of course. Let me grab the key.'

THE TEN-MINUTE WALK WAS PLEASANT; the sun warmed their backs. They had brought jackets but soon removed them as they walked. The agent introduced himself, Paul Smith, and chatted about the area and what events and activities took place there.

They approached the large imposing building, and suddenly Freya was afraid. This was a huge step, and the feeling of vulnerability crept into her once again. Rosie noticed immediately. She placed her arm through Freya's and kept them moving towards the entrance.

Paul punched a code into the door release mechanism – a modern fixture in an otherwise period façade – and pulled open the door, holding it for both Rosie and Freya. The main entrance was much larger than the photos had implied, the ceiling high and the room wide. It was freshly painted here too, and the faint smell of paint hung in the air.

'The flat is on the third floor and towards the rear of the building. Would you like to take the stairs or the lift?' Paul asked as he glanced at the caged lift.

It looked as vintage as the rest of the building, and Freya wasn't sure she trusted it. She smiled. 'Let's take the stairs. I'm not sure how reliable that is.'

'It's in good working order, I assure you,' he said quickly with a chuckle, 'but yes, let's take the stairs. I know I could use the exercise.' He touched his stomach, which Freya noticed did bulge a little over the top of his trousers.

They walked along the quiet corridor towards the door at the very end. Paul pulled a small cluster of keys from his pocket and opened the heavy white door.

'It's not been lived in for a couple of months, but it's newly decorated so in turn-key condition,' he said as he held open the door for Freya and Rosie to enter the flat.

Freya walked into the small entrance way and then straight through the doorway to her left, which took her into the living area. A large window filled most of the wall opposite. The room was indeed as small as it looked in the pictures. Apart from the original metal window and the old-style radiator beneath it, there were no period features here. No ceiling architrave or any other indication of the history of the building. She'd have to have some sort of futon or pull-down bed, but the space was pleasant and appealed to her. She wouldn't have to find too many pieces of furniture, and it would be easy to heat when needed.

Paul walked towards the archway at the furthest corner of the room, next to the window, and pointed. 'The kitchen,' he said.

Freya had to stifle a laugh as she walked into this room. If she held out her arms, she could touch each wall. 'There's no room for you,' she said with a giggle as Rosie tried to tuck herself in to join her.

'This is very compact,' Rosie agreed, and they both chuckled as they turned on the spot to take it in. 'But look, you have room for a microwave on the countertop, a couple of cupboards, a washing machine and an oven.'

'Yes, and look at the lovely narrow counter-to-ceiling window,' Freya said with a burst of laughter at the absurdity of the size of the room.

'I get it, ladies,' Paul said. 'It's very compact.'

'It's a shoebox,' Rosie countered with a smile.

'But I still like it,' Freya said, glancing around, thinking of all the possibilities this place had to offer. 'It might just be the one for me.'

6

Moving day began at six thirty in the morning with a breakfast of bacon rolls from the café near the flat, washed down with large cups of coffee while Freya, Rosie, Ben and Ben's friend Jon decided who would be doing what. Everyone pulled together to help Freya move in. Her parents had promised to travel from Surrey to help and bring a selection of household items that they'd offered to Freya – utensils and kitchenware they had duplicates of and no longer used.

Freya had spoken with her parents once she'd decided to take the flat, to let them know that her marriage was over rather than her merely taking a break from it. They were disappointed, obviously, they loved Liam, but they were supportive and accepted her reasons for the split. She'd spoken about arguments, tension, and their relationship irrevocably breaking down, but kept his abuse from them, for now. It would be too much information for them to deal with. That was the excuse she told herself anyway. There were probably a few emotions for herself to contend with too on this matter: embarrassment that she'd allowed someone to treat her in such a way, and a good dose of shame, but one thing she was sure of was that this was not a conversation to be had yet. Perhaps in the future when she was more settled and had more strength to share the horrors she'd been through. Their desire to come and help was enough for her to know she was loved and supported.

Rosie had taken out the lease of the flat in her name once they'd agreed Freya would be easily traceable if she did it in her own – plus the fact her credit rating would be on the floor, as she'd never purchased anything in her own name since she'd started her relationship with Liam all those years ago. Rosie helped with the deposit, as she had promised – something Freya would be grateful for for many years to come. After the lease had been agreed, Freya and Rosie spent their spare time at the flat, measuring up for furniture and deciding the basics of what she'd need, given that she was starting from scratch.

They bustled together in the living room, bringing the few boxes that she had, and then they set to work scrubbing and polishing every surface in the flat with buckets of soapy water and cloths, wanting it to sparkle so that it would feel more like home. The living room was long, enough to be able to section it so that she could have the area closest to the window and kitchen space for a small table and chairs, keeping the middle of the room for the sofa and TV, and the opposite end of the room as her bedroom area. A nice little screen could further divide the room, if she wanted, but that was something she could do once she'd settled in. The ability to have those choices made butterflies dance in her stomach, reflecting the possibility of an independent future, carving out a life of her own. But for now, she had to focus on the essentials, which included a sofa, TV, and bed.

She'd found a good deal online for a small double bed and had spotted a couple of pretty striped bedding sets in the homeware section of the local supermarket, together with some new cutlery and crockery. Rosie and Ben's friend Jon had donated a sofa that had rarely been used, and Rosie and Ben had given her an old flat-screen TV that had been stored under their bed, for a 'just in case' situation.

Freya's emergency nest egg had depleted to a couple of hundred pounds, but the gratitude she felt towards everyone who had been willing to help was stronger than the feeling of guilt at the burden she'd become when deciding to leave the life she'd had. A life that had included the nice little luxuries of a comfortable existence, as long as she could endure the acts of violence that came with it.

Freya had just finished cleaning the kitchen when Jon and Ben inched into the room with the sofa. She noticed the little beads of sweat that had formed on both their foreheads from the effort of climbing the stairs. There had been no chance of jamming this piece of furniture into the antiquated lift.

'Here, let me get you guys a drink,' Freya said as they placed it down where she wanted. She grabbed a couple of cans of lemonade from the fridge and handed them out.

Both men took them gratefully and drank. Jon's gaze had rarely left Freya all morning. It was now so noticeable she was sure she must have something on her face. Perhaps he'd heard the story of her life, perhaps he was trying to contemplate why she'd had to suffer the way she had, perhaps he was just a starey kind of person, but she ignored it, grateful that he'd let her have such a large piece of furniture for free.

Once the sofa was settled in place, Jon made noises of having to leave, so Ben offered to walk down with him to collect another box.

Freya thanked him again, but was not unhappy at him leaving, not wishing to be in his sights any longer.

The intercom buzzed as Rosie came out of the bathroom carrying a bucket of cleaning products, her hair scraped back into a ponytail and her pink cheeks an indication that she too was feeling the heat in this small place.

'Drink?' Freya asked.

Rosie nodded gratefully as she answered the intercom, letting in whoever was on the line.

Freya checked out the window, a habit that had followed her here too. 'Who is it?'

Rosie crossed the room towards Freya. 'It's just Mum and Dad,' she said with concern in her eyes. 'Are you okay?'

Freya breathed out. 'Yes, of course. I just keep thinking about Liam.'

'Did you think I'd let him in?' Rosie asked.

'No,' she said. 'Ignore me. I'm just a little overwhelmed. Today is a big day for me.'

Rosie hugged her. 'It is, but it's a good day and one that we're going to celebrate. I understand that you're anxious, but we're not going to let anything happen to you or allow the thought of him to ruin your day.'

Her parents' bickering grew louder the closer they got to the flat. Freya and Rosie laughed as they listened to her mum admonishing her dad over something trivial.

They knocked on the door as they continued their discussion, and Freya went to answer.

'Mum, Dad, come in. We heard you from the hallway.'

'Darling,' her mum said as she wrapped her arms around

her, 'so good to see you. Are you okay? Poor thing, look at you.'

Her dad followed behind. 'Hello, love,' he said with a smile.

She hugged her dad too and took them both into the main room, gesturing with her arms. 'Well, this is it.'

Her mum scanned the room quickly. 'Well, it's very nice, darling.'

'It's a start,' she said, 'and it looks a lot better now that we have the sofa and bed in place. I just need to find a unit to keep the TV on, and then this space will look fine. A nice rug and some long curtains and it'll be really homely.'

'It's lovely,' her mum agreed. 'You seem to have many plans. What about the house in Southampton?'

'No, we're not going to discuss that today,' Rosie said firmly. 'That will sort itself out in good time. Today is about celebrating the new start for Freya.'

Her mum smiled, but Freya saw the disappointment in her mum's eyes at what her daughter had given up.

'Where's your kitchen?' her dad asked, picking up the box he'd brought in.

Freya tipped her head to look inside the box and saw all the donated kitchenware. 'Over there,' she replied, pointing to the archway in the corner of the room. 'It's massive, so please don't be overwhelmed.'

Freya and Rosie glanced at each other and smiled.

Ben returned to the flat carrying a box filled with the purchases she'd recently made. 'All right, ladies, where do you want this?'

'Now, there's one more box downstairs in the lobby,' her mum said. 'Shall I go and get it, or does anyone else fancy getting it for me? There's also the dining table set, if anyone is feeling strong.'

Freya smiled. 'I'll grab the box.'

'And we can get the table and chairs, but maybe we should get some lunch first? Have a break?' Ben replied.

Her mum looked around and then at her watch. 'We all must be ready for something to eat. Let's go out for lunch, check out the local pub.'

'Sounds great, give me a minute, and then we'll go,' Freya called out as she shut the door to her flat. She strode down the corridor, mindful of where she was going, the place still new and unfamiliar. The box was small and light enough to carry easily up the stairs. A door shutting in the distance and then footsteps made her pause on the first flight. She wanted to wait until whoever was coming had passed by. Colliding with one of her neighbours would not be the best introduction, so she chose caution.

She looked up to see a man jogging down the stairs towards her, his brown hair brushed back off his face in waves and a day or so's worth of stubble.

He smiled at her. 'Hello, are you moving in here?'

Feeling her cheeks flush, from nerves and irritating shyness, she smiled back. 'Yes, that's right.'

He stopped and leant against the handrail. 'I'm Elliot. I'm in number nine. Well, me and my wife, Ava. What number are you in?'

She didn't want to disclose that to a stranger, feeling safer keeping herself to herself. 'Erm, well... just along that corridor.'

He nodded and, by his expression, seemed happy to not pursue her answer. He'd either picked up on what she wasn't telling him, or he did not care much to know the details.

Her eye went to two finger-long scratches on his forearm, something he noticed too when he reached across and covered it with the palm of his other hand. 'Well, it's really nice to meet you,' he said. 'We're a nice bunch here. I'm sure you'll settle in in no time... er...'

'Well, thank you,' she deflected quickly. 'It's nice meeting you.'

He held up his hand and continued with his descent down the stairs. 'Have a great day. If you need anything, give us a knock. Number nine.'

She called out her thanks again and with an eye roll climbed the stairs. Could her first encounter with someone in this block have been any more awkward? And did she have to stare at the scratch on his arm like some sort of skin police? She groaned, mortified that she'd been such an idiot. Why couldn't she just be friendly? Was sharing her flat number or name so impossible for the sake of friendliness? She remembered Liam and decided that yes, actually it was impossible at this stage. It would only take another 'friendly' conversation between him and Elliot and, bam, all of her details would be given out in a moment.

She padded up the stairs and towards her flat, deciding not to share this brief but awkward encounter with one of her new neighbours, keen for something to eat and preferably a large glass of wine.

———

IT WAS eight o'clock when everyone had disappeared for the day, amidst a sea of hugs, kisses and well-wishes, and once alone, she shed her clothes and stepped into the shower, wanting to wash away the day's sweat and dust that clung to her skin. For the first time in five years, she was alone, completely and utterly alone.

The bathroom was long and thin with a window that was a little too small to properly light the room, but the sanitary wear was new, and with a brand-new shower curtain, lots of brightly coloured bottles of toiletries, and a small house-plant her mum had given her sitting on the white-tiled windowsill, the place was brightened up nicely. Moreover, it was all hers, a feeling as joyous as it was terrifying.

Understanding how appliances worked in a new property had never been as challenging as figuring out the shower in this place. She'd turn the dial for the hot water, and it came out cold, and turning it just slightly to cold morphed it into skin-peeling heat. When she'd managed to get a temperature that wouldn't cause third-degree burns, she languished under the stream. Her body felt good too. No bruises anymore, but no constant aches either. Was that real, or was it that she just had a more positive outlook now? She didn't care; she felt good.

Letting her hair dry naturally in the evening heat and dressed in shorts and T-shirt pyjamas, with flip-flops on her feet, Freya poured hot water from the kettle into a mug and chucked in a teabag. Leaning down to grab the milk from the old fridge that sat under the counter, she wondered how it ever kept anything cold. It whined and popped and made a few clunking noises that made her question its lifespan.

She positioned the chair from the small dining table her parents had gifted her, a delightful unexpected extra, in front of the window and glanced over the immaculately kept gardens that ran parallel to the high street adjacent to it, a line of tall, evergreen shrubs separating the two. She couldn't stop herself looking for him, and convinced herself in the moment that he would be looking up, waiting for her to notice until she had no choice but to hide from his impenetrable gaze.

But there was no one, just the odd passer-by out for a walk in the hazy evening sun, or a group of friends who chatted animatedly as they walked, perhaps just out of the pub and onto the next. She told herself to relax and be thankful that she had found herself here. She'd never delighted in the sense of invisibility before now and cherished this moment of calm.

She hooked her leg up over the table, something Liam would have aggressively smacked away had he noticed such blatant bad manners. But she could do whatever she wanted now. If she chose to dance on the table, she could, but dancing was alien now to her, when once it had been something she loved to do. She cradled the mug in her hands and glanced into the windows beyond.

More thrillingly, she'd found that with a twist of her head, she could see into the windows of the flats that protruded from the end of the U-shaped building, a curved turret-like end punctuating the architecture of this old building. Located on the third floor meant there was only one additional floor above hers, but it was in these exquisitely crafted double casement windows that she saw the living spaces of the flat above and the one level to hers. Immediately drawn in, she gazed inquisitively, never expecting to unlock an undiscovered part of her personality – that of a voyeur.

She smiled. She only wanted to pass the time, a little bit of people watching while she settled in and drank her tea. Where was the harm? She let herself continue, even though she ensured she remained discreet.

In the top flat, she saw an old couple who spent a long while watering the myriad of plants in their window, strewn everywhere and hanging from the frames in places too. He was slight, white haired and chatting happily. Although Freya saw the wife, small, and equally as slight, she felt that the husband was talking more to the plants than with his significant other, although she could be wrong and told herself not to be so cynical.

Next floor down, and on the same level as Freya's flat, a woman in her mid to late twenties stood at the window, staring out across the skyline with a cup in hand too, attractive, with hair falling in long spiral curls in a mix of browns and blonde, and milky skin. Freya watched as another person came into view, someone she recognised. Elliot, the man she'd met on the stairs. So that was his wife, Ava, if she remembered the name correctly. A smile on his lips, he sidled up behind her and placed a kiss on her neck. Ava tilted her head to allow him to continue, and smiled too, moving her lips to say something to him before turning to face him. A cute greeting of two people in love and, from their age and enthusiasm, probably just starting out on their journey together.

Feeling that voyeurism wasn't all it was cracked up to be, and that intruding on a private moment between the happy couple was probably not the best way to move forward with her life, she glanced away and down at her phone instead.

She googled the town and its surroundings. The place felt alien to her and so different to where she'd come from. Although she was excited about this new transition, she didn't yet feel comfortable to go out exploring and would let the internet pick this up for her, for now.

She found that there were plenty of eateries and coffee

shops on the high street, and some clothes shops and chemists. There was a small convenience shop nearby and a large supermarket about one mile from here. Walkable, at some point. She made imaginary orders from the menus she'd downloaded from the nearest coffee shop and imagined the lovely pastries and cakes that were on offer, together with the hot lunch options such as paninis, toasties and soups.

The phone rang as she held it, and she had to catch it as it slipped from her grasp. It was Rosie.

She hit the button. 'Hi.'

'Hey, how's it going?' Rosie asked. 'I know I always struggle in a new place. Everything feels weird and wrong for a while.' She paused. 'Sorry, that was insensitive. I shouldn't have been so thoughtless. You're going to feel all those things more than most.'

'It's fine, and yes, it does feel weird and wrong, but I'm also kind of excited.'

'That's great news, sis.'

'I know. I am happy, I think. My body feels better today somehow too.'

'Really, that's even better news. How's your painkiller intake?'

'Doing just fine, thanks.' Freya laughed, deciding to omit the fifteen milligrams of diazepam she'd be taking later to help her sleep. No point causing more worry.

'Sorry, but I feel kind of responsible, as Mum and Dad have gone home now.'

'Well, you don't need to. I'm doing just fine.'

Rosie audibly inhaled. 'That's great news. Really great.'

'I'm just imagining what I'll order from the little coffee shop up the road.'

'Oh, there's apps for that; you can totally order in, now.'

'Well, if ever there's a sentence that makes me feel like I've just flown in from the moon, that's the one.'

Rosie laughed. 'Sorry, didn't mean to make you feel like that, but I'm serious, you can order whatever you like.'

'I know. Liam did allow a takeaway now and then, and I know he used a couple of apps, depending on what we wanted.'

'Oh dear, I really scored an own goal with that one.'

'Don't be silly, you're just trying to help, and I love you for it.'

'Okay, so in a bid to salvage this conversation, what are your plans for tomorrow? Resting, I hope?'

'Yeah, I've got lots of supplies and endless amounts of tea, so I'm going to chill out here and get used to my surroundings.'

'Check out the TV, too. Ben fixed up a box. Freeview or something like that. Get cosy and watch TV. Have a sleep if you need it.'

'Sounds divine.'

'Absolutely, and I'm more than a little jealous.'

'You could always come and join me. We can snuggle up like we used to as kids. Kids' TV and hot chocolate after school, remember?'

'Of course I do, and if I didn't have a backlog, I'd definitely be there. Enjoy it though. You deserve it. All of it.'

7

Freya's morning started uneventfully, and the afternoon disappeared into a blissful oblivion of sleep too. Freya woke on her sofa, a blanket draped over her and the TV quietly playing. She opened her eyes and saw the evening news playing out. She reached for the remote, switched channels and sat up.

Feeling hazy, she stretched, stood, then wandered into the kitchen. The sun shone its last beams of the day, giving the room an orange hue. The diazepam in her system made her particularly drowsy, and she couldn't remember if she'd taken a second tablet in the middle of the night or if she'd just dreamt that she had. She opened the fridge and pulled out some salad and the whole cooked chicken her mother had brought with her yesterday, which took up most of the middle shelf of the small fridge. She hummed quietly as she cut a couple of slices of the breast meat and filled a plate with the salad, adding some potato salad on the side, still adjusting to the fact that there would be no Liam returning home, ready to start a fight because of the food or whatever else he took offense to. It was just herself in her own space. She pulled out a glass and filled it with tap water and went back to her sofa.

She sat and switched on her TV and happily ate while she flicked through the channels until she found a channel playing old American comedy shows. The writing of the show was dated, but funny, and she found herself laughing out loud more than once as she enjoyed her food. Once finished, she left her plate in the sink and made herself a cup of tea. Her mealtime was as uneventful as her day, and the fact that she had no one to answer to filled her with a sense of peace. It didn't matter that the plate wouldn't be washed and put away immediately following dinner, and it didn't matter that she'd not spent hours preparing a meal from scratch that would then be critiqued harshly until she no longer wanted to eat what she'd cooked.

With tea made, she went to the spot that was fast becoming her favourite place. Shielded well enough from full view of the high street by the tall line of shrubs, she gazed out over the communal gardens to the front. Curious about her neighbours, she then glanced across the building to see if there was anything new to be found.

Elliot and Ava were there, but this time there was no sweet affection. They were arguing, and by the way hands gesticulated wildly, flying into the air, with raised bitter voices, angrily. A world away from the loving embrace they'd been locked in only a matter of hours ago.

He held out his hands to hold her arms, and she moved, trying to escape his hold. They scuffled for a moment until Freya felt it necessary to open one of her windows, hoping to hear more. She didn't like the way the argument was heading, and she'd been party to too much violence not to recognise the many red flags.

Although she could hear them shouting, she couldn't hear what was being said. She watched until they were out of view and waited nervously for the sound of crashing furniture or the bump of a body hitting something it shouldn't.

Apart from some door slamming, there was nothing else to note, but the hackles on the back of her neck had been awoken, and suspicions of how violent this man could be wouldn't leave her mind. She remembered the scratches. Perhaps Ava had tried to protect herself from him. She shuddered and waited for more, but there was no more to be heard since the final door slam. Still, she sat on her chair and told herself that another cup of tea was in order, even though the thought of it was not enough to pull her from the chair.

When the night claimed her view, she felt compelled to close the window and draw the curtains, wanting to shut out the world, feeling protected and shielded by the fabric. Safe from a world that included Liam and his prying eyes.

She went back to her sofa and picked up her phone. A habit she'd formed quickly after receiving it, finding it necessary to check every hour or so to see if any messages had been received from an unknown number. From him, toying with her. Ridiculous, she knew, but something about his total lack of contact frightened her.

A loud bang from outside in the corridor pierced the silence, jerking her from her seat and flipping the phone from her hand. Her heart thumped as she waited for footsteps to approach her door. When she finally got her body to move, she rushed across the room to the door, wanting to check that she had remembered to lock and bolt it. She had, of course she had; there would probably never be a world in which she could ever forget such a thing.

She felt the need to rest her head against the door, to listen out. If he was here, he'd be calling her, goading her, waiting for her to crack and open the door and plead for his forgiveness, in a bid to avoid any further punishment. He'd taunt her, mock her, and then drag her home somehow, and there would be little she could do to stop it.

Voices sounded in the hall, angry voices, a man and woman, but as she listened, it became clear it was not Liam. The woman was begging for the man to stay while he said he wouldn't, he'd leave whether she liked it or not. She apologised over and over. The sound was pitiful. His voice was harsh, punishing, and did not relent. Freya heard thumps down the stairs and then the faint sound of the main door opening and closing.

She rushed to her window and pushed back the curtain enough to see the man – Elliot – stride angrily down the path towards the street, not bothering to look behind.

The woman must have remained in the hallway, judging by the sound of her pitiful sobs.

Freya wanted to open the door but couldn't. She couldn't face the thought of what was happening. She couldn't cope with having to deal with another woman's ordeal at the hands of her partner. Maybe one day she would. Maybe one day she'd find the courage to help. But not today. She needed to level out her breathing and distract her mind from the throbbing in her head and ears. Her body throbbed too, as if it were remembering all the beatings she'd suffered in the past. Triggered, as everyone refers to it these days.

She sat and waited for the woman to return to her flat,

quietly hoping it wouldn't be too long. Her nerves couldn't take too much more of this.

When the hallway was finally silent, Freya sat back on the sofa, realising she'd been rigidly upright. Her muscles ached, and her mind buzzed. She needed to get it under control. She went to the kitchen and opened the small cupboard above the oven where she'd put all of her medications, meticulously saved and readily available for whenever she needed them. There, she pulled out her diazepam and popped one tablet from the foil. She swallowed and then cupped her hand under the tap at the sink and slurped the water from her palm. She went back to her sofa and waited for it to take effect, staring at the TV, but not registering whatever was playing. She didn't care; she just needed to focus on herself and calm her mind.

The warm feeling from the sedative releasing its chemicals into her body relaxed her muscles and soothed her mind. Once again, she was surrounded by an artificial cloud of tranquillity that dampened her anxious mind and kept her safe.

She moved to her bed and lazily pulled the blanket over herself, not wanting, or able, to fully undress and get under the covers. The woozy peacefulness that the drug gave her meant nothing else mattered, she would just exist in this moment as the world and all its evil fell away from view, and sleep came for her.

A LOUD NOISE pulled Freya abruptly from her sleep. An unfamiliar noise in her unfamiliar surroundings. She sat up, tangled in her blanket, and looked around. She rubbed her face and pulled her hair back, tucking it clumsily behind her ears. It was morning, and late. She glanced at the door and relaxed when she saw it was still chained as she'd left it. Her heart pumped but didn't race as it had yesterday.

She rose from the bed and went to the bathroom. Her head throbbed, suffering the post-sedative hangover that always lingered the next morning. She'd have to counteract that with painkillers.

She'd need to be careful, aware that she could easily slip back into the routine of taking them a little too regularly, as she had early last year. When Liam was particularly stressed at work, he'd been even more agitated and violent, if that was possible, and she found that the drugs were the only way to keep herself out of his way. It was only when he became angry that he couldn't hold a conversation with her – or, more importantly, when she couldn't fully engage when he wanted sex – that she realised she'd have to reduce her intake.

She went to the kitchen and flipped the kettle for a cup of tea and opened the curtains in the living room. It was a lovely day and an indication of the warmth that was coming. Unable to stop herself, she glanced over towards the couple's flat and saw Ava standing at the window, cupping a mug in her hands and gazing out towards the street. She had a sadness that Freya recognised, and in that moment, Freya wanted to go to her, to help her. Be her friend.

She snapped her head away with a tut. Of course she couldn't do that. She couldn't leave this flat, and what good is someone who can't even do that to someone who has very serious issues in their relationship. Maybe, if she ever got out of her flat, she'd convince the woman to leave, just like she had. Escape into the unknown with the hope that her husband would let her go. Maybe they could disappear together.

She went back to her tea and considered the idea that maybe now was the perfect time to venture out of the flat. She'd been cooped up in here for a couple of days now. If she didn't leave and go outside, would she ever? A shudder went through her at the thought, but she forced the idea to remain, thinking through the benefits of getting outside in the sun and fresh air. She remembered the agent saying there was a park close by. Perhaps she could get to the park and return home straight away. Going out in small increments might be what would work best.

But as soon as she considered the reality of leaving the flat, the sense of being in an unfamiliar town became overwhelming. She was out of place here; this was not her home. But it was all she had.

She paced the room. Yes, she should get outside, at least unlock the door. If she could do that, then that would be a win. Still in yesterday's clothes, she ran a hand through her hair. She walked to the front door and took a deep breath before sliding the chain through the catch, letting it hang against the doorframe. Slowly, she turned the thumb-key and then pushed down on the handle. The click of the door opening set off her heart until all she could hear was the blood pumping in her ears.

She pulled back the door and leaned her head into the corridor. No one was around, but a door closing prompted Freya to dash back into the safety of her flat. She flicked the thumb-key, replaced the chain and stayed there, leaning her head against the door while she waited for her breath to return to its normal pace.

She would not be leaving today.

8

Three days had passed since her attempt at leaving the flat. It had also marked two more occasions where she'd witnessed a fight between Ava and Elliot. Frustratingly, she never saw him strike Ava, but she heard it, the alarming thuds of a physical scuffle and the cries and the worrying silence that always followed.

He would leave, too, after he'd inflicted his damage on her, and Freya would always watch him walk away – only feeling safe once he was out of the building and no longer a threat to anyone. He was another Liam, dangerous and unstable.

Today, showered, hair washed and in fresh clothes, she felt stronger. More able to cope. The day was pleasant and seemed to scream to her that she should use it to take the step out of her cave. She grabbed her phone and stepped into the trainers by the door. This was more than she'd ever done before, and she really believed that she might be doing it this time. She might actually get out the door. She'd managed to do without the diazepam since her last pill too and was thankful that it wasn't seemingly taking hold of her. She resolved to only use it in emergencies.

'You can do this,' she murmured to herself as she turned the lock and released the chain.

She grabbed the keys for the flat that hung from the little hook on the wall and pulled back the door with as much confidence as she could. As she stepped out into the corridor, the floor seemed to wobble beneath her, and she struggled to level out the feeling of light-headedness. Her confidence was a world away from when she'd had her family with her on moving day. Now, she was alone and no longer had the safety net of others around her.

She breathed. She *could* do this.

She pulled the door shut and double-locked it, tucking the keys into her pocket. Gripping her phone in her hand, she walked slowly down the corridor, her breathing fast and uncontrolled. She needed to get it under control. Reaching the top of the stairs, she rested her hand against the wall and took some deep, steadying breaths.

When her vision normalised, she made her way down the stairs and into the large lobby. She could take a break and sit on the large black, leather-look sofa with white piping positioned by the window, next to the large palm plant in a shiny black planter, or she could really go for it and take a walk outside to the park.

She kept going, surprising herself, and walked down the path and past the row of shrubs that she'd only ever stared at since arriving. Not knowing where to go, she turned right and continued, checking over her shoulder intermittently. The feeling she was being watched – something that would probably never leave her – became more intense with each stride. Remembering an article she'd read about looking confident, she tried to look as though she had somewhere to be, that she had a destination and wasn't just wandering around, unsure, and a target for anyone who might want to take advantage of that.

The end of the road was punctuated by a junction.

A man hurriedly strode past her, brushing against her arm and making her stumble. He didn't look back, probably didn't even realise what he'd done, but it was enough to wipe out the small shred of confidence she had left.

She turned and marched back towards her block of flats as tears stung her eyes. Overwhelmed, the noise of cars, horns, buses and the sheer number of people were enough to make her break into a run until she was back at the entrance of the mansion block. She punched in the numbers, then rushed through the door as the buzzer released it. She lingered in the lobby for a moment and took the opportunity to sit on the sofa she'd disregarded earlier and waited for the turmoil inside to settle.

Wanting to feel safe within her own four walls, she stood and went to the stairs, heading up to the two flights to her floor. She rounded the corner of the staircase and hurried up, rushing to turn into the hallway that led her to her door.

Moving quickly, she saw the haze of another person before she collided with them. She clamped her eyes shut, anticipating the impact.

'Hey,' the man said.

She opened her eyes and saw Elliot standing there, as surprised as she felt. She stepped back and looked at him, the man who beat his wife.

'Oh, hello,' he said with a pleasant smile. 'Are you okay?'

'Yes, er, I'm fine...' she stammered as she moved away from him. 'Sorry, I have to go.' She turned and hurried along the corridor and clumsily pulled the key from her pocket, watching as it fell to the floor. She reached down to grab it.

'Are you sure you're okay?' he asked again with a look of concern as he watched from where they had collided.

She eventually got the key into the lock on her door and turned it, pushing it open. 'Yes, I'm fine. Goodbye.'

She slammed the door shut with the expression on his face etched into her mind. What would he think of her after their first meeting and now this? *The lady in flat twelve is a bit of a character,* she imagined him telling the other residents. *Ran right away from me.*

'But that's because you're a monster,' she mumbled as she hung the key on the hook and put the chain across the door. 'And I've met your type before.'

The one opinion she didn't care about was that of a wife-beater.

She went to the bathroom and thoroughly washed her hands and face, needing to get the outside world off her skin, needing to feel clean in her space. She couldn't contaminate the inside with outside-world dirt and even decided to change, putting the clothes she had been wearing into the washing machine for a quick wash.

She grabbed her blanket from her bed and wrapped it around herself to watch TV. She couldn't contemplate eating right now and just needed to lose herself in something other than her life and her feelings.

The room was stuffy. She went to the windows and opened them, letting the warm air refresh the room. The sound of the street was mainly drowned out by the trees absorbing most of the noise, and she enjoyed the quaint tranquillity it offered in such a busy part of London.

Needing to know if Ava was doing okay, she glanced over towards their flat. It looked empty and shut-up. No one home. Or perhaps, as Freya had needed to do, maybe the woman was healing, hiding from everyone until her bruises had faded and her cuts healed.

9

R osie, as promised, arrived to visit Freya. She must have thought that Freya wouldn't notice her glance around the room as she walked in, or the way she casually checked out the kitchen. All things to indicate whether Freya was coping or not.

'I'm fine, you know,' Freya said with a smile. 'I can see what you're doing.'

Rosie muffled a laugh. 'I'm sorry, I just want to know that you're okay.'

'I'm doing really well, actually,' Freya said with a hint of defensiveness.

'I can see that. The place looks really nice.'

'Well, it's clean, and I keep it tidy. Goodness knows I don't have anything else to do.'

'Have you been out yet?' Rosie asked.

'Once. Managed a walk down to the end of the road, but that's it.'

'Where?'

'That way,' Freya said, gesturing towards the right.

'Stopped by the junction where the fitness studio is, had a massive panic attack and then came home.'

'Oh, sweetheart,' Rosie said. 'That bad?'

Freya nodded.

'Well, if you're interested, I found out there's another fitness studio just around the corner that are running some fitness lessons. It's a little closer, and a new course is starting. Perhaps we could do that?'

'I've kept myself alive so far, in pretty dire circumstances. I think I'll be fine.'

'Yes, but this might help you feel more confident. You know, living alone and stuff.'

Freya nodded. 'Maybe.' She saw Rosie's face and sighed. 'Okay, give me the details.'

Relieved, Rosie pulled a piece of paper from her bag. 'It's all here, look. Next Tuesday at seven in the evening.'

'I don't know,' Freya murmured. 'I mean, I'll have to go out at night. I'm not sure I can do that.'

'I'll be with you. I think it will do you the world of good, and I need to get fit again.' Rosie patted her stomach. 'Getting a little too comfortable.'

'You're gorgeous,' Freya scoffed. 'I'll think about it.'

Rosie pecked a kiss on her sister's cheek. 'That's all I ask.'

The open windows did nothing to hide the voices raised in argument from outside.

'What's that all about?' Rosie asked, looking out the window.

'My neighbours,' Freya said. 'Elliot and Ava. He's knocking her about.'

'What?'

'You know, like Liam. Using his fists on her.'

'Yes, I get the gist,' Rosie said. 'Have you seen it?'

'No, not exactly. I haven't met her yet, and I've only seen them scuffle, but I know what it leads to. He always leaves when he's done. She's left alone to pick up the pieces.'

'You don't know that.'

'Don't you think that I know how these things work?' Freya spat. 'I've had it happen to me so many times I've lost count.'

'Whoa, whoa, it wasn't a criticism. I know what you've been through. I know it's been hell for you, but take a minute to think about this. You haven't actually seen him be violent towards her.'

Freya shook her head.

'And have you seen her afterwards, you know, with bruises or injuries?' Rosie asked.

'No.'

'Well, maybe you might want to consider this a little more,' Rosie warned. 'I mean, these are your neighbours.'

'I'm not going to rush into anything,' Freya replied. 'But maybe in some weird way, I found this place and found them so I could help them.'

Rosie frowned. 'Freya—'

'Yes, I know that sounds crazy, but maybe fate is a thing; maybe I'm meant to be here.'

'Maybe.'

Freya glanced up and saw the elderly gentleman who lived above Ava and Elliot appear at his window, an anxious expression on his face as he lingered, rubbing his chin with his fingers, seemingly listening to what was unfolding below.

'Look at him,' Freya burst out. 'He's checking them out too.'

'Freya, he could be doing anything.'

'No, he looks like he's heard it all before. I'm telling you, he knows something is not right.' She'd never seen him do this before, but she was convinced he was as concerned as she was.

'Look, what about the police?' Rosie asked.

'Not an option. Not yet anyway. I can't make myself known to the police. It's too risky, especially with Liam looking for me. He probably has his little minions out looking for me as we speak.'

Rosie reached out and held Freya's hands. 'Calm down, sis. Do you really think he'll have people on it?'

'I wouldn't put anything past that man,' Freya said. 'I've left him. He'll be angry about that and will not let it go until he's found me.' Freya broke the contact she had with Rosie and sat down on the sofa. 'He'll stop at nothing. I've defied him, you see.' She rubbed her arms, feeling the chill in the air. 'He's out there, waiting. I know it.'

Rosie sat with her sister and wrapped her arm around Freya's shoulder. 'I believe you. You know the man more than me, and you endured things I couldn't even imagine. I understand your fear.' She paused for a moment. 'And you really think this man is being violent to his wife?'

'I really do.'

'Well, there are ways around this kind of thing. You could call the police anonymously, or I could.'

Freya nodded but felt no ease at Rosie's suggestion. Something about Liam made her feel that even calling anonymously, he'd know, and he'd find her, and she'd be trapped with him again.

Rosie stood up and went to the window. 'Is that him?' she asked, pointing.

Freya strode to the window. 'Yes, that's him.'

They both watched as Elliot stood looking out the

kitchen window, a cup in his hand as he held his phone to his ear, engaged in conversation. He laughed, continued to chat for a little while longer and then hung up the phone. Seconds later, Ava came into view, her hair covering most of her face, but she went to him and wrapped her arms around him. When he reciprocated and placed his lips on hers to kiss her deeply, Freya and Rosie both looked at each other, their brows raised.

'I see what you mean,' Rosie murmured as they turned their attention back to the couple. 'That is definitely a man with something to hide.'

Freya slapped her sister's arm. 'No, this is what they do. They argue and make up. Really. We can't see her face. She could be hiding all sorts of bruising. She could be hugging him to placate him. You don't know. You really don't.'

Rosie turned her attention to Freya, a look of concern on her face. 'You know you can talk to me. You've been through so much, and things have moved very quickly since you've been here,' she said gently. 'Could it be that perhaps what's happened to you has kind of tinted your view of others?'

'No.'

'I mean, people fight,' Rosie continued. 'It happens, and sometimes it can be spiteful, bitter, and might be perceived as being violent.'

'What about the cries, the sounds of violence?'

'But you haven't *seen* that, have you?'

'No,' Freya said, doubting herself. 'But I just feel something about them. Something wrong.'

'Keep an eye on it, then, but be careful. You don't want to get yourself into something either. Poking around in someone's business could cause you more trouble. You need to

keep yourself safe, too, however much you might want to
help. Okay?'

'Okay,' Freya muttered angrily.

ROSIE KEPT to her word and arrived at six thirty to collect
Freya for the fitness class. She took her by the arm and led
her into the room – a boxing studio, punchbags dotting the
edges of the room, suspended from the ceiling. Mats sat
stacked against the wall in the corner, and the distinct smell
of sweat hung in the air.

'Come on, it'll be fun,' Rosie said, laughing. 'You can get
all that silent aggression out of your system.' She pointed to
one of the punchbags. 'Think of that as Liam and knock it
senseless.'

The room was stuffy too, and Freya was keen to leave, but
she smiled as she crossed the room with Rosie and noted the
other women arriving. 'I'm worried if I do that, I'll never
stop.'

Rosie chuckled. 'True, true, but you'll feel a million
dollars once you've done it.'

'Maybe.'

Rosie shrugged off the backpack from her shoulders and
hung it on one of the rows of pegs on the wall in the corner
of the room, with the other bags and jackets.

Everyone was in sports gear, and Freya felt exposed
dressed in one of Rosie's outfits. A black sleeveless vest
top and multicoloured leggings that hugged her legs.
She'd not worn such tight-fitting clothes in a long time, as
Liam never wanted her body on show to anyone but
himself. Not that she dressed like a nun, but each outfit

had to be scrutinised by him before they could start the day.

The trainers she wore were comfortable though, and Freya considered getting herself a pair, when she had the money, of course.

A tall, muscular man strode into the room, holding a large gym bag, which had a water bottle clipped to the side. 'Good evening, ladies,' he said in a friendly, confident tone.

The women all chimed their greetings, including Rosie, but Freya remained silent, still uncomfortable being here.

'Okay, so let's get a mat each, and we'll get started.' He discarded his bag and grabbed the water bottle, bringing it with him as he strode over to Rosie and Freya. 'Hi, ladies, and welcome to the class. So which one of you is Rosie?'

'That would be me,' Rosie replied with a smile.

'And that means you're Freya, right?' he said, shooting her a friendly smile.

'Yes, that's me,' Freya said, not feeling at all comfortable with her real name being used. She'd have to discuss that with Rosie later.

'So, I'm Jake, and today we'll be going through the basics – a circuit session, some cardio, and some stretching. Are there any medical conditions I need to be aware of?'

They both shook their heads.

'Anything you'd like to ask?'

Again, both shook their heads.

'Great, well, let's get started, and if you have any concerns during the sessions, just give me a shout.'

Rosie raised a brow as he walked away and smiled at Freya before blowing out a sigh.

'Stop it,' she murmured, unable to stop herself from smiling too.

He was young and handsome and perfect for the job he did. His vest top hung loosely and barely covered his firm and muscular body, revealing the many tattoos across his chest and down his arms. He had a nice smile, and his close-cropped fair hair suited his skin tone.

Freya turned away when she realised she'd been staring and went to get a mat for herself and Rosie.

They started out with a warm-up, which was enough to leave Freya breathless, but she did as best she could with the instructions. She engaged in the class and did all of the sets requested, ignoring the sweat and the way her face flushed with rosy heat. He watched all the ladies as they worked, and kept a particular eye on herself and Rosie.

They spent time working in pairs for the stretching techniques, and Freya and Rosie had fun laughing at the absurdity of positions they managed to get themselves into.

At the end of the session, the other ladies drifted away until it was just Rosie and Freya left.

'Thanks, er, sorry, what's your name again?' Rosie asked.

'Jake,' he replied as he wiped a towel over his face. 'Jake Evans.'

'Well, thanks, Jake. It was fun.' Rosie smiled and glanced at Freya.

Freya ignored her sister and mumbled her thanks before grabbing Rosie's arm and turning her away to leave.

'Don't even go there,' Freya warned once they were out of the room and earshot. 'Do you think that romance is something I'm looking for right now?'

Rosie frowned. 'No, of course not. I'm sorry. He's just gorgeous, and I thought he might be a little distraction we, or rather you, could admire from afar. No harm in looking.'

'The only distraction I want right now is what TV show

I'm watching or podcast I'm listening to with the meal I'm eating.'

'Fair point,' Rosie replied. 'But you won't always feel like that, and, well, this is a good way to get you "out there".'

'I don't want to be anywhere but my little flat, thank you.' Freya linked her arm in Rosie's. As they walked down the street, she monitored their surroundings with periodic glances over her shoulder.

'You don't need to do that,' Rosie said kindly. 'If he has the nerve to show up here, I'll give him a piece of my mind.'

It was sweet that Rosie thought she could handle someone like Liam, so she chose not to disagree, instead pulling her closer to lean her head on her shoulder. 'Thanks, sis.'

'No problem. Now what are you going to do when I leave?'

'I'm going to take a long, hot shower, and then I'm going to watch TV, eat something and sleep for a week.'

'Has this taken it out of you?'

'For sure. I haven't done so much in a long time. But I definitely need the exercise.'

'Well, I'm glad we went, then.'

Freya locked and chained the door when Rosie left, and treated herself to that hot shower. Humid air from the heat of the day filled the flat, so she decided that tonight she'd be brave and leave the curtains and windows open to let in the cool night air.

Dressed in her pyjamas, she made eggs on toast and settled on her sofa and switched on the TV. Voices drifted through the air, angry, argumentative voices. Knowing who it would be, she went to the window and listened.

The man's voice was louder – Elliot's – and she could

hear Ava's although only intermittently. Sure enough, they were locked in an argument again, and this time he held her shoulders as he shouted in her face.

The woman laughed, right at him, and Freya held her breath, ready for the fist that would surely follow. If she'd ever done that with Liam, he would have knocked her into another dimension for being so bold. Ava wiggled out of his hold and went to walk away, but seemingly furious, Elliot grabbed her arm and pulled her back. She yanked herself free and strode away, and that was when they disappeared from view again. Then, silence.

She watched and waited for him to leave, to disappear into the night, as he had done so many times before, but he didn't appear. Something about this bothered Freya. She couldn't put her finger on why it bothered her, but something was different this time. She turned and noticed the lights were out, but the windows were still open.

She stepped back, anxious about what to do next. Should she go to them? Knock on the door? A groan of frustration slipped from her lips. Her inability to make a decision annoyed her. She looked down as she wrung her hands together and looked out the window again. Nothing had changed. Lights off and windows open. She should do something. Yes.

She slipped on her jeans over her pale blue pyjama bottoms and went to her front door. Lifting the chain, she hesitated and lingered there for a moment. With a breath she pulled open the door and looked out. They were on the same floor, so all it would take was to walk along the long corridor to the other side of the building and knock on their door. She could do that. Maybe knock, maybe call out, she wasn't sure, but she couldn't let indecision fester in her body any longer.

She grabbed the keys and shut the door. Slowly, but with purpose she took one step in front of the other. If one of the other residents chose to walk out their door right now, they'd be met with this strange woman wandering down the corridor at a snail's pace, dressed in jeans and a T-shirt that was obviously sleepwear by the 'dreamtime' wording and the series of Zs that trailed beneath. If they saw her, she would forever been known as the crazy lady, but right now that was the least of her concerns.

She hesitated, momentarily paralysed with fear and indecision. What the hell was she doing? She wasn't cut out for this. Jesus, she was the least qualified to help in this situation, and if she was witness to any more violence, she'd probably have a PTSD episode right on their doorstep, but something inside encouraged her on, and she approached the doorway with caution.

She held up a balled fist to knock on the door and heard their muffled voices through the door – whispers, crying. Ava's tears, her sadness. She heard her whisper how she was sorry, and Freya felt the rage bloom inside her. She had often said the same. Sorry for angering him, sorry for burning the dinner or spilling the drinks. Always sorry. Always her fault. The man said nothing. He'd probably done enough.

The clank of the lift as it kicked into action snapped Freya back to reality, and she ran, darting back along the corridor to unlock her door and disappear inside. Laughter carried along the corridor outside to fade away on a closed door.

Freya held the phone in her hand and considered that now was the time to call the police, whatever the outcome. It would not help her cause, she knew the danger she'd be in, but maybe an anonymous message would be enough. Perhaps an online form? She wasn't sure what to do.

As if wanting to force a reaction, the phone rang, buzzing in her hand. Freya jumped and let out a strangled cry. But it was only Rosie. She answered as her heart pounded and her stomach churned.

'Rosie, what's—'

'Freya, listen to me,' Rosie snapped. 'Are you alone?'

'Of course, why?'

'It's Liam. He's just paid us a visit.'

'What?'

'Yes, just now. Ben saw him off, but you need to know that he's here in the area.'

'Oh God.' Freya gasped as she switched off the lights in her flat. Under the cover of darkness, she crouched low to drag the curtains together and ran to the sofa.

'Are you locked in?' Rosie asked. 'Ben wanted to come over, but I said that it's too dangerous. Liam could be waiting out there for one of us to do just that so he can follow.'

'Yes, of course, good plan,' Freya said breathlessly. 'I'm locked in. He won't be able to get in the main entrance. At least I hope not.'

'But listen to me,' Rosie said. 'Something's off about him. He was too calm, concerned for you. It was weird. I was expecting him to throw threats around and be angry, demanding, but there was nothing like that. He was *nice*. He's up to something, I feel it.'

'Doesn't surprise me,' Freya said, one ear listening for any noise outside her door, as if he explicitly knew where she was hiding and was already here. 'I had all the hearts and flowers after he'd beaten me black and blue. How sorry he was. How he'd change. All of it. He's probably putting on the same performance for you too.'

'Probably,' Rosie agreed, 'but it only makes me suspicious.'

'Of course it does. He's a corrupt little soul and capable of anything.'

'I saw a side of him that actually frightened me. The calmness hid something – something behind his eyes. Something cold.'

'Tell me about it,' Freya said.

'I just can't believe how long you had to put up with that. It must have been terrifying. I'm so sorry I didn't help sooner.'

'Nope, don't go blaming yourself,' Freya soothed. 'I could have come to you sooner. I could have told you the truth of what was really happening. How bad it had got, but I was ashamed. I felt bad for wanting to believe that he would change. For giving him all the second chances. So I kept quiet.'

'Oh, Freya,' Rosie gasped.

'It's hard knowing that someone who's supposed to love you could cause so much pain.'

'I'm so sorry.'

'You have nothing to be sorry for.'

'But I'm your sister. I should have protected you.'

'What could you have done? He would have hurt you too if you'd got involved, and I couldn't let that happen. I'd got myself into that mess, but you? You had nothing to do with it, and I couldn't live with myself if anything happened to you or Ben.'

'Well, I'm here now, and I will do everything I can to protect you, okay? Ben feels the same; he's sitting next to me and agreeing. We're here for you. Mum and Dad too, if you let them in.'

'I will, but it's difficult.'

'They care, but they don't do emotions very well; we both know that.'

'Yes, I know, and I know that they love us in their own way. Maybe I'll discuss it with them. When this is all over.' She rose from the seat, agitated. 'Damn it, I knew this was too good to be true. I knew he'd find me.'

'He was bound to come here at some point, and I guess it's a good thing that he has, because it shows that, actually, you're not as easy to find as you think you are.'

Freya sighed. 'Maybe, but you say he's too calm. I don't like calm. It hides something dangerous. He's up to something, I know it.' Feeling safe enough to switch on a light now that the curtains were closed and she was hidden from view, she paced the floor. 'He'll have someone watching your place if he's not there himself and will probably do that for a couple of days yet.'

'I'll keep a lookout for anyone suspicious,' Rosie said.

'I'll do the same,' Freya replied, her mind racing with what she should do next as she wished Rosie goodnight and hung up the call.

Freya sat in silence, her phone in her lap. She couldn't even allow noise from the TV and had muted it, leaving the images to play out quietly. She listened to every creak and knock in the old building, fearful of making a noise that would reveal her hiding spot, exposing herself to the enemy.

Her eyes fluttered, and her head lolled slightly, her body and mind exhausted from the earlier exercise and overdose of adrenaline this evening's discovery had released. She fought the sleep her body craved, her senses alert to anything that could indicate his arrival.

MUFFLED footfalls sounded outside her door. She froze, listening for him, for his voice singing her name, begging her to let him in. She wanted to cry or scream, but she was mute, unable to do anything except stare at the door, her body tense and her hands clammy. Frantic, she considered what she could use as a weapon but remembered that these could, and would, be used against her. The knife that sat in her drawer was useless to her, more likely to pierce her body than protect her from him.

She waited for what felt like days, but no one knocked, and no one spoke. She could have imagined it, the fear in her mind playing nasty games, but whoever or whatever was out there did not harm her this time.

10

H aving spent a week hiding, too scared to go outside, Freya finally felt able to leave her flat. Feeling trapped in the small space, she needed to get out, breathe different air and feel part of the world again. She'd created a self-imposed jail for herself, and it was time to break free.

Dressed in one of her sister's borrowed dresses, a white cotton shift with a chain of embroidered flowers running along the hem, she decided that she'd wander up the high street, familiarise herself with the place she now called home, and do a little window shopping while she was at it. Clothes that she could buy some day when she had money of her own. Rosie and Ben had been so kind to her, paying her rent and food. She would be eternally grateful for all they were doing for her, but she needed to get out there again, back into the working world.

Liam had wasted no time in suggesting that she give up her job when they moved into the small two-bedroomed flat they'd rented in London before his grandmother passed away and bestowed him the house in Southampton, taking her further away from all her family and friends. She'd laughed at him when he'd said it as they ate their red Thai curry takeaway at the end of moving day from the dishes carefully laid out on top of unopened packing boxes. They'd been sat in the middle of the disorganised clutter of their new living room, and she'd thought he was joking.

But he was not joking, far from it. His wife-to-be would not be part of the working world. He wanted her at his beck and call, no questions asked, and at first the sentiment made her feel special, wanted, *needed*. She thrived on that, enjoying how it felt to make a difference in someone's life, playing the role of a stay-at-home – cooking and cleaning, weekly visits to her favourite shops to buy furnishings from the endless supply of money he'd happily provided; cute little ornaments to prints in frames for the walls, a new rug or a cushion or two – making a home for them both. She never once considered that it was an act of control over a person, or that his intentions were anything other than loving.

But that was before the violence began. In the weeks after her wedding, the reality of her marriage was soon reduced to anger and hard fists, resulting in a plethora of injuries that required hiding herself away while she healed. And when he dislocated her shoulder, she understood that he never joked about anything concerning her as she cried out in a mix of shock, horror and pain at what her new husband had done to her. Returning from their honeymoon in Malaysia, the discovery of his capacity for violence shattered the last of her idyllic memories of their marriage in the blink of an eye. Worse to come was the shock of knowing that he only grudgingly took her to the hospital when it was clear the injury wouldn't heal on its own, her arm left hanging in an agonising position that made it impossible for her to move; otherwise he would have left her to deal with it herself. She'd given up crying after the numerous doors she'd 'walked into', the copious amounts of burns to her skin, either from hot appliances or liquid, in the days, weeks and months that followed.

And later, the constant push-and-pull in their relationship – her threats to leave and his promises to change – meant she knew she had no capacity for a full-time career that involved facing customers every day.

So it meant she left the job she loved. A restaurant manager in a Grade II–listed red-brick eighteenth-century hotel, just inside the M25. Built on a site once home to Henry VIII with an imposing stone triple-arch entrance, the hotel lay hidden in the Surrey countryside, within well-manicured grounds and an impressive lake. The stylish hotel with a family feel had been her place of work for six years before she met Liam. She never thought she'd leave. Even in her darkest moments she only really considered her absence a temporary one, that Liam would actually change and relent, or that she would leave him instead, taking herself back into her career with no permanent damage, to herself or her career. But that was five years and countless numbers of beatings ago, and she'd since forgotten most of what she'd learned. That, and the continual upgrade of technology, meant she would take longer than most to retrain.

Having sat in the lobby of her new building for a minute or two, using the area as her safety zone, her bridge from the outside world to the inside, she needed to move, to take the next steps. She breathed. She could do this. Yes, she could. Standing, she strode towards the entrance, pulled open the door and stepped out.

She told herself that Liam wouldn't be around still, that he couldn't be, knowing how much his work ate into his time, and that it would have dragged him back to Hampshire long ago, but it did nothing to relieve her discomfort at feeling so exposed and vulnerable. She continued along the pavement, undeterred, but when she passed a shoe repair shop that had a pedestal of baseball-style caps and hanging lanyards outside on the pavement, she grabbed a hat, a black one, and went inside to pay.

With the cap pulled down enough to shield her face, but not so much to make her look conspicuous or odd, she continued on, feeling a little more secure. She would not let him continue dictating what she did with her life and reasoned that, yes, he had come here, but with the intention of speaking with Rosie. He would not have necessarily come to the conclusion that Freya had set up home just around the corner from her sister, and that Rosie and Ben had stayed away the moment he was on the scene.

But he is a detective, she thought as her confidence took a sudden nosedive that made her legs wobble. *That's what he does. He investigates the unknown until he has his answer.*

She glanced over her shoulder and kept her pace while she considered the implications. She reasoned that if he was here now, he'd waste no time making his presence known.

After a few moments of convincing herself of this fact, she breathed a little easier and found comfort within her place in the crowd – hidden. She wandered past a small clothing shop and doubled back to check out the mid-length blue striped linen dress on the mannequin in the window, little wooden buttons in dots down the front. Fifty percent off and she was drawn to it. She wanted to go inside and try it on, but she didn't have the money, so what would be the point? Pensively, she stared at it, checking out the rows of clothes hanging from chrome brackets in the shop, the mirrored walls and polished wooden floors, and the music emanating out before she continued on. Maybe one day.

The aroma of coffee pulled her along the high street until she saw a board on the pavement outside a nice-looking café with a striped awning protecting customers from the midday sun. She had enough money in her purse to grab a coffee and headed for the door. As she pushed it open, she glanced at the paper sign taped to the window that gave details for a part-time worker – twenty-five hours per week.

She dismissed it as quickly as the little bell above the door finished its welcoming chime, but once she picked up on the warm atmosphere and chilled-out music, she instantly changed her mind.

She walked towards the counter and looked up at the large chalkboard that decoratively listed all of the variations of coffee, other hot drinks, smoothies and cold drinks that were on offer.

'Hi, what can I get you?' the woman behind the counter said pleasantly as she wiped down the coffee machine with a blue cloth.

She was tall and dressed in black trousers and a white T-shirt that had a small logo of the café on the upper left-hand side. Her lilac-coloured hair was cut short and styled to hang over half of her face. The woman had a confident air about her that told Freya she was the owner of the place.

'I'd love a latte, please.'

'No problem,' the woman said as she began to prepare the coffee. 'Have in or takeaway?'

'I'll have it here, thanks. That window seat looks great.'

The woman nodded. 'It is,' she replied as she handed the mug to Freya. 'Best seat in the house.'

Freya paid and went to the table by the window. Whilst it was a lovely spot, the sunlight warming whoever sat there, she suddenly felt too exposed. Too visible. Instead, she moved to the table in the corner. The vantage point from where she sat provided just as good a view out the window, giving her the opportunity to still people-watch. Something she hadn't done for such a long time. As she sat there watching strangers pass by, all with their own agendas and lives, she felt the little bubble of excitement in her stomach at how good it felt to be out in the world again and no longer trapped in a marriage and a life that never felt like hers.

An old lady wearing a long raincoat, even in this summer heat, pushed open the door and negotiated a wheeled shopping cart through the door. She was followed by a woman who pushed a swanky pram. Casually dressed, she looked immaculate, her blonde hair scooped up into a messy bun that looked as if she'd just stepped out of the hairdresser's, all the honey and gold strands swirling on top of her head and glinting in the light, and she wore cut-off denim shorts and a cute off-the-shoulder top. Effortlessly unfussy. She could have come straight from an Instagram shoot; she looked so amazing. The baby was perfect too, from what Freya could see. Sitting in a back-facing chair, and able to look directly at her mother, she looked angelic with her blonde curls hitting her honey-coloured skin. Not a sound escaped from her rosebud lips, and she seemed happy to watch everyone watching her.

Freya looked down at herself, and although her dress was pretty and fit her well, she felt inadequate next to someone so magnetic. Her hair needed cutting, she could definitely use a facial, and as always in situations like this, her body felt as if it were exposing all of the bruises and injuries Liam had given her over the years, displayed on her skin for all to see.

The ladies both requested their takeaway orders, and the woman behind the counter worked efficiently with a friendly smile for everyone, including the young girl, whom she handed some frothy milk in a takeaway espresso cup after she'd got the okay from the mum. A babyccino, Freya thought she heard them say.

The little girl was delighted and held it carefully in her chubby little fingers, and the two women smiled when they saw the milky moustache on her lip.

Freya liked it here.

When Freya had finished her coffee, she went to the counter. 'I wondered, is the part-time position filled?'

'No.' The woman sighed. 'Lots of applications but no one I really liked. Why? Are you interested?'

'Maybe,' Freya said. 'Although I haven't worked in a while.'

The woman stopped what she was doing and dried her hands on her apron. 'What's your background?'

'Er, well, I was in hospitality,' she stammered, nerves making her stumble over her words. 'A hotel, but I've been out of the game for around five years.' She took a breath and licked her dry lips, trying to turn this around. 'I've just moved to the area, and I need something local.'

Freya saw the expression on the woman's face. Not hopeful.

'Why don't you drop in a copy of your CV, and I can have a little think about it.'

The way the woman began tidying and wiping down the

countertops indicated that she'd perhaps already made her decision, but Freya asked for her contact email anyway.

Freya headed home. She would be going to another self-defence session with Rosie later, and she wanted to ensure she ate in good time before the exercise.

Rosie badgered her to keep it going and informed her what time she'd be round to collect Freya. Freya didn't mind; she looked forward to it. It felt good to release the tension in her body, and Jake and the other women were friendly and welcoming, making it an easy way to spend an evening.

———

Rosie's text saying she was outside the back of the building and hidden from the main street prompted Freya to head down to meet her.

Freya jogged down the corridor and headed towards the back staircase, the fire exit route for the building, and noticed Ava wandering towards her. She had no visible injuries, her hair was pulled up into a neat bun, and she wore a mustard-coloured cotton top and navy-blue shorts that looked clean and pressed, but her slow movements and the purple shadows under her eyes emphasised her exhaustion. Freya understood everything, that she'd be sapped of energy just keeping things together, to heal and appear normal, as if nothing were wrong. One of the hardest acts to do.

Freya blurted out her greeting before she had time to change her mind, and it startled them both. The woman looked at her, confused.

'Sorry, I didn't mean to scare you,' Freya said. 'Just thought I'd say hello. I've recently moved in here.'

'How nice for you,' Ava said blankly as she continued with her route. 'I wonder how long you'll stay. It's a strange place full of strange people.'

There was no warmth in her voice, and what she said sounded oddly threatening, but Freya didn't mind. She knew the maelstrom that would be raging inside the poor woman. She also knew the need to watch the clock and keep moving in order to return home and not engage with anyone. More control imposed on her.

'I'm Freya, by the way, and definitely not strange,' Freya replied as lightly as she could, but Ava had already disappeared around the corner and probably wouldn't have heard.

'Let's go,' Rosie said as Freya pushed open the door and walked out into the small courtyard area at the back of the building.

'I'm coming,' Freya replied as she pulled the rucksack that contained everything she needed for the class – water bottle, small towel and a packet of glucose sweets – over her shoulder. 'You're early tonight, and why meet me here?'

'Just quicker, that's all,' Rosie said, then pointed to the black cap. 'What's this all about?'

'My security blanket,' Freya replied. 'You ready?'

Rosie nodded, and at her encouragement, they ran the short distance to the venue.

Freya shot plenty of side-eye to her sister when they were the first to arrive.

'Okay,' Rosie conceded. 'It's early, and we didn't need to rush.'

Freya frowned. 'Why the hurry, then?' she asked, suspicious now.

'It's nothing. Honestly.'

'Well, now you have to tell me, or I'm going to think the worst.'

Rosie sighed. 'Look, don't get uptight, but I wanted to get here and away from the flat as quickly as possible. I've had another call from Liam.'

'You're joking,' Freya said.

'Wish I were.'

'I convinced myself earlier that he'd be back in Hampshire by now.'

'Yes, I think he might be, but I still have the feeling he knows that you'd be here with me, and it's making me feel uneasy. Ben wanted to come along tonight, but he knew that might completely spook you.'

Freya sat down. Any conversation that involved Liam still zapped the energy from her body. It angered her. She rested her head in her hand. 'Maybe I should meet him. I should tell him it's over and that he's not to contact me. At least draw a line in the sand.'

'Do you think that would work?' Rosie asked as she joined Freya and sat.

'I don't know. No, probably not.' She sighed. 'Maybe if you and Ben were with me? That might work.'

Rosie sat down next to Freya. 'He may have calmed down and accepted things now. Perhaps having that conversation will give you both closure of some sort.'

'I don't trust that he won't try every trick in the book before he accepts I no longer want to be with him.'

'It's worth a shot. Think about it, and we'll be there, if that's what you want.'

Jake strode into the room, his face lighting up when he saw them both. 'Evening, ladies,' he said through his smile. 'Keen tonight.'

Freya smiled. 'Got to keep those black clouds away.'

'Damn right,' he replied. 'Like the hat, by the way. Suits you.'

Freya instinctively pulled it off and tucked it in her bag, not comfortable with the compliment.

Undeterred, he seemed happy to chat with them while he prepped for the class and they waited for the others to arrive.

Freya couldn't help but notice his physique. He kept himself extremely fit. Somewhere, deep within her, a long-forgotten part of her found him pleasant to look at. Attractive. To admire a man again, especially one as appealing as he was, instead of cowering from a man about to strike, was strangely agreeable. It gave her hope for her future. The toxic, sticky glue that bound herself to Liam, against her will, seemed to be losing its strength. She felt her soul breathe, believing that freedom from him and his violence might yet happen for her, finally.

Her face flushed, and her eyes darted from the view when he caught her staring, but instead of bursting into laughter, finding hilarity that someone like her would be attractive to someone like him, his smile was gentle, kind, as if he was genuinely happy that she'd done what she'd done. Feeling suddenly too hot, she took a step back.

'Is there a window we could open?' she asked, realising too late that the question was only compounding the situation, making it obvious that she was affected by what had happened when she'd only intended on changing the conversation.

Jake turned and looked around. 'Yeah, I think there's some over there that I could crank open. I'll go and take a look.'

He crossed the room as Rosie looked at Freya, a glint in her eye. 'Bloody hell, what was that?'

Freya gently swatted Rosie's arm. 'Shut up; it was nothing. I don't even know. I was just... I don't know. What? Just stop it.'

Rosie shrugged. 'I'm not doing anything.'

'Good, because I'm ending this conversation right now.'

'Okay.'

'What is that supposed to mean?'

'Nothing!' Rosie said, laughing. 'Just chill out; he's coming back.'

Freya felt her face flush as he approached again, so she turned away and crouched down to pull the water bottle from her bag. She didn't need this. She didn't need, or want, any misunderstandings in her life right now. Yes, he was attractive, and she'd been caught peeping, but that was as far as it would go. She was content with her new flat and her hard-fought peace that had been absent in her life for so long.

She wasn't going to jeopardise any of that. It was too precious.

THE LESSON WENT WELL, and Freya enjoyed the exercise and the release of endorphins in her body, but she held back when he focused his attention on her, and shoved Rosie forwards whenever he asked for a volunteer.

He actually looked disappointed when Rosie stepped forward, clearly wanting Freya instead, but she told herself that he didn't know her. If he did, he wouldn't be so interested. A broken, unsuccessful woman approaching her mid-thirties with nothing to show for her life except the mental and physical scars that haunted her every day, living off the charity of her sister for food and lodgings. No, once he knew the real Freya, he'd run a mile, and she couldn't blame him. Who would want someone so in need, so damaged, and with enough baggage to sink a ship? It was for the best if she knocked this on the head right now before she made a fool of herself.

The session ended with Jake informing them all that he had to move the next session to the Monday rather than the Tuesday due to a double booking, and although she was polite to him and took the time to note the amendment to the date in her phone calendar, she only kept it to the bare minimum in the conversation. He looked a little confused but kept his composure. She only noticed him watching them leave when she turned to check she had everything she'd come with.

'What's going on?' Rosie asked as they walked out into the late summer air. 'He was nice. There's nothing wrong with talking with someone. He's not going to bite.'

'Awkward turn of phrase,' Freya said, as a scar the shape of Liam's upper jaw hidden in her hairline – a bite given to her purportedly in the heat of passion, but really a mark of ownership and dominance – began to twinge.

Rosie looked at her, confused.

'Doesn't matter,' she replied quickly. 'I know there's probably no harm, but it's too soon. I have to get my shit together first before I can even contemplate anything like that. Jesus, I haven't even got a job.'

'Don't worry about that, me and Ben are happy to support you.'

Freya linked her arm in Rosie's. 'I know, and I thank you

sincerely for it, but I need to find a job. I need to earn money. I can't be rattling around that flat all day, however tiny it may be. I need to be busy, and I need to think about what I'll do about Liam.'

'Well, I agree that it's a good idea to be busy. A job would be good for you, but take things at your own pace. You need to remember where you've come from. You need to heal.'

A car horn startled them both, and although they had a little laugh at their joint reaction, they still walked a little quicker to Freya's flat.

'Are you going to be okay?' Rosie asked when they reached the rear of the building.

'I'm going to be fine,' Freya said, 'but thanks for making me do this. I feel good. What about you? Is Ben coming to walk you home?'

'Yeah, he's on his way.' Rosie pointed at Freya, suddenly remembering. 'Oh, and you're all good for Sunday, yes? Dinner at mine with Mum and Dad?'

'Wouldn't miss it,' Freya said. 'Let's hope we're not interrupted by any uninvited guests.'

'Don't worry, we'll chase him away if he dares to darken my doorstep.' Rosie hugged Freya hard. 'Call me later if you need anything, okay?'

'I will. And thank you.'

'For what?'

Freya smiled. 'For everything.'

11

After a plentiful Sunday lunch at Rosie's of roast beef, roasted potatoes, vegetables, Yorkshire puddings, all washed down with a deliciously mellow red that Ben had chosen, the whole family trudged themselves and their overly full bellies out into the garden to sit and enjoy the late afternoon sun.

Her mother fussed and tidied around them as they chatted and reminisced over family events from the past.

'She's getting the broom,' her dad said as he watched his wife venture back into the kitchen and pull a broom from the tall cupboard at the end of the counter that housed all of the household cleaning items.

'Not the broom,' Rosie said in mock horror. 'There'll be no stopping her now.'

Her dad stood and went to the kitchen, where he gently prised the broom from her mum's grasp. 'Why don't you take the weight off for a moment. The floor is fine.'

Her mum stopped and smiled. The lack of resistance she put up at the idea, and the speed at which she discarded the broom, proved to them all just how much she wanted to relax and join them too.

By the time the sun rays had fallen behind the large oak tree at the bottom of Rosie's garden, her dad checked his watch and started making noises about needing to beat the traffic if they were to get home before nightfall.

Freya waved them off and watched as her dad negotiated his old silver BMW up the residential street. 'They don't make them like this anymore,' she remembered him saying fastidiously when asked if he'd ever sell it. 'Built like tanks, these babies.' He crawled along in the centre of the road, past the parked cars that lined the street, and disappeared around the corner.

Her mind wandered back to the business of her rebuilding her life, and she thought about the job at the café. She'd been mulling it over for the last couple of days, deciding if it was right for her, and although it was far from where she'd come from, she considered it might be the perfect place for her to begin her career again.

Still full of food, wine and dessert, the three of them settled in front of the TV together. Rosie had offered Freya the sofa for the night, to which Freya had wasted no time in accepting. She was coming to love her new home, but there was nothing quite like being with people. Rosie and Ben cuddled at one end, and Freya settled at the other, her legs tucked underneath her, and her head resting against the cushions. She closed her eyes, enjoying the moment of peace.

Sitting in the coffee shop, having opted for one of the tables in the window, she laughed at something funny Jake was telling her, his hair shining in the sun and a jovial glint in his eye. She twisted her coffee cup against the saucer as she listened to his stories that made her clasp her sides with laughter, her cheeks wet with tears. His gaze warmed her as it lingered on hers, and it triggered a sense of belonging in his company. He continued with the funny stories until she was begging him to stop, her stomach aching and sore.

But he wouldn't let up, and everything became hazy as the sun that had shone through the window pleasantly enough soon became too bright, hurting her eyes and making her squint. She looked at Jake as he laughed through his conversation, seemingly unaware of the blinding light that had faded and whitened everything in view. He laughed and laughed and threw his head back in an odd maniacal way, as if hysterical. He laughed as he paled into the sunshine too, his features disappearing into the light.

When the sun lost its intensity and she could see again, there was no more Jake, only Liam, and he too, was smiling. Laughing at something funny until he looked straight at her and stopped, his face settling into bitterness, disappointment and then rage. He reached out and grabbed her arm, his lip curling to snarl something she struggled to make out. His fingers bit into her skin, marking it no doubt, and she squirmed to release herself, without success.

He dragged her arm towards himself, pulling her into the table. 'You're never leaving me again; do you understand?' he said as he released his grip on her and pushed her away. She tumbled out of her seat and onto the floor.

The woman behind the counter, normally so pleasant, began to laugh too as Liam rose from his seat and took a step towards her to reach down and grab her hands.

'Time to go home, Freya,' he said, his voice thick with malice. 'Time to go back to where you belong.'

The laughter was loud and filled her head until she

could no longer breathe. She began to thrash as he pulled her to her feet and clutched her close to his body.

'Freya. Freya. Wake up.'

She jolted and snapped open her eyes, her body clammy with sweat and her heart racing.

Rosie smoothed Freya's hair as she sat perched on the cushion closest to Freya, and Ben stood behind her, staring, his brow furrowed.

'You're all right,' Rosie soothed as she continued to smooth her hair. 'Just a bad dream. Everything's fine.'

Freya swallowed, aware of the fast pace of her breathing, and tried to calm her body and mind. 'Yes,' she panted. 'Just a dream.'

THE NIGHT OF RESTLESS SLEEP, Freya too afraid to fall deep enough to dream, left her with a pounding head and eyes that were sore and swollen. She crumpled a little more when she remembered that Jake had moved this week's session to today. She made a few noises about cancelling, but Rosie shook her head.

'We are definitely going to the session with Jake today,' Rosie said while she prepared breakfast for them both.

'But how am I going to face him?'

'It was just a dream, and you need to get over it and forget it, or you'll never go back. And that would be silly, especially as you're really benefiting from the fitness, and he literally will have no clue that you dreamt about him.'

'But it's not just that. It's obvious he's interested.'

'So? Just take it as a compliment.'

'It's awkward.'

'You don't have to act on it unless you want to, and it won't do you any harm to release all that negative energy that's pent up inside you.' Rosie scraped scrambled egg from the pan and tipped it onto two plates of buttered toast and took them to the table where Freya sat, her head in her hands. 'You need to get whatever happened yesterday out of your system.'

Freya couldn't disagree that that sounded good, to exercise her body hard enough for exhaustion to take over. 'Yeah, all right. I'll do it.'

Rosie smiled as she lifted her knife and fork to eat. 'I have a pretty full day, but you're welcome to stay here.'

'Thanks, but no. I'll go back to the flat. It'll be good to freshen up, get a change of clothes.'

'Okay, but I'll come by just before seven.'

FREYA ARRIVED home after she and Rosie had taken a convoluted route back to the flat in an attempt to mislead anyone who might have been following or monitoring them.

The evening had started pleasantly enough, but it had quickly morphed into worrisome territory when Jake had eyed her on her arrival and made his way over to her, making a friendly enough comment about needing a volunteer, which scared Freya off like a deer caught in headlights, sending her bolting to the bathroom to control her breathing. He was just being pleasant, but Freya's mind told her that he had spied her looking the other day and had taken that as an invitation to show his interest too.

He was nice, and she couldn't even consider bringing

him into her world of fear and distress. She'd messed up. He wasn't to blame. This was all on her.

In the lobby, the sound of a man and a woman arguing could be heard, their voices carrying in the silent air. Freya knew immediately that it would be Elliot and Ava. She recognised his voice, the sharp intonation, the angry reasoning. Compelled to know more, she found herself climbing the stairs, with no intention of heading right towards her flat, but instead heading left towards the sound of the fighting. Their voices became louder, more intense, and Freya felt her heartbeat begin to race in her chest as she neared their door. She had no business doing what she was about to do, no business at all, but she was unable to stop herself as she balled her hand into a fist and knocked on the door.

Immediate silence followed, an unwelcome interruption no doubt, but she was here now and had to take her chances with whatever consequence might come her way.

Footsteps approached the door from the other side, and then the lock clicked, and the door opened.

The man blinked his surprise at the sight of this relative stranger, another resident of the building, showing up at his house. Barefoot, his shirt pulled at the collar and his hair dishevelled, he glared at her and then turned to look over his shoulder.

Freya cranked her head through the crack in the door, keen to catch sight of Ava, to check that she was all right and if there was any evidence of violence. She was interfering, massively overstepping, but she had to know.

'Can I help you?' Elliot snapped.

'You remember me,' Freya blurted out, flustered and unsure. 'I'm just down the hall. I heard noises, that's all. I just wanted to check everything was okay.'

'What the hell has it got to do with you?' he said coldly, his voice laced with fury at her meddling.

The door pulled back, and Ava appeared, dishevelled too, her face shiny, her eyes swollen and watery, her lashes clumped together.

'Leave it, Elliot,' she said, clutching at his arm and ignoring Freya. 'Just close the door.'

Freya held out her hand to stop the door from closing. Never had she been so bold, or out of line, but something in her couldn't let this drop. 'I just need to know everything is okay.'

'Are you the police?' he asked.

'No, of course not.'

'And are you a relative or someone in our family?'

'You know I'm not; it's just—'

'Then I suggest you get your foot out of my doorway and get the hell away from me. I will call the police for harassment if you decide to linger here any longer. Do you understand?'

The anger in his eyes made his threat more dangerous than before, and without hesitation, Freya backed away to have the door slammed shut hard in front of her.

She'd made a mistake; she saw that now. He'd likely punish Ava more now for what she'd done, and that was foolish of her, and unforgivable.

Freya hurried back to her flat and locked and chained the door behind her. She left the lights off and rushed to the window, where she looked out towards their flat to see more, if she could, of their argument.

The woman stood with her back to the window, talking, maybe pleading, but Elliot was not in view. Ava seemed engaged in an argument of sorts, and Freya couldn't remember a time she would have been able to do such a thing, but she reasoned that everyone was different, and perhaps this woman was early in the relationship, when she still had fight in her soul. Before it would be beaten out of her. Elliot came into view and then disappeared with Ava following close behind. After that, she saw no more of them nor heard their raised voices.

Unsettled, she poured herself a glass of water and sat down on her sofa. Jittery, and finding it unhelpful to be seated, she paced the room instead, occasionally glancing over towards their window to catch anything more. She'd be ready. She'd phone the police and intervene. So many times had she wanted someone to do that for her, to step in and help when things got so bad that she was sure she'd die at his hand.

There would be no sleep tonight, feeling as if she needed to keep watch, so with a blanket, she positioned herself near the window and prepared for a long night.

12

Freya stepped out from the shower and pulled on another one of Rosie's dresses. She decided that she'd get out today; she needed some space to clear her head. The night had been uneventful, and she considered what Rosie had said. Maybe she was projecting the horrors she'd lived through onto this couple. Maybe she had no business getting involved.

She'd managed to go another night without the diazepam too and felt that was cause for celebration. She'd take another walk down the high street and visit the café again, maybe chat with the owner. She had her CV printed out and ready to go, having used Rosie's computer and printer. She'd be forever indebted to her sister, and getting a job was the first step to no longer being a financial burden on her.

She combed her hair back into a low ponytail and slid the cap on. Hopefully Liam or his cronies wouldn't recognise her now – a stone lighter, hair longer and wearing someone else's clothes.

She jogged the last couple of steps into the lobby and jumped at the sight of Ava pacing back and forth by the entrance.

Ava noticed immediately. 'Are you okay?' she asked.

'Yes,' Freya replied with a smile as she laid a hand on her chest to steady her heart. 'You startled me, that's all.'

Ava smiled. 'I'm sorry about that.' She looked over her shoulder and back to Freya, bristling with excitable, nervous energy. 'I'm actually alone right now, so would you like to pop up for a cup of tea?'

Freya hesitated.

'It's just that the way we met before wasn't a true reflection of who I am, and it would be nice to get to know you a little better. I always think it's nice to know our neighbours here. It's almost like a family, and I was rude and aloof on both the occasions that we crossed paths, and I'm sorry for that.'

'Well, I was just going to pop out.'

'That's perfect. I can join you,' Ava said cheerily as she linked her arm through Freya's and strode towards the doors. 'I will show you around, and you can tell me where you're off to. It'll be a great opportunity to get to know one another.'

Freya wasn't sure she wanted to get to know her, and the cheery, effusive woman was jarringly different to whom she'd met before. It made her uncomfortable.

Ava glanced at Freya and laughed. 'I know what you're thinking, but really, it's fine. I just want to have some fun. We're around the same age, I'm guessing, and God knows we're probably the only ones in this building who are, so come on.'

'And Elliot is okay with this?' Freya hated asking it, but she knew it was important.

'He's fine. He's out, so what he doesn't know won't hurt him.'

THEY STRODE down the high street, and Ava chatted happily, careful with the questions she asked Freya – where she'd come from, was she single, how long did she intend to stay at the flat. Information that was easy to ask, and easy to give. She never delved deep enough to question Freya's relationship status or history, but still managed to elicit just the right amount of information out of her so that soon enough she was acting like a lifelong friend of Freya's, with a familiarity formed out of years of knowing one another rather than the minutes they actually had. It was endearing rather than weird, even though Freya struggled to understand her motives, but God knew Freya needed a friend, and in time, her guard came down slowly. It was impossible not to when Ava seemed so happy. Maybe something had happened between Elliot and Ava; perhaps they'd turned a corner in their relationship. It hurt Freya's head to think too hard about it, so she just rode the wave that Ava had created, letting herself be pulled along, finding that she was beginning to enjoy it.

They passed by the shop that had the nice striped dress in the window, and Freya slowed to check it out again.

'You like it, don't you?' Ava said, watching Freya with a smile, her eyes playful, her long curls brushing over her shoulders, catching on the slight breeze.

Freya nodded as she stared at the outfit. 'Can't afford it right now, though. Maybe soon, if it's not snapped up.'

Ava lunged for Freya's hands and pulled her closer to the door of the shop.

'What are you doing?'

'Let's go and try it on,' Ava said excitedly.

'No,' Freya protested. 'I can't afford it.'

'Doesn't stop us from dreaming.'

Ava laughed and released one of Freya's hands to push open the door before dragging Freya inside. She headed straight for the counter and smiled at the woman working there.

'Can we try that dress, please?' Ava said, pointing at the mannequin in the window. She looked Freya up and down. 'I'd say a size ten, no, an eight.'

'Of course,' the stylishly dressed woman said as she sashayed from behind the glass-fronted counter that was full of jewellery and over to a rack of dresses. She pulled a hanger from the abundance of dresses and held it out.

Ava grabbed it. 'Thank you. Fitting room?'

The woman pointed behind, and Ava grabbed Freya's hand and walked her to the small cubicle at the back of the shop with a red velvet curtain.

'Go on,' Ava said. 'But let me see it even if you hate it.'

'I can't do this,' Freya whispered as her heart began to race as she caught the woman watching them.

Ava stared at Freya, serious. Desperate. 'Look, I know this is crazy. I know it. But I just want to live. I want to forget what's waiting for me at home. Just for a moment. Please.'

Freya looked at her and the hopelessness in her eyes. A smiled tipped her lips. 'Okay, but only if you promise me one thing.'

'What's that?' Ava asked, her happy expression returning.

'You have to try something on too.'

'Deal.'

Ava rushed to the rack of dresses and picked out a long, velvet spaghetti-strap gown in a beautiful emerald green. 'If we're going to do it, we're going to do it well. You go first, but we have to swap. We both have to wear each outfit.'

'Deal,' Freya repeated.

Freya pulled the curtain across and slipped out of her dress and pulled the striped dress around her shoulders and began buttoning the dress together.

'Well, how does it look?' Ava asked from the other side of the curtain.

Freya pushed back the curtain and walked out, giving a little twirl.

'Very nice,' Ava said.

It was perfect, just as Freya had hoped it would be. It fitted Freya like a glove, the flattering V-neck, the way it cinched her waist and flowed to her knees. It was cool and perfect, and Freya didn't want to take it off.

'My turn,' Ava said, dipping into the cubicle.

Freya waited patiently as Ava shuffled around inside the small space before finally pushing back the curtain.

She looked stunning, the gown gliding over her hips, showing off her slender figure. The green picked up the colour in her eyes, and her hair fell over her shoulder and down her back.

'Wowsers,' Freya said. 'You look amazing.'

Ava did a twirl, holding the sides of the dress in her hands. 'Thank you. I feel amazing.'

A small bruise cupped Ava's left shoulder. She covered it with her hand when she noticed Freya looking at it. 'We need to swap,' she said quickly, returning to the cubicle.

Freya stood open-mouthed while she waited. What

should she say? Should she ignore it, try to talk about it? She didn't know what to do. When Ava came out dressed in her normal clothes, her mood had changed.

'I'm not sure I feel like swapping,' Freya said, picking up on it immediately. 'How about we pop to the café just a couple of doors away. I wanted to pop in there anyway; there's a job there that I have my eye on.' She paused. 'Well, I'm not sure how successful I'll be. The first interaction wasn't hopeful, but I want to try again. Why don't we grab a drink. Perhaps you can give me some tips on how to smooth talk the owner into getting the job.'

Ava nodded, and Freya took the opportunity to go and change too.

———

WITH THE CLOTHES shop behind them, they walked in relative silence along the high street to the café, squinting in the heat of the midday sun, the air hot and oppressive. Freya pushed open the door and let Ava go in first. They both ordered coffee and a fancy cookie and found a table.

The other customers' chatter compensated for the fact that Ava and Freya suddenly had nothing to say. It was now or never, Freya thought, and she leaned in.

'I know what you're going through,' she said. 'I've been where you are. A forceful partner. I just want you to know that you can trust me. We may not know each other very well yet, but I can be your friend, and I can help you if you ever need it.'

Ava smiled so sadly that Freya wanted to hug her. 'It's not what you think,' she said, staring at the cookie in front of her. 'It's passion. That's what he says. We're young and foolish, and we're making mistakes along the way.'

'You shouldn't be hurt because of it.'

Ava shook her head. 'I'm not, no more than I deserve.'

Freya fought the urge to scream. 'You don't deserve any of what he's doing. You deserve respect and love and care.'

'He does love me, and I love him,' Ava said. 'But in our own way. We understand each other. We need each other. I can't leave.'

Freya didn't know what sort of twisted love story Ava might be telling herself, but Freya knew that she wouldn't be able to reach her until she was ready.

'Just know that I'm here for you. And I'm just down the hallway. You can come over whenever you like.'

Ava smiled, her playfulness glinting in her eyes. 'That's the best news. Now, what can I do for you to make up for it?'

Freya stared, not expecting anything in return. 'Nothing.'

'I know,' Ava said, jumping up. She went to the counter and started chatting to the woman. They discussed something that Freya was unable to make out, but she kept watch while they both glanced her way.

When Ava came back, all smiles, she giggled as she sat down. 'Well, that was a really interesting conversation. Seems like the woman would be very interested in having a discussion with you. I've told her all about your job at the hotel and how you're looking for something new to get your teeth into. If you'd like to go up and see her, you can work a few things out.'

Freya sat wide eyed. 'Really?'

Ava giggled again. 'Yes, really. Go on. That job is yours; now go and get it.'

Freya walked up to the counter, her mouth dry and

hands clammy as she hurriedly tried to prepare what she'd say. She'd wanted to put in her CV, and that was what she had intended to do when she woke up this morning, but this turn of events had her on the back foot and unsure of how to deal with it. With a dry mouth, she smiled her best smile and held out her hand to properly introduce herself.

She would get this job.

———

THE UNKNOWN NUMBER on Freya's phone startled her, and her stomach dropped. She stared at the screen as the phone chimed, and waited for the answerphone to kick in. Sure that this was an omen, she felt the unease creep in that he'd found her and was on his way.

When the message beeped to indicate a voicemail had been left, she hesitated before hitting the button to listen to it. Better to know now; being prepared would help her if she needed to move quickly to leave and start somewhere new.

Surprised to hear the woman from the coffee shop asking her to come in for a discussion about working hours and pay, she tried to regulate the feelings of intense panic to hopeful excitement. She was to call when she could to arrange a mutually convenient time.

Without realising, a smile had crept over her lips at the thought that another piece of the puzzle was about to slot into place in rebuilding her life. This could be it. Maybe Liam would let her go, maybe she could have the conversation Rosie had suggested, and maybe he'd accept it.

She spent the morning deciding which of Rosie's outfits would suit the meeting. It couldn't be too formal or too casual, so unsure of what to do, she settled for some black trousers and a blouse patterned with small white flowers and some sandals. It was too hot to consider shoes.

When she pushed open the door and caught the same delicious aroma of coffee and sweet treats, it felt right, where she was supposed to be, and the smile she gave to the woman as she approached the counter was genuine and wide.

They discussed her employment history and experience, and although it was perfectly clear that she was, on paper at least, overqualified for the role, this would be the perfect way to get her back into the working world once more.

Freya spent an hour in the café looking over the facilities, how things were arranged out the back and how the stockroom was stacked. All things she could work with and places she could add value and help to improve. It felt good to use her brain in this way again, focused on something other than a husband who liked to create an atmosphere of fear. She felt free for the first time – really free – and although she maintained her professionalism, she could have hugged this woman who chatted away showing off her business, completely unaware of the opportunity she'd given Freya.

When Freya returned home, she walked on air, excited for what lay ahead. A new future awaited her, and she was ready to begin.

She skipped up the stairs and ran through the food options she had in her fridge. Tonight would be a treat night perhaps. She'd get a takeaway, maybe a small bottle of wine. Something to mark the occasion.

She entered her flat and went straight to her cupboard to change into comfortable slouchy clothes. She enjoyed the thought that soon she'd have a little bit of her own money to go out and buy things that she liked; even though

Rosie's wardrobe was more than suitable, it was about the independence of it. The knowledge that what she wore was entirely her choice. Not Liam's, not anyone's, and that felt so good.

She leafed through a couple of takeaway apps and decided on the filthiest burger with fries and a dangerously calorific drink. What the hell. She deserved it. She sat and ordered and opened her phone while she waited for the food, researching the best skills she could bring to her new role. This was just the start, after all. Then she decided to call Rosie, share her good news.

A loud crash pierced the quiet in her flat, and she jumped up – an automatic response to any loud noise since she'd known Liam, and instinctively went to the window. Sure enough, Elliot and Ava were arguing again, and this time, Ava was crying, extremely distressed.

With her heart beating, she looked back for her phone. In the time it took to grab it and return her gaze to them, Elliot had both his hands gripped on his wife's wrists, and they fought and swayed in a strange dance until he dragged her from view.

'Okay, that's it,' Freya murmured. 'No more violence.' She dialled for the emergency services. At that moment the notion to protect herself wasn't at the forefront of her mind; instead it was the need to protect her new-found friend. No one understood what Ava was going through as much as Freya did right now. The safe-thinking, logical part of her mind did flag a warning, but she chose to ignore it, resolving to figure it out if or when the time came. She spoke clearly about what she'd witnessed and requested police visit the couple to ensure the woman was all right. She declined giving her name or contact details, and instead shared she was a neighbour in the same block. No lies there and no harm done.

Her food delivery arrived at the same time as the police. She realised she'd have to go and collect it from the lobby of the building and hoped, no, prayed, that she would manage to avoid any confrontation. They'd know it was her, surely, and that might make Elliot even more angry and unstable, and while she was prepared to help her friend, she didn't yet feel anywhere near strong enough to come face to face with a new aggressor.

She grabbed her keys and ran down to the lobby. She took the paper bag of food from the driver, gave her thanks, and scurried upstairs as quickly as she could.

As she reached the top of the stairs and was about to head down her hallway, she saw in her peripheral vision a couple of police officers outside Elliot and Ava's doorway. Ava was crying, and Elliot's voice was raised and angry, demanding to know why they were there. The officers, one male, one female, were trying their best to de-escalate the heat of the moment, ordering everyone to calm down. Part of Freya bristled at the command, and the next decision she made came from an inner need to protect another human being in danger.

She turned and headed towards the voices and manoeuvred herself into the officers' line of sight. 'Excuse me,' she said, her voice shaking.

One of the officers spun around.

'Can I help? Ava is my friend.'

Elliot lifted his arms in the air in exasperation. 'Jesus, what the fuck does she want now?'

The officer held out his hand. 'No need for that,' he warned Elliot. He turned to Freya as Ava disappeared back into the flat, still visibly distraught and, in Freya's eyes, almost hysterical. The female officer followed her in.

'Are you aware of the situation here?'

Freya nodded. 'I am, unfortunately.'

Elliot let out a sigh. 'Officer, she has no fucking clue what's going on here.'

The officer turned to Elliot. 'I won't tell you again,' he snapped before turning his attention back to Freya. 'What can you tell us?'

'That they argue all the time, and I'm beginning to worry for Ava's safety.'

Elliot let out a laugh but said nothing.

The commotion that followed blurred in Freya's mind as the officers discussed Elliot going down to the station, his reticence to do so, and Ava's reappearance to plead for everyone to leave them alone. Freya was caught up in a torrent of emotion as they all spoke over each other, their own point to make, including the police officer. He finally took control of the situation and ordered Elliot to go with him, and asked Freya to remain with Ava, which she agreed to immediately. But Ava was having none of it and still demanded to be left alone. Freya felt the painful distress in her cries as she begged everyone to go.

It was only when Ava agreed to call a family member to come over that the officers were happy to leave, and at that point they told Freya she was free to go back to her own flat and that they'd take it from there.

So caught up in the moment, it took a second to realise a sixth person had rocked up behind them all. She felt it, but ignored the significance, feeling conflicted – still wanting to stay, but also wanting to get back to the peace and safety of her home.

'You need a hand, Officer?' The man from behind spoke, full of confidence and authority.

The sound of his voice turned her legs to jelly and forced a cry from her throat.

The voice was unmistakably Liam's.

Her world collapsed around her as the unthinkable happened. She turned to look as she struggled for air.

He was here. He'd found her.

13

Freya turned and stumbled backwards, dropping her bag of food as she attempted to get as much space between herself and her tormentor as possible.

'We've got it from here, sir,' the officer replied. 'We're going to take a trip down to the station, let things cool off a bit.'

Liam smiled, a smug expression plastered all over his face as he nodded to his colleague. 'Good plan.'

He didn't look at Freya, but she stared at him in disbelief. He was dressed in a smart suit and had the calm demeanour of someone in total control of the situation. A hundred questions rushed through her mind as she struggled to keep her legs from crumpling. He should be in Hampshire, not here. What was he doing working in London again, and what would be his next move? She flinched, sure he would wrap his arm around her right now and take her away to dish out his punishment for her wrongdoing.

Freya was sure she was dreaming or having a nightmare as she stood in the hallway, cornered with the officer on one side, Liam the other. She wanted to run but was stuck as they waited for the family member to arrive.

A woman in her sixties rushed up the stairs, her blonde hair similar to Ava's, dressed in a slouchy T-shirt and jeans, clearly not expecting to have to run out at this point in the evening. She went to Ava and hugged her tight as Ava cried in her arms. The woman, who Freya could only assume was her mum by age and demeanour, soothed Ava as she guided her back into the flat and closed the door, ignoring them all.

The officer prompted Elliot to go with him, the female officer following them.

'Wait,' Freya blurted as she reached for the handle of Ava's flat and wiggled it desperately, pointlessly. Panic caused her heartbeat to jump in her throat. 'Don't go yet.'

The officers turned to look at Freya.

'It's all right,' Liam said calmly to the female officer. Friendly, even, as he picked up Freya's bag of food from the floor. 'I'll handle this; you carry on.'

Freya went to move away from him, but he just laid his hand on her arm, preventing her from going.

'You're sure?' the female officer said, watching.

Freya opened her mouth to speak, but Liam interrupted her, whispering to her.

'Do you want these plods to know what's going on between us?' he asked. 'Do you want them all to know?'

She paused, looking at him, terror filling her.

The female officer filled the silence, her eyes laced with doubt. 'I'll wait downstairs, sir. Make sure you don't need anything further here.'

Liam nodded, keeping his emotions under strict control. 'Much appreciated, Smith. Wait for me down in the lobby. I'll be a couple of minutes, that's all.'

She nodded and disappeared from view.

Alone with him now and feeling shaky from the adrenaline that had been released into her system, she stepped away from him and cleared her throat. 'Keep away from me.'

'It's okay,' he said calmly. 'I'm not going to hurt you.'

'I know you're not, because you're going to leave right now, or I'll scream, and that officer will be straight back up here.'

He smiled. 'Look, can we start again?' he asked, his hands palms up, in negotiation.

'No way. I'm never going back there again.'

'No, Freya. I know that.' He looked down the hallway. 'Can we go to yours? I assume you live here too.'

'Do you think I'm stupid? I'm not letting you anywhere near my home.'

'Listen, five minutes, Freya. Just give me five minutes. That's all I ask.'

She remained silent, staring at him and breathing quickly, her body in defence mode. Mindful of the officer downstairs, she considered what would work for her. She could deal with this now, with the relative safety of another police officer, or she would have to live with the option he could turn up here unannounced again and potentially catch her off guard and in a worse position. Her body was tired from feeling constant tension, and she knew she was fed up with looking over her shoulder. 'We can go downstairs, if we must. In the lobby.'

'I know I'm the last person you'll ever trust again, but I give you my word that I am not going to do anything. I just want to speak to you.'

'Why should I trust anything you have to say or do to me?'

'You don't, but you must want some sort of resolution too?'

She bit her lip in frustration. She didn't want any of this, but he'd found her, and this was happening. 'All right. Downstairs. Five minutes, but I want your guarantee that you won't show up here ever again, for what it's worth. I want you to say it out loud.'

'You have my word,' he said without hesitation. 'I won't contact you, and I won't come here.'

She nodded and chucked a finger out to indicate that he could get moving, which he did. She followed, feeling safer that way.

The officer, Officer Smith, Freya recalled, stood by the doors, staring out into the evening light. Liam went to her and spoke quietly. The woman looked at him and then at Freya and nodded and then left the lobby and waited outside. Freya could still see her; she hadn't left, she was just giving them some privacy. What he'd said to her, Freya would never know, but she was thankful that the woman stuck around.

Liam strode to the sofa by the entrance and unbuttoned his suit jacket as he sat and placed his phone and her bag of food on the table. 'Do you want to sit?'

'No, thanks, I'll stay here,' she said, keeping her distance.

'Fair enough,' he said with a nod.

She clasped her arms around herself, a sense of protection, despite her standing far enough away from him. She checked the officer outside, who stood with her back to them.

'I know you're afraid of me,' he began, watching her. 'And I'm here to say I'm sorry.' He rested his arms on his legs and linked his fingers together. 'I understand that you had to do what you had to do. You ran. You'd had enough. I get it.'

'You're lying.'

'No, I'm not, but I don't expect you to believe me. Why would you after all I've done.'

'That's right, I don't believe you.' She glanced at the door only a few strides away. 'Why are you even here? You should be down in Hampshire.'

He shrugged. 'I've been looking for you for weeks now, and I just want to know what's going on. You can't blame me for that.'

She stared at him, her mind becoming fatigued from the fear and adrenaline.

'Okay, so maybe you can,' he murmured. 'I got a transfer back here when you left. I didn't know what else to do. I wanted to find you; I wanted us to talk. I thought I'd come back to where I first started out, here at the Met, and then I'd try to convince your sister to tell me how to contact you.'

'You need to leave her alone,' Freya snapped, an overwhelming need to protect her sister from harm. 'She has nothing to do with this.'

'Well, that's not strictly true, is it,' he said. 'I mean, she must have helped to get you settled in here.' He glanced around the lobby. 'It's nice. Very vintage.'

'Get the hell out of here, Liam,' she spat with far more confidence than she'd ever spoken in a long time. She wondered if he'd bite and give out a quick punishment before he left. She was ready to run, to leap for the door.

He studied her for a moment. He looked the same, well turned out, smart suit, nice hair. Perfectly groomed. If only what was inside was as pleasant to look at, but only she knew how rotten it was. How dark and twisted.

'You look good,' he murmured as his eyes scanned over her. 'This definitely suits you.'

'Because I've been able to heal,' she spat. 'No bruises on my skin for weeks now. No pulled muscles or injured bones.'

He blinked, caught off guard. 'Okay, I deserved that.'

You deserve a whole lot more.

'Why are you here?' she asked again. 'Specifically, tonight.'

'I was on call. Thought I'd join the plods to see what was going on. Take a look around.'

He could still spout the bullshit; that hadn't changed. This wasn't about the warring couple or joining the plods. This was about putting two and two together and knowing that this place was around the corner from Rosie's and a female neighbour had called in. This had pricked his detective sensibilities enough to make a visit, and sure enough, his hunch had paid off.

'Well, you found me. Big deal.'

'I think it's a very big deal. I'm glad, although I'm sensing you're far from it.'

'You beat me black and blue, Liam. I needed to get out of there. I left everything behind. That's how prepared I was to get away from you. I never wanted to see you again.'

'I know,' he said as he stood.

She tensed and immediately stepped back, glancing at the woman outside. 'Stay where you are. I mean it.' She held out a trembling hand.

'Hey, I'm not going to hurt you,' he said as he watched her. 'I just want to talk. That's all.' He sighed and shook his head. 'I accept that we're over. I didn't want to, not for a long time, but I've come to realise that you must have been desperate to do what you did. To disappear like that, and all because of me. That was a hard pill to swallow. But I know there's no going back with us. I fucked up. I'm sorry.'

His words didn't touch the tough armour she'd built around herself, but if he was willing to take responsibility for his actions, then she'd accept it, even though she deserved so much more.

'So what do you want?'

'Well, now that we're here, I'd like us to discuss how we go about our separation and ultimately our divorce. That's what you want, right?'

'Yes, that's what I want. It's the only option. You knocked all the love I had for you out of me.'

He looked to the floor. 'Ouch.'

'Truth hurts?'

He looked up at her. 'Yes, Freya. It does.'

His expression knocked her off balance because what she saw looked like genuine remorse. She checked herself. *All an act. Don't fall for it.*

'Well, we do need to discuss the formalities, I suppose. The house. I still have possessions there. My clothes and stuff. Unless you've burned them?'

'No, I haven't burned them,' he replied with a gentle chuckle. 'They're all just as you left them. Neatly stored away.'

'Well then,' she said, 'we can arrange a meeting, I guess. Maybe with mediators or something.'

'Will you let me have your number?'

'I will not,' she blurted. 'I will call you. I assume you still have the same number.'

He nodded.

'Okay, well, I think it's best for you to leave now,' she said, wishing him gone.

He moved towards the door. 'I'll wait for you to call me, then,' he said as he opened the front door, prompting Officer Smith to turn around. 'It's really good to see you again.'

She waited until they had disappeared down the pathway before she turned on her heels and ran upstairs to her flat, shakily opening the door. She threw down the bag of cold, greasy food she'd retrieved from the table and rushed to the toilet in the bathroom to throw up the contents of her stomach.

FREYA HAD BEEN MUTTERING to herself for most of the afternoon. She had been wringing her fingers constantly for most of the day until they ached, and paced her living room as her heartbeat fluttered in her chest. It was the first time she'd been back at her home since she'd seen Liam.

She'd retreated to Rosie and Ben's the minute she could get a taxi to take her to their place, and it had taken them a few hours, at least, to calm her once she arrived. Midnight conversations over tea tried to alleviate the stress that tensed her body, discussions on why he had returned to London, and the consideration from Rosie that perhaps he might have changed. Freya dismissed that line of thinking immediately. There was no way someone like him would ever change.

She couldn't relax and struggled to get a full lung of air. She didn't know why she'd agreed to meet with Liam, but she had, and now the nerves were threatening to take over. She'd called him the very next day after their confrontation in the foyer, her mind in a hurry to be rid of him, and had arranged to meet him the following week, which had come around far too quickly.

Rosie was certainly against it, as was Ben, and when Freya declined any help or support in case Liam turned nasty, she saw the disappointment in their eyes. But she knew that if they were spotted, Liam would become like a cornered animal, caught in the wild, and would change to attack mode in an instant. This was the only way to ensure he felt like the situation was on his terms and minimise the risk of injury to anyone else involved. But she did tell them where she'd be, at what pub she'd be going to so they knew where to find her if she changed her mind.

She'd spent the morning cleaning Rosie's house, trying to occupy her mind, and then had arranged another taxi to bring her home. She showered and changed, dressed in jeans and a navy T-shirt, nothing over the top, or to appear as if she was trying too hard, but an armour of sorts, none-theless, giving her the confidence to face up to the man who had torn her down for so many years.

She arrived at the pub early to allow herself time to settle and prepare – not too far away for a nightmare journey, but not too close to home either. A public place where she'd be safest from harm. Her nerves jangled, and she needed this over with more than anything else in the world. It was neces-sary if she was to move on. He wouldn't leave her be now that he'd found her. He'd use every trick in the book; she was well aware of that. All the apologies, all the promises to change, the flattery, and the care. He'd done it all before. He'd even soothed the bruises on her body with the same hands that caused them, a strange juxtaposition of both cruelness and tenderness.

She ordered herself a mineral water from the bar and

found a table at the back of the room where she felt most comfortable. The perks of being early. It was both suitably visible by other patrons but quiet enough that they could talk freely without worrying about being overheard. She noted the exits and where the toilets were, should she need to get away, and then watched others come and go as she fought to quieten her jiggling leg, a symptom of too much nervous energy surging in her body. She scrutinised the chalkboard that advertised the live music and quiz nights, and also went through the list of cocktails listed on a board nailed to the exposed brick wall behind the bar, deciding what she'd have if she were here in different circumstances. Anything to distract and calm her mind. The sun was hidden behind clouds today, but the air was humid, and the ceiling fans in the bar were doing their best to circulate the heavy air. She listened to the laughter, the boisterous conversations.

Everything faded though when he pushed open the door, dressed in a casual shirt and jeans and a confident smile. She focused her mind. She'd prepared for this as much as she could, but still she felt nervous. She noted the looks from the other women who watched his arrival, a few of the men too. *Yes, he might be pretty to look at,* she thought, *but never touch. You'll burn if you do.*

He glanced her way and gave a half smile as he crossed the room to her. 'Freya,' he said as he approached. 'Thank you for coming.'

'I wasn't sure I wanted to.'

'I know, and I appreciate it. You don't owe me anything after the way I've treated you, so it's a pleasant surprise to see you here.' He pointed to her glass. 'What are you drinking? Can I get you another?'

'Mineral water, and no, thanks, I'll stick with this one.'

'Of course, I'll just go and grab a drink.'

He returned with a tall glass of cold beer, the condensation already bubbling on the outside of the glass, and placed it on the table. 'So where do we start, eh?'

'I don't know.'

'Look, I know you're hating this, but I just want to talk, that's all.'

'Okay.'

'So how have you been keeping?' he asked. 'I mean really.'

'I'm fine,' she said.

He nodded. 'I'm glad. Happy for you. For the record, I was worried about you, you know. You just vanished off the face of the earth. I had no idea where you were, or if you were hurt.'

'Would you have cared?'

'Of course I would have,' he murmured regretfully. 'In fact, it was you doing a runner that made me realise how terrible things had become.'

How terrible you'd become, more like, she thought to herself.

She glanced down. 'I had to get away, Liam. I couldn't take it anymore. You were killing me, slowly, painfully. I didn't know what else to do. It was like my mind took over and got me out of there.'

He reached out for her hands and then withdrew them, instead cupping his glass. 'I'm so sorry. I don't know how many times I can say it to make you feel it.'

'They're just words,' she murmured with her eyes cast to the table. She wanted to say how she felt, she *needed* to say how she felt, but her nerves wouldn't allow her to make eye contact with the man she was still so afraid of. 'And I don't know what you're expecting, but you need to know that we're long past the reconciliation phase.' She lifted her glass to her lips with shaking fingers and took a drink to allow herself a moment to pause. 'We're here to discuss finishing this marriage and beginning divorce proceedings. That's all.'

'And that's what you really want?'

'I travelled hundreds of miles to get away from you, Liam. To start a new life somewhere new on my own. That's how much I wanted it. And I didn't want you to find me, but you did, and now here we are. So yes, I think you can believe it's what I really want.'

He nodded ruefully. 'Okay, I understand. You're angry.'

'Yes, I *am* angry, but I'm also tired. You took things from me that I'm not sure I'll ever get back. But I'm finally starting to heal, Liam. I am no longer in pain. Not just the immediate bruises but the long-term pain of the damage your fists have caused. The ache of anxiety is easing every day too. I have to protect that.'

She glanced at the clock, wanting out of this place.

He sighed. 'I thought we could work it out.'

'Really?' she said. 'You thought I'd want to go back there.'

'No, not there, but I thought we might start again. We had some good times, at the beginning. We loved each other. Is there no way we can't get back there?'

'No, Liam. Too much has happened. It's over.'

He tapped his finger on the table, eyeing her as he processed all she'd said. 'Okay, if that's what you want.'

Her body remained as tense at it had on his arrival. She needed to be wary. He could end this anytime he liked. It would be nothing for him to reach across the table, grab her by the wrist and walk her out of the pub without anyone noticing the force he used. One snap decision and a litany of violence to back it up would ensure she'd regret ever agreeing to meet with him.

'I'm glad you finally see it.'

'I'll speak to a solicitor, and I suggest you do too, I guess,' he said resolutely.

'Fine, that's exactly what I'll do.'

'What about the stuff at the house?'

'I only want what's mine,' she said. 'You can box up and return my things to Rosie and Ben's address. I know you know where that is, especially after your recent visit there. It avoids any unnecessary contact that way.'

'You really *are* angry,' he murmured. 'You really want me to do that? You're not going to share any contact details? Even your number?'

'No, I'm not. It's enough that you know where I live. I'm not giving you any more details. And please don't track me or delve any deeper into my life. I'm here and giving you this time, but don't think for a minute I won't disappear again overnight if I have to. I'll make sure you never find me next time. Do you understand?'

She felt as powerful as a mouse standing up to a lion, but she'd make her point before she'd leave. He needed to know how serious she was about this. That she meant every word.

'Perfectly,' he said. 'Although I'm surprised you think I'd stoop so low to use my position in the police in such a way.'

She huffed out a silent laugh. The lengths he'd stoop to were so low one would have to be a limbo dancer to match it. She rose from her chair, her legs shaking. 'I'll be in touch soon, then.'

He stood too. 'Thank you.'

'For what?'

'For giving me this time. For not taking my head off. You'd be totally entitled to do so after how I've treated you.'

'Well, I'm not like you. I'm not a monster.' She didn't give him time to reply before she strode to the door and out into the street.

It was only when she had put enough distance between herself and the pub did she allow herself a moment to stop and breathe. She tucked herself into the small alleyway between two shops in the high street, away from the passing crowds, and leant against a wall, her body still trembling. She licked her lips, her mouth dry, and talked herself down, breathing until she was calm.

She'd shocked herself at how she'd spoken to him. So bold. So clear, even though she'd been terrified. It was obvious that in the time since she'd left him, she had found her voice again.

14

Freya pushed open the door to the coffee shop and was met with a warm smile from Lucy, the owner. Today was her first day in the café and three days since she'd met with Liam. She needed to put it behind her, move on. The diazepam, however, had won again, and she'd taken it the night Liam had returned and every night after that. Despite wanting more, she had to be careful not to take any prior to her first day at work. Being drowsy and in a post-sedative fugue was never a good impression.

'Hi, Freya. Welcome,' Lucy said. 'How are you today?'

Freya managed a smile, but her nerves were already jangling, and her body had begun to crave the medication it needed to remain calm. 'I'm good, thank you,' she said, telling herself that faking it was the only way to get through the day.

'Great,' Lucy replied. 'So come on over; pop your bag under here,' she said as she grabbed the neatly folded and brand-new apron with the café's logo on the front. 'This is for you.'

'Thanks,' Freya replied as she slipped her bag in the recess in the back of the counter and took the apron. 'Where would you like me to start?'

'Dishwasher needs emptying, please, and then we need some cake cutting into slices and putting onto a covered cake stand. Coffee and walnut, today, I think.'

'Perfect, leave it with me,' she said as she pulled open the door of the dishwasher and stood back to let the large plume of steam billow up to the ceiling.

Once all the cups, mugs and saucers were stacked on the shelf on the wall behind her and the cutlery placed in each stainless-steel container, Freya pulled out a large coffee and walnut cake from the tub underneath the counter and sectioned it into slices, placing it on top of the glass-fronted counter in a pretty covered stand ready for their next customer. It looked delicious, and her mouth watered.

'So, how are you settling in around here?' Lucy asked while the place was temporarily empty of customers, a lull in the afternoon following the lunchtime rush. 'Do you like it?'

'Yes, I do. The area seems nice, and my sister is just around the corner. My flat is feeling like home every day.'

'I know the block,' Lucy said. 'Very impressive place, that.'

'Yes, well, I wish my flat were as impressive. A tiny one-room flat is not what you'd expect from the outside, but it's cosy enough for me.'

'Southampton, is that right?' Lucy asked. 'Where you were before.'

'Yep, that's right, although Surrey is where I grew up, and London, here, was home for many years. I moved down to Hampshire for my ex's job.'

'Ah, I see. I note the fact that you have an ex, so I'm

guessing the split brought you back here.'

'That's right,' Freya said, keen to divert the conversation elsewhere before any uncomfortable questions were asked.

'And who's that? Man? Woman?'

'Man, but probably more like a rat, to be honest.' They both laughed, and Freya took the opportunity to ask a question of her own. 'How long have you been here?'

'About three years. Moved down from Yorkshire to set this place up just before Covid hit. I thought we were gonna fold, but the residents around here kept us going with takeaways, home deliveries and the like. They were amazing. It was tight, I lived hand to mouth, and it wasn't pleasant, but I got through it, just.'

'Wow, that sounds tough,' Freya said.

'It was. Were you affected?'

Freya thought back to how her life had remained unaffected by the lockdowns of twenty-twenty. Liam had enforced his own on her for years, so apart from a few changes in his working pattern, life went on unaltered. Liam was crankier and quick to anger because he had so little freedom outside of work, and living around him was a lottery as to whether he'd lash out or not. It was no lie that she'd had some of the most brutal of beatings during that time, and the oppressive claustrophobia that came with living with such a volatile person all day every day without reprieve was almost as bad as the violence.

'No, not really. I didn't work, you see, so life was pretty much the same.'

Lucy stared a little, perhaps trying to read Freya, but Freya just turned away to grab a cloth and a spray so she could set to work wiping down before the next batch of customers filtered in.

'At least you have more colour in your cheeks than when you first came in,' Lucy said. 'White as a ghost then.'

Freya smiled. 'I'm still adjusting, but thanks.'

'Do you have anyone here other than your sister?'

'No, I'm afraid not. I lost touch with all my old friends when I moved away.'

'That's a shame.'

Freya shrugged. 'It happens,' she said as she remembered how cruel Liam could be when she wanted to go and visit her friends in London, and on more than one occasion had caused an injury, spilled boiling water from the kettle on her hand, or pushed her into door hard enough to bruise her face. Injuries that would keep her home. A ploy designed to ruin her plans and prevent her from seeing friends once more. They just became bored of rearranging every time and stopped asking. Not their fault. They didn't know. Perhaps she should have confided in them, perhaps they could have helped, but she believed the threats Liam made should she ever do that and so always refrained.

'I'm off out tonight, if you're interested,' Lucy said with a smile. 'Just a few drinks at the local pub with a few friends. Do you know the Old Frizzle, just around the corner?'

Of course she did. It was where she'd first met Liam. She nodded.

'Should be a nice evening if we can grab a table outside. Do you fancy it?'

'Oh, no, I couldn't, but thanks for the invite.'

'Okay, well, if you change your mind, just come along. Here's my number,' Lucy said as she pulled out the phone in her apron pocket and dialled Freya's number. 'We could toast your first day back in the working world.'

'You must go,' Rosie said over the phone.

Freya leant against the kitchen counter as she dipped the teabag in and out of her mug. Her feet hurt, her back too, and she just wanted to lie on the sofa now that her shift was over, and relax for the night. 'No, I don't think so. Why would I want to do that?'

'Because it will be fun, and you'll meet new people, that's why.'

'I couldn't. I can't remember when I last had to make conversation. I'd be rubbish at it and would make it weird.'

'We're all weird, Freya; it's just how well we cover it up that determines what people think of us.'

Freya laughed. 'I suppose.'

'Would you like me to come with you?'

'You'll come with me, like a child on their first day of school.'

'Seriously, I can, and then I'll just disappear when you're happy.'

Freya sighed. 'I don't know. Is that weird? Do people do that?'

'Of course they do. It'll be fun.'

'No, it's fine... but maybe. Oh, I don't know.'

'Let's do it,' Rosie said. 'Be ready in an hour.'

Freya pulled on some black jeans and a black floral blouse that she'd wear with some ballet flats. Her feet could not cope with any type of heel tonight, so that would have to do.

Rosie rang her phone to let her know she was there, and Freya grabbed her bag and met Rosie outside.

The pub was busy, but not crammed. Freya spotted Lucy

immediately at the bar with two guys and another woman. 'I'm regretting this already,' she muttered under her breath as Rosie kept her walking forward.

'It's going to be fine. A couple of drinks, that's all.'

'Freya!' Lucy exclaimed as she spotted them walking her way. 'You came.' Lucy turned to the others. 'Andy, Jim, Sally, this is Freya, my new assistant.'

They all greeted her warmly.

Andy and Sally stood next to each other, and from their close proximity, Freya assumed they were a couple. Sally was plump with twinkling blue eyes and blonde hair, and Andy was cleanly shaven, face and head, and towered over them all. Jim looked to be much older than the others and could be a parent of one of them, perhaps. Although Freya couldn't determine whose.

'This is my sister, Rosie,' she said, heat flushing her cheeks.

'Fancied a sly weekday drink, did you?' Andy said with a smile and a wink.

'You got it,' Rosie said confidently. 'In fact, why don't we go get another round. What are you all drinking?'

'Thanks, Rosie,' Andy said. 'I'll have a beer.'

'Me too,' Jim replied.

'White wine for me and Sally,' Lucy said.

They shuffled in closer to the bar and waited to be served. With a tray full of drinks, they all decided to go and find a table outside in the small garden out the back. Freya followed, concentrating on balancing the drinks, aware of how clumsy she could be. That was what Liam always said, anyway.

They spent the next hour or so chatting, and although pleasant enough, Freya was finding the constant need to show interest and fully engage exhausting. She wanted to follow Rosie, who'd told them all that Ben needed her at home about half an hour ago when she'd wanted to escape too. She'd been here long enough and willed a plausible excuse to pop into her head.

'Can I get anyone another drink?' Freya asked, interrupting the conversation.

Only Andy piped up, which suited her depleted finances, so she headed for the bar with his request for another beer. She stood next to an imposing character while she waited, and when she stared at her reflection in the mirror on the wall opposite, she realised the person was Jake. He was looking straight at her too.

They both turned to each other.

'Small world, eh?' he said with a chuckle. 'Having a good night?'

'Yeah, out with some friends. I'm a bit over it though, the thought of my sofa, an unhealthy meal, and a night of TV are calling me.'

'I get you. Midweek drinking is not my sort of thing anymore, but I'm here under orders from my brother. I have to include socialising in my calendar instead of working all the time, apparently.'

Freya smiled. 'If you love what you do, it's easy to fall into that, I guess.'

'Yeah, I get a bit passionate about it, and if I'm not teaching, I'm at the gym or planning my next training courses. It's a bit of a problem, if I'm honest.'

'I'm guessing your brother is older than you.'

'You'd guess right.'

'Then I completely understand. Rosie dragged me here

too. Telling me it's time to get out there and meet new people.'

'Is that what you're doing? Meeting new people?'

'Yeah, although I'm not sure I'm these "kind" of people. Lucy, my boss, she's lovely, but the others? Well, they're all into their careers, which range from fine art painter, a GP, to a full-time mum. I don't have a clue about any of that, and it seems they have degrees and diplomas in the subject. Rosie's even gone home now.'

'So coming up to buy a round was a blessing.'

'Absolutely, and they're really nice, and I shouldn't be so ungrateful, but I'm not sure I want to go back.'

'Why don't you tell them you've met a friend you weren't expecting.'

'You?'

'Yeah. See, you have friends.'

She smiled. 'I suppose I do.'

Freya took the beer back to Andy and made her polite excuses, explaining that an old friend had just come in. Jake did the same, and they managed to hide away in a corner of the pub, aware of the likely social faux pas they'd made, but not caring.

———

'WOULD you like me to walk you home?' Jake asked as they stood and left their empty glasses on the table.

She glanced out the window. The night was drawing in, the navy sky darkening the streets around her. It had been pleasant spending time with Jake, but she trusted him no more than anyone else. 'I'll be fine, thanks; I might grab a taxi. I don't feel like walking now.'

He studied her. 'You don't feel safe walking out at night.'

'I'm just tired,' she lied. Of course she didn't feel safe walking at night. She didn't feel safe at any time of the day. She didn't even feel safe in her own skin.

'Listen, why don't I walk you back. It's such a short distance, the taxi will fleece you for the fare. Why don't you save your money.'

Her heart rate increased. She didn't need this stress. 'No, don't worry, I'll be fine.'

He looked at her with sincerity. 'Look, I understand. It's why I run the class I run. You can trust me,' he said with a smile. 'And I've shown you all my best moves; you'll know exactly what to do if I try anything.'

'No, I really don't think it's a good idea.'

'You're in control, I promise. I feel responsible to ensure you get home safely. Like I said, you can trust me.'

She sighed and looked around. Enough people were spilling out into the street from the bar to make her consider the option of safety in numbers, and she didn't want to walk alone. That frightened her more, especially with Liam knowing where she lived. She'd make a big enough scene if anything were to happen, enough to draw attention to them both, and that would be very damaging to his reputation if he was seen hitting on a woman at night, with the police checks he had to maintain to run a business such as his.

'Okay,' she said finally. 'But just to my flat. I won't be asking you in for coffee or anything like that.'

'No problem,' he said. 'I didn't expect that.'

'Good, I just want to be clear.'

'I understand.'

They chatted easily as they walked along the pavement to her block, and he asked if she was happy for him to walk her up to the main entrance. She appreciated him asking and agreed.

'Well, I had a blast this evening,' he said with a smile as they stood outside the entrance to her building. 'If this is what socialising is about, then I'm all in.'

'Me too,' she replied.

They lingered for a moment, but Freya wasn't ready for anything else to happen. It was right to end here. They were friends, he'd proved that so far, and that would be as far as it went. He would not be getting a tour of her flat or the use of her bed.

'Well, goodnight, Jake. Thanks for walking me home.'

'It was a pleasure,' he said without any hint of disappointment that the evening was ending here. 'Will I see you later in the week at the session?'

'Yes, I'll be there.'

'Great, well, I'll look forward to it, then.'

She let herself in and turned to wave at him once she was in the lobby.

He raised his hand back and turned to walk away, soon disappearing from view.

She wondered where he lived. Was he close, or would he have to catch a train, a bus, or both to get home? The wonder of being able to walk alone at night, safe and not needing to check over one's shoulder, made her jealous. She'd never consider doing that, always opting for a taxi or joining others to do the journey together.

She climbed the stairs to her flat, exhausted from such a full day, and clasped the handrail for additional support. The place was quiet, now late, with everyone probably settled in for the evening, and she thought she was alone until she heard the muffled thuds of someone walking down the hallway. As she reached the top of the stairs, Elliot appeared.

She gasped, startled by his sudden appearance, and shifted her position to face him. A small bruise above his eye caught her attention. Perhaps Ava had fought back, and the thought pleased her. Freya had done the same a couple of times too, when a beating had become so vicious that her survival instinct kicked in and caused her to lash out in defence.

He moved closer to her, making the hairs on the back of her neck prickle.

'What do you want?' she said curtly.

'I want you to back off. Calling the police on us? Who the hell do you think you are?'

'I'm someone who cares about your wife. She's my friend.'

He laughed bitterly. 'My wife is not the one in danger.'

'Is that a threat?'

The sneer on his lips faded into hostility as his eyes narrowed. 'You can take it exactly as you want, and you're going to stay out of my business from now on. Do you hear me? Am I making myself understood?'

'Perfectly,' she murmured as she felt her body cower away from his overbearing posture.

'Good, then I'll let you be on your way.' He held out his hand to gesture her to walk on by.

She moved immediately out of his path and straight for her flat. Her hands trembled as she tried to force the key into the lock, and despite knowing that he'd be watching, she didn't turn around to check. She did not want to make eye contact with him that could provoke him into acting on his threat.

15

Freya had not been home for more than five minutes after her shift, her third ever, and had just kicked off her shoes when her phone rang. 'Hi, Mum.'

'Oh, Freya. The worst has happened,' she said, her voice wrought with anguish.

'What is it?' Freya asked with concern for her mum.

'We've been burgled.'

'What the hell,' Freya gasped. 'When? Are you and Dad all right?'

'Yes, yes, we're fine, but the place has been ransacked. It's a total mess. I can't tell what's actually been taken. Whoever did this wasn't happy to steal, they wanted to wreck the place as well.'

Freya checked her watch, grabbed her bag and stepped into the shoes she'd just discarded. 'I'm leaving now. I'll jump on a train and be there in an hour or so. Have you called the police?'

'I'm just about to do so. I am just so shocked I didn't know what else to do.'

'It's okay; hang up and call them. Have you called Rosie?'

'No, not yet.'

'No problem, I'll do that, and if she's free, she can come with me.'

Freya heard shuffling sounds in the background and realised her mum must be sorting through the chaos.

'It's such a mess,' her mother said as her voice cracked.

'It's okay, Mum. It's just things. The most important thing is that you're all right.'

'I'm not sure I am right now.' Her mum sniffed.

'I'll be there as soon as I can.'

FREYA NEGOTIATED the tubes and trains, which hadn't yet filled up with commuters, as it was only one in the afternoon, but it was heavy enough to irritate Freya. She hurried across platforms and dodged the meandering tourists taking snaps of everything they passed, the groups who walked in such a way that they filled the platform spaces, making it difficult to negotiate, and anyone who pushed a buggy or pram. She'd messaged Rosie, shared the basic details and asked her to call, but she had no idea what her schedule would be and if she'd be free to talk at all.

After a series of train hopping, jumping off one to join another, she was soon at the station in Surrey. She hurried along the main road, half jogging, half walking whenever she was out of breath, until she reached the close where her parents lived. The entire journey had been spent worrying about her parents and not fretting about the vulnerability of doing the trip alone.

A police car sat outside the house, on the road of the cul-de-sac, and the presence of it reassured her. From what Freya knew, the police rarely visited after the report of a burglary, so this was progress, and she allowed herself to hope that their quick reaction might aid the recovery of some of the stolen items.

She hurried to the door and rang the bell. Her mother answered, and that was when Freya saw the true devastation of the home behind her mum. It looked as though the entire contents of the house had been tossed out of drawers and cupboards and strewn about the floor. The mess was incredible, and any original usage was hard to recognise from the damage caused.

'Oh, Mum.' She hugged her mum hard and let her cry on her shoulder for a moment. 'It's okay.'

They trod through the mess, careful not to cause any more damage to her parents' things, and went into the kitchen, where her dad stood talking to the police – an officer and a man in a suit – both with their backs to her.

The man in the suit turned and smiled at her.

It took a second for her to register who it was, but when it did, she let out a shocked gasp. 'Liam.'

He walked over to them both. 'Just awful,' he said heartfeltly. 'I heard the news and recognised the names, so I decided to come here too to check out what's happened.' He touched her mother's arm and gently caressed it, his expression stricken with regret. 'I'm so sorry.'

'It's okay, Liam,' her mother replied as she affectionately patted his hand. 'I'm glad you're here. I wouldn't trust anyone else with this mess, believe me.' She glanced at Freya. 'And maybe you two can have a little chat at some point. Now that you're both here.'

'Mum, this is not the time or the place,' Freya said, taking a step away from them both.

'It is lovely to see you, Freya,' Liam said with his best smile. The one he used when he was on his best behaviour. 'How are you?'

'Exactly the same as you found me before,' she responded icily.

'Freya,' her mum said, 'there's no need to be rude.'

He smiled and said nothing, instead moving to the police officer, who had moved away from her dad and was now busy noting down information. They talked quietly in the corner as the officer shared information with Liam, who listened and nodded as if to prove how engaged he was. Of course, he wouldn't be entirely engaged in that conversation. Freya knew that he'd be scanning the room, assessing everyone's body language, and would have half an ear listening to their conversation.

'Mum, really? Now?' Freya hissed as she grabbed her by the elbow and moved her closer to her dad.

'Well, there is no need to be rude, and you two need to chat at some point, darling. You're never going to work things out if you don't.'

'It's not as simple as that.'

'Darling, it can be,' her mum replied. 'Look, I know your relationship is a volatile one, always has been, but he is clearly still in love with you. It's written all over his face.'

Freya clenched her fists by her sides. 'Mother, you really don't know what you're talking about; we need to stop this discussion before it gets out of hand. Now is not the time.'

'I just think—'

'No,' Freya said assertively, 'end of conversation.'

Freya turned to her dad, who busily picked up the

contents of the drawers that lay scattered across the floor. She walked towards him, needing his calming presence. She always did after conversations about Liam with her mother.

'Hi, Dad,' she said.

'Hi, lovely girl,' he replied sadly as he scanned the area. 'Just take a look at this mess.'

She wrapped her arm around him, and he hugged her close. 'We'll clean it up, get it nice again,' she said as she leant her head on his shoulder. 'At least you weren't hurt. Either of you.'

'Yes, we will, and you're right, we're unhurt.' He glanced at his wife. 'Your mother giving you relationship advice again?'

Freya smiled. 'Yes, she's in love with Liam more than me, I think.'

He chuckled. 'She's always liked him. He couldn't be more perfect in her eyes for a son-in-law.'

She hugged him close. 'Do you feel the same?'

'Not necessarily. I'm only happy if you're happy.'

'I wasn't happy at all.'

'Yes, that's the impression I got,' her father replied. 'And I know you'll tell us the real reason why when you're ready, but it must have been bad enough to run back to London.'

'He's bad news, Dad.'

'Then you must do what's right for you. Your mum will understand when she hears everything you have to say.'

'I wish she would just take my word and that be enough.'

Her dad patted her arm. 'Give her time. She will.'

Liam broke their conversation by appearing again. 'Right, I think we have everything we need to go from here,' he said. 'I'll hand things over to the local force, but I'll keep an eye on everything, make sure to keep everything moving, and keep you informed.'

Freya's mother went to him and clasped his hands in hers. 'You are so kind. Thank you, Liam.'

'Anything for my wonderful in-laws,' he said with a sickening smile.

Freya felt her stomach turn.

Liam and the other officer left them in peace to begin the clean-up task properly. Not having to stop continually to answer questions or wait for areas to be dusted by the forensics team that showed up, focusing on surfaces most likely to have been touched, but found nothing of value and then left. To really get into the task of making the place look like a home again.

The next time the doorbell rang, it was Rosie, who arrived hot and flustered, her cheeks pink. 'I'm so sorry I took so long; the bloody trains were delayed.'

'It's no problem,' her mum replied. 'We've had the police, and Liam assures us he's going to monitor the situation.'

Rosie looked at her mother and then Freya. 'Liam? He's been here?'

'Yes, he left about half an hour ago. So helpful,' her mother said. 'Thank goodness for people like him.'

'Did you know that he'd be here?' Rosie asked Freya.

'No, that was a surprise for me, too.'

Rosie walked to Freya and took her by the arm into the other room. 'What the fuck, Freya. Are you okay?'

'I'm fine, except Mum's been simpering over him the whole time. She refuses to believe and accept it when I say we're over. I swear to God, she'd still find an excuse for him at my funeral when he's behind bars for murdering me.'

'Come on, it's not that bad. You know how she is. She

can't face up to the fact that he's out of your life, and now theirs.'

'Yeah, I know. I'd just like some support sometimes.'

'You need to tell them,' Rosie ordered as she hugged her hard. 'They need to know all the dirty details of what he's done to you. I guarantee she'll change her tune when she knows everything.'

'It's just so... hard.'

'Why?'

'Because I feel stupid and ashamed for letting him control me for so long.'

'Well, I think you're brave enough to go through everything he did to you, so you're brave enough to tell the people who love you without feeling shame. In the meantime, you have me and Dad. And Ben. And who knows, maybe Liam won't ever be Mr Perfect, but he might be telling the truth. You doing a flit back up to London might have been the wake-up call he needed.'

They all worked together getting the house back in shape, washing everything down, wiping away the residue left by the fingerprint powder the forensics team had used. Liam had done a thorough job, and it bugged Freya that she had him to thank for it. No wonder her mother had a skewed version of who he was. To her, he was a strong, masculine energy that made her feel safe, and who wouldn't like that and want to cling onto it? Especially now, when her home had been invaded.

It was evening by the time the house was restored to a home, and although Freya was shattered, the hard work had been worth it to see it back to the home it was. It would take time for her parents to adjust to living in a house that had been ransacked by an unknown assailant, but she hoped they would get through it and not feel the need to move somewhere new, as so many victims of crime did. Herself included.

Rosie and Freya shared the train back home and sat in relaxed silence as they picked at the cocktail sausages, cherry tomatoes, tortilla crisps and apple slices their mother had given them for the journey, packed up in small, lidded plastic pots like they were children again. Even in an emergency, her mum could still whip up some finger food from the contents of her fridge, the one place the burglars had not touched.

———

JAKE'S FACE lit up when Rosie and Freya entered the gym. They were late, and the session had already begun.

'Ladies,' he chimed as he noticed their arrival and walked over, his happy, glinting eyes focused on Freya.

'A little frazzled, but we're here,' Rosie said, chucking her bag down with the others. 'Our parents were burgled, so we've spent the afternoon involved in the clear-up.'

'Oh, what a nightmare,' Jake replied, the smile gone from his face. 'Are they both okay?'

'They will be,' Freya said. 'And thankfully, they weren't in when it happened, so apart from being shaken up, they're fine.'

'Thank God for that,' Jake said as he made the bold move of reaching out to gently rub Freya's arm. 'Are you okay?'

Freya discreetly edged away from his gesture of affection. 'I'm fine, but thanks for asking. Rosie too.'

'Wasn't sure we'd make it tonight,' Rosie said, picking up

on the sudden change in mood, 'but the train gods were kind to us.'

He moved his hand away swiftly, picking up on her unspoken command. 'Cheers to the train gods, then,' he said with a smile. 'You can join in at the next break, so just relax for now, and I'll call you when we're ready to begin the next round of circuits.'

He walked away and continued with his instruction as the other women milled around him.

Rosie turned and looked at her. 'Why did you do that? He was being sweet.'

'I don't think sweet or anything else is a good idea at the moment.'

'But from what you've told me, you two were getting along so nicely at the pub. He seems pretty infatuated with you.'

'That's just it. I don't need someone infatuated with me. It's too complicated. Liam was infatuated too, and look how that turned out.'

Rosie's expression softened. 'I know, I understand, but not everyone is like Liam.'

'What if I don't care? And what if I don't want Jake pulled into this mess? Can you imagine what Liam would do to him if he ever saw that I'd moved on with someone new?'

'You don't know what Liam would do.' Rosie glanced over her shoulder at Jake. 'But you may want to let him down gently. I think he's keen.'

'I will,' Freya said with a sigh. 'I shouldn't have had that drink with him the other night. That was stupid of me. I'll speak to him later.'

'But if you want to turn him down,' Rosie said, 'please take a minute and remember that you need people around you. Even if you're just friends. Don't push him away completely. You can't live holed up in that small flat forever, alone.'

'No, maybe not, but it's just fine for me now.' Freya knew that what Rosie was saying was true, she was already starting to feel the small beats of loneliness in her heart, but it was safer this way. No complications. No misunderstandings and no harm of being hurt again.

———

WITH ROSIE WAITING for her outside and the last of the stragglers leaving the gym, Freya went to Jake, struggling to find the right words.

He stopped packing up his bag and turned to her.

'Hi,' she said nervously. 'I'm sorry about before. I was a little stressed with all that's been going on.'

He tossed the bag that he'd been packing down on the floor. 'It's all right, no harm done,' he said kindly. 'I probably overstepped. I shouldn't have made assumptions.'

'It wouldn't be a problem in any other situation, but, well, I've been through a lot recently, and I kind of have a lot of baggage.'

'Yeah?'

'Yeah. And I still have stuff to work through. I've been hurt badly in the past.'

He shot her a glance as he ran his hand through his hair. 'You have a problem with mobility in this arm, which is just beginning to soften,' he said, pointing to her left arm. 'So I'm guessing perhaps a dislocation or a fracture at some point.'

She glanced at the floor and nodded. The arm had never felt right since Liam had dislocated it, but it was true, the exercises she was doing in these sessions were helping a lot. 'You'd be right,' she murmured. 'About the dislocation.'

'And the way you flinch at every loud noise, it's enough to see that you've been through something significant.'

Again, she nodded.

'Well, in that case,' he said, 'I think whatever you've been through, the bravest decision you've made was leaving,' he said, his eyes soft and kind.

'I know, although I don't feel brave most days.'

'Don't be so hard on yourself.'

'I took the coward's way out. I just disappeared. No explanation, nothing.'

'Sounds like whoever you left didn't deserve that kind of honesty.'

'Maybe not, but I should have faced it. Faced him.'

'I think in your heart you knew the danger that would have caused you.'

His understanding of the situation overwhelmed her. He was far too close to the truth. She stared at him and then cleared her throat. 'I should go.'

'Yes, of course, but, Freya, I'm here if you ever want to talk.'

A small flutter of butterflies danced in her stomach. She crushed them immediately; they had no business playing with her like that. 'Thank you.'

Rosie leaned against the railing as she waited outside and stood up straight when she saw Freya push open the door. 'Everything okay?'

'Everything's fine,' she said, blinking back the tears that pricked her eyes. 'We talked. We know where we stand.'

'Oh, I see,' Rosie said disappointedly.

Freya linked her arm in Rosie's, and they walked away.

'It's the right decision, really. He knows what's happened to me.'

'What?'

'Well, he figured it out. The basics, anyway. He saw it in my mobility, apparently. Guessed I'd had an injury.' She laughed. 'If only he knew how many there had actually been.'

Rosie blew out through her cheeks. 'Bloody hell, Freya.'

'And he's a good enough person not to push it with any more questions or make me feel like some sort of freak.'

Rosie hugged Freya close. 'You'd never be that.'

'Doesn't change the fact that this is how it has to be. I have enough to worry about right now with Liam back on the scene. I need to remember what's important.'

They strolled back to Freya's, and whilst they chatted and planned out just how they'd deal with whatever the future held, a strange sensation crept over Freya. An awareness that grew with the beat of each footstep – a subtle sense of being watched, of someone's eyes on her, observing. And despite her best efforts to dismiss it, the feeling grew and grew until the only thing she could do in response was to quicken her pace.

16

The commotion outside infiltrated the quiet sanctuary of Freya's flat until she could ignore it no longer. A man shouting, banging against what she assumed was the doors of the main entrance. She heard other voices too, residents perhaps trying to reason with him. Her first thought went to Elliot and whatever he might be up to, but whatever or whoever it was, she was glad to be locked up in her flat, safe from the chaos.

She just wanted a peaceful night. After a couple of long arduous conversations with her solicitor about the divorce process and who was entitled to what, none of which bothered her, she just wanted out of the marriage, her decree nisi had been granted. Although most people would be happy to mark this first process of a divorce by celebrating, Freya just wanted it to pass quietly by. She had no desire to celebrate anything about this part of her life, a time that had been filled with hurt and hatred, and a loss of something within her – a lightness of being – she feared she'd never get back.

When the voices from downstairs grew louder, she found

herself leaning in at the window to check outside to see who it might be.

Banging on her door pulled a cry from her throat as she spun around to stare at the door and whoever might be on the other side.

She inched closer. More banging. Her heart raced.

'Freya?' someone shouted. Elliot. No doubting his voice.

'What do you want?' she shouted back, still refusing to open the door.

'There's someone downstairs who says they know you. They want to see you, and they're not going away. You need to come down and sort it.'

'I don't know anyone who'd act like that.'

'Freya, I don't have time to stand here and argue the point to a fucking door. Are you going to go down and sort it?'

'All right!' she shouted, more to make him go away than anything else.

She needed to think. She paced, and when there were no more bangs against her door, she assumed Elliot had left her alone.

She stepped into her sandals and grabbed her keys. Hesitantly, she opened the door, hoping that Elliot hadn't remained, waiting for her, keen to knock some sense into her too. But the hallway was clear. She walked the length of the hallway and went down the stairs.

Her stomach dropped as she recognised Liam's voice and realised it was he who had been causing the disturbance. If her neighbours didn't already have a negative impression of her, they would now.

Liam looked straight at her through the doors, a look of relief at seeing her. The expression caught her off guard. She couldn't remember a time when he'd been pleased to see her.

'Freya,' Liam mumbled, 'let me in, please.' His slurred words indicated that he was drunk, and she immediately tensed at the thought.

'What do you want?' she demanded. 'Because I've got nothing to say to you.'

'I just want to see you,' he slurred as he managed to lose his balance just standing still. 'Got the paperwork through.'

'You have no need to be here,' she said resolutely. 'You're drunk and need to go home. I'm not letting you in as you are.'

'Yup,' he said with a shaky nod. 'Of course. That's the right thing to do. Well done. I'll go. I just wanted to see you. Stupid of me to think that you'd want to see me. I'll go. I'll go.'

She sighed. She could let him into the lobby at least, a public space with people passing through. It would get her neighbours off her back, which was double the incentive. 'All right, just wait a minute.' She buzzed him in, and he stumbled through the door and into the lobby.

He sat on one of the leather sofas in the lobby, his shoulders slumped, and his suit ruffled and creased. He looked a sorry mess, and for a moment she felt sorry for him.

He looked up as she approached and had to squint through the alcoholic haze to see her. 'Freya.'

She sat on the arm of the sofa at the other end, which he noted and nodded. 'Good shout,' he murmured. 'Keep your distance from me. Best policy.'

Although he'd done significant damage to her either drunk or sober, right now there was something about him that looked broken. In this state it didn't look possible for him to inflict any damage at all. 'What do you want, Liam?'

'What do I want?' He laughed. 'I want my wife back, my old life back, and not all this fucking mess around me.'

'I think you should go and sober up.'

'Yes, you're probably right.'

'I am right.'

He cast a bloodshot glance her way. 'I like this new assertive you, Freya. It's like you were when I first met you.'

'Before you knocked it out of me.'

'Touché. I deserved that.' He ran his fingers clumsily through his hair. 'I really deserved that. I just wanted to see you, that's all. Mark the end of our marriage.'

'I can see you've already done that,' she said. 'How much have you had to drink?'

He shrugged. 'Stopped counting.'

'So now you've seen me,' she said. 'Here we are marking the end of our marriage. That's it. Done. I can't help you any more than that.'

'I just wanted us to part as friends if we could. Stupid really to think that, but I realise I fucked up, and I wanted to let you know that I know what I've done. Drunk or sober, I realise I lost the best thing that ever happened to me. All my fault too.'

'I loved you so hard, Liam,' she said, feeling strangely numb. 'I would have forgiven that first beating if you had stuck to your promise that it would never happen again. Most women would have disappeared, but not me. I loved you enough to stay, and you took advantage of that love until it was only fear that kept me with you.'

'I know, I did terrible things. If I could change things, I

would. I ruined our relationship. You did nothing to deserve what I did, and I'm sorry for hurting you like that.'

'It's in the past,' she said coolly, knowing that it would be etched in her soul for a while yet. A crude carving of pain. 'It's time to move on.'

'I'm going to miss you,' he murmured as his eyes glistened with what looked like tears. 'Is there no chance?'

He was so broken, so sad, she felt pity for him for the first time. 'That chapter is closed. We're done, but I'm glad you can admit to what you did. I hope you get the help you need. I hope you don't treat anyone else the way you treated me.'

'I have learned, Freya. I was evil, I know that now.'

'Well, then that's a good thing to come out of this, us.'

He swiped away an errant tear from his cheek. 'I'll go.'

She stood as he did the same. As she did, she caught sight of his other hand, which had a line of blood snaking down to his fingers. 'You've cut yourself.'

He looked down and struggled to focus his gaze on his hand. 'Ah, yes, I thought I'd caught my hand on something. Can't remember what.'

'Was it a fight? Did you get into a fight?'

'Jesus, no,' he said indignantly. 'I told you, I'm not that person anymore. I must have done it coming over here. I think I fell. I can't remember.'

The blood still trickled a little as she watched him mop it with a finger, only to smear it further over his skin.

Oh, Jesus, she thought. *I can't believe I'm about to do this.*

'Why don't you come up quickly so that you can run that under water or something.'

His face lit up at her suggestion. 'Really?'

'Five minutes, no more, and then you'll leave. I must tell you that I have plenty of things up there that I can use to defend myself, and the neighbours across the hall are my friends now. They'll hear my screams if you try anything, so don't go getting any ideas. I'm not the frightened little thing I once was. I will fight back.'

'It's okay. I'm not going to harm a hair on your head. I promise.' He held up his fingers as if doing some sort of Scout's honour.

She helped him up the stairs and towards her flat, steadying him as she opened the door. Once inside, she flopped him down on her sofa and went to the kitchen. Keeping an eye on him, she filled a bowl with water and grabbed the roll of paper towel standing upright on the counter and then pulled out the small first aid bag from the cupboard. She sat next to him and balanced the bowl on her lap and guided his hand into it, watching the thin trails of blood curl in the water.

'Thank you,' he said quietly. 'I don't deserve any of this.'

'No, you don't.'

The mood had calmed, and Liam seemed more lucid with each minute that passed.

'That man earlier, downstairs,' Liam asked. 'Does he know you?'

'Elliot. No. Well, kind of. We're neighbours. He and I have argued a little. I don't like the way he treats his wife.'

Liam nodded thoughtfully. 'Does he intimidate you?'

'Sometimes. They're a strange couple, always fighting, then making up. No one really believes that he's dangerous. Rosie thinks I'm jumping to conclusions, but he's bad news, I know it.'

'Then I believe you,' he said. 'You always figured everyone out way before me, and I'm the detective.'

She smiled. 'Sometimes.'

'Has he ever threatened you?'

'No, not directly, but I keep myself safe.' The words left her lips, but they were dead words; she didn't feel or believe them.

Liam nodded again, watching as she tended to his wound. 'Good, I'm glad you keep yourself safe. You know you can always call on me, if he scares you. I can help. I don't like to think of you in harm's way with someone like that.'

'Then why didn't you think like that when I was with you?'

'Because I'm an idiot who needed his head seen to.' He placed his other hand on hers in the water. 'I want you back, Freya. I want to make amends, please.'

She looked him in the eye and shook her head. 'You know, I really believe you do.'

He nodded.

'But it's too late. The trust has gone, Liam. Can you understand that? I will always be waiting for you to lose your temper or come home in a mood. I'll always be on edge waiting for the first blow to come my way.'

He looked down, sadness in his eyes. 'I really blew it.'

She lifted his hand from the water and gently patted it dry. Selecting an appropriately sized plaster from the box on her lap, she covered the wound. 'There, all done.'

She placed the bowl on the table and stood, taking his hand to help him to his feet. 'Right, you're all patched up. Time to go.'

He shuffled to his feet and let her walk him to the door. 'Thanks, Freya.'

She opened the door and faced him. He gazed at her, and it took her straight back to their early days when life was good, when they had fun. When they were in love.

He gently held his hand to her face and caressed her cheek with his thumb. 'I was so stupid. Hurting someone as lovely as you.'

He was gentle, his hand warm, and the part of her that would have pushed him away and out the door without a second thought was shooed away by the part of her that yearned for the touch of another, even his. She gazed at him too, not sure why, but knowing that she couldn't stop. She stared at his hair that tumbled over his forehead, his plump lips and his eyes that were soft with alcohol and desire. He was pulling her under, and she felt herself struggle to breathe.

'Let me stay, Freya, please.'

She hesitated, and he took his chance and edged closer. 'Let me try again,' he murmured, his face close to hers. 'I love you.'

She stared at him, speechless, and he leant in closer, close enough to place his lips on her neck, enticing her with gentle kisses against her skin.

Her heart fluttered as she stood motionless, letting him take his time, planting kisses wherever he chose. A small sigh escaped her lips, and she felt his mouth twist into a smile between the kisses. His hands reached around her waist, pulling her closer to him. Again she gave no resistance, her mind unable to process all that was happening and the magnitude of what she was about to allow to happen.

He murmured her name, and as if smacking her back to reality, memories crashed into her mind of all the violence, the damage he inflicted, the pain. A means of protection to remind her of what could happen if she let him back into her life and her bed.

Seeing clearly again, and the harsh reality of what waited for her if she chose to travel down this path, she laid her hands on his and pulled them away and took a step back. 'No, Liam. This isn't what I want. You have to leave now.'

'You're sure?' he asked, his eyes bright with desire.

'I am.'

Disappointment covered his features, but he nodded and walked away.

Needing to be sure that he would actually leave, she followed him to the main entrance and let him out, watching as he stumbled down the pathway to disappear from view.

She needed air too, a sudden desire to break free from the world she inhabited. A sense of bravado filled her. She'd confronted the man she had been so terrified of, saw him weak, drunk and full of guilt. Yes, she'd let him into her home and wondered if that had been a mistake, but she'd stood her ground and didn't cave when he tried it on. She'd told him no and asked him to leave, and he'd listened and done as she'd asked with no resistance given. She might suffer a backlash from that rebuttal, but the more she considered it, the more confident she became that he was unlikely to remember it, and very likely to continue downing significant quantities of alcohol before the night was through. It bolstered her into wanting more, more freedom, more independence.

She found herself returning to her flat to gather up her things and leave the building, striding out onto the street and into the dusky evening light, determined to live freely.

She hadn't travelled far when the sense of bravado faded as quickly as her building slipped from view. The feeling of being watched surrounded her, just like the other night with Rosie, and although there were plenty of people around –

couples enjoying an evening stroll, dog walkers, parents with restless kids – she felt the need to keep checking over her shoulder, just to be sure he wasn't there. Despite her best efforts, part of her felt vulnerable at being followed by him, or anyone else.

When the feeling didn't subside, she turned and headed for home, unable to continue on without feeling panicked. She'd made a mistake, lived momentarily in a fool's paradise, and now just needed to be home again, and safe, tucked away in her flat. With the building back in her sights, she hurried towards it and turned quickly into the grounds and onto the pathway that would take her to the entrance.

A figure lingered by the door, and she felt the fear tingle in her spine. Why she thought it would be anyone to do with her, she couldn't fathom, but the heavy sensation in the pit of her stomach wouldn't lift.

17

It wasn't Liam, he had been wearing a suit, and this person was in denim shorts and a white T-shirt. Regardless, it was a man, and in her world they were a threat, known or unknown. Hesitating for a moment, she slowed her pace, wanting to be sure she could negotiate her way past this man and get back into the safety of the building.

He turned as she approached, and she blew out a sigh, immediately recognising him.

'Jake,' she said quickly, 'what are you doing here?'

He smiled. 'Hi, Freya. I thought I ought to return this to you. You left it at the gym the other day.'

He handed her Rosie's borrowed black hoodie that she had indeed left behind. 'Ah, thank you.'

'I wouldn't have come to your home, but I was passing, so I just thought I'd stop by on the off chance you'd be in. Rosie also said it would be okay. I think she may have been trying to let you know.'

Freya glanced down at her phone and saw the five missed calls and a text that she'd missed, having knocked it unknowingly into silence mode. 'Oh, yes, I see she's tried to call.' Feeling sheepish, she understood his discomfort to be here, not wanting to break any trust they might have been building, together with his need to see her.

'I also wanted to check you're okay. I was worried about you after the other day, but if I'm out of line, I apologise.'

She smiled. 'No, you're not out of line. Thank you for returning this. Do you want to come up? A coffee or tea?' She smiled, cringing at the awkwardness.

'No, I'll let you enjoy your evening,' he said, returning her smile. 'I just wanted to return this.' His smile faded as he glanced at her shoulders. 'You're shaking.'

She wrapped her arms around herself self-consciously. 'Yeah, just a little overwhelmed, I suppose.'

He looked confused.

'Liam, my ex, turned up here earlier. He was steaming drunk. All regretful and wanting to reconcile, if I'm not mistaken.'

'Oh, wow.'

'Yes, and so I went out for a walk, feeling on top of the world that I'd managed to confront him, but that feeling didn't last, and I soon felt vulnerable again, so I came home.'

Jake hesitated, went to speak and then stopped.

'What?' she asked.

'Look, you can tell me to back off or mind my own business, but would you like to go for a drink? Just round the corner at the local. You can tell me about it if you want?'

She thought for a moment. 'Actually, I'd really like that. But instead of the pub, can we go to the coffee shop? Where I work.' She checked her watch. 'Probably got forty-five minutes before Lucy closes up.'

His smile brightened his face. 'Okay, sounds great. Let's go.'

They made the walk to the café in a few minutes, and Freya caught sight of Lucy the moment she pushed open the door. Lucy had decided to keep the café open later into the evening during the summer months to catch the passing trade of dog walkers or the like who might decide a coffee was a better alternative to a pint or glass of wine.

'Freya,' Lucy said with a smile, 'lovely to see you. You do know you're not down to work this evening?'

'Yes, I do. I'm here with a friend.'

'Ah, well, come in and grab a table,' Lucy said. 'Coffee?'

Freya looked at Jake.

'Sounds great,' he replied.

They found a table tucked into the corner, and Lucy brought over two large cups of coffee for them and then left them alone. Only a couple of other passers-by came in, wanting takeouts, keeping the place a quiet sanctuary.

Jake stirred his coffee and took a sip. 'So what caused your ex to show up at your flat today, if you don't mind me asking?'

It wouldn't hurt to open up. She didn't have to share all the details of the hell she'd been through, but she could give him the outline and where they were now. 'Decree nisi came through today, which means he would have received it too. He obviously wasn't happy about it and decided to get drunk and come and visit me.'

'Was he violent?'

'No, I don't think he was capable of it, either.' She stirred her coffee. 'He seemed so broken tonight. So empty. He wasn't around for long. I soon sent him on his way, and to my surprise, I think he might stay away. Well, I'm hopeful anyway.'

'As he should.' After a pause, he continued, 'He hurt you badly, didn't he?'

'Yes, he really did.'

'Would you like to talk about it? If you want to.'

She shrugged a little. 'I'm like a lot of other women out there. I met someone, fell blindly in love and missed all the red flags.'

'The violent red flags?'

'The violent, the controlling, the gaslighting. I could go on. There were more flags there than at a semaphore flag convention.'

'And then they promise you that it will never happen again.'

She smiled. 'You seem to know the basics well enough.'

'I knew someone who used to get knocked around a bit. I watched it destroy her little by little. I tried to help. I tried to *get* her help, but it was painful to watch all that she went through. One of the reasons I started the classes specifically for women.'

'So you understand that when they're violent and then promise that it'll never happen again, we believe them because we're so desperately in love and want to get back to that time when they would do anything for us. To bask in the warmth of their love again.'

'Yes, I do.'

'And in time, that desperation becomes fear until you're completely trapped because you start to believe them when they tell you that you'll never make it in the outside world without them. Or worse, that they will find you and kill you, and you believe that over everything else because you've seen their rage and the brutality that is inflicted at their hand.'

From his expression, Jake looked to be holding on to his anger by the finest thread. 'When did it start, if you don't mind sharing?'

'Soon after the wedding,' she said, placing her mug down after taking a drink. 'The arguments grew fiercer until they spilled into beatings. Then came the apologies, the care, the promises. He was so gentle then. A completely different person. I so wanted to believe him, and at first I put it down to stress at work. He's always been prone to stress, you see. He strives for perfection, and that means that he always has a long way to fall when it doesn't work out. It was slaps at first. A few shoves, but these turned into full-force punches, always to the body. Somewhere it wouldn't be seen. I was still working at this point, so he had to ensure I could leave the house with no one asking questions. Things gradually got worse and worse until I had to leave my job in hospitality, which I loved. There were some days where my eyes would be so swollen that they'd close, and I'm sure he broke my nose on one occasion, even though he never took me to get it looked at.'

'What?'

'More control. He made sure it was he who made the decisions about the care I would receive. Not me, not my pain. And the times when he did relent and get me to a hospital, he always tried to stay in the room with me so I'd keep my mouth shut.'

'Did the hospital not intervene?'

'They tried when they could. They knew the process and knew what to do to get rid of him enough to ask me if I wanted help. But it was pointless. I could tell them everything, but it didn't mean they could protect me when I was alone, back at the house.'

'I'm so sorry,' Jake whispered as he held out his hands to hers.

'For what? This had nothing to do with you.'

'I guess for the evil that men do. I know it happens. I've seen plenty of women come to my classes, and I see the bruises, although I never say anything. I make sure they have the tools to build their strength physically with the hope that they can also get their strength mentally in order to do whatever they need to do, be it leave or stay and remain resilient.'

'Then you are one of the good ones.'

'It's not much, but it's something.'

She leaned forwards. 'And let me tell you, it is something. Everything helps. That's all I wanted. Someone to recognise what I was going through and help me. Not with leaflets or details of organisations. Real help that would enable me to fight back, however that may look. I feel so much physically stronger, and although I could never win a fight with Liam when he's in one of his moods, I could have recovered quicker or found the strength to leave sooner. It matters.'

'You matter.'

She smiled. 'Thank you, and yes, I do, but it took me a long time to realise that.'

'Your sister seems like a great help.'

She sat back in her chair. 'She's been totally wonderful. Her and Ben. I couldn't have got the place over there without them. I'll be forever in their debt.'

'She seems like someone who would do anything for you.'

'She's the best, that's for sure.'

'And your parents.'

She sighed. 'That's a little more complicated. They know something's not right, I'm sure they do, but I haven't told them. I can't.'

'Why?'

'I don't know. They loved Liam, still do. At first, I thought I was strong enough to handle everything that was going on between Liam and me. I didn't want to give them cause to worry. Then I *couldn't* admit to it. I couldn't open up to them. It had been such a long time. They were so happy their children were settled, and I felt so ashamed of what I'd become. It became easier to just let them believe what they wanted.'

'But something changed.'

'Oh yes, it did. The last beating was so bad I really thought I would die.'

Jake gazed at her, pulling the information out of her.

She rested her fingers on her throat. 'He choked me and fractured my eye socket. I blacked out completely, and I thought my life was over. When I came to, I got myself to hospital and realised that next time, it might be. I went home, realised nothing would change, and it made me revaluate what I needed to do, so I left. I had a bag packed, hidden, ready to go, and that day, when I was discharged home and alone, I bolted. Straight out into the world. As easy and as hard as that.' The horror on his face stopped her. 'Would you like to talk about something else? I get that this is a little heavy to deal with. I shouldn't have shared. It's not your problem.'

'No, I just can't—' He looked away, and she noticed his

leg tapping and his fists balled, seething with anger. 'I can't believe that he got away with it for so long. The absolute bastard.'

'It's okay. It's over now.' She said the words out loud in the hope that she'd begin to believe it too.

'You're very strong. Very brave,' he said, composing himself now. 'I don't know anyone who could deal with something so terrible and sit here as you are now.'

'I'm no different to any other woman who's left an abusive relationship. We're alive, and that's all that matters. We can cope with anything once we escape.'

'It's really that simple?'

'No, of course not. There are days when the flashbacks are so bad you can't get out of bed, or the fear of being dragged back to that place overwhelms you, and that's aside from all the physical scars and damage you have to deal with on a daily basis. They're fading, but I still have headaches, and my back twinges now and then. I need tablets to help me sleep.'

He shook his head, clearly shaken by their conversation.

'I'm sorry, I feel I've said too much.'

'No, you have nothing to apologise for. I'm sorry you had to live that life. What about the police? Have they ever been able to help you?'

She shrugged. 'Liam works for the police. He's a detective, you see. He makes it difficult, no, sorry, impossible. They can't help me.'

'What about injunctions?'

'Wouldn't help. He'd find a way to get to me. He'd kill me if I ever tried anything like that. Sheer anger would ensure I was dead within a week. He wouldn't care about the consequences, just the punishment. But I'm guessing he'd get away with it. He always seems to land on his feet.'

Jake blew out a sigh. 'Men can be monsters.'

'Yes, they can. But not just men. Women are capable of it too.'

'Agreed. It's all so fucked up.'

'We're all animals; it's just that humans are at the top of the chain.'

'Whatever I can do to help you, you know that I will. I am here for you, as your friend.'

'Thank you, I need plenty of those, that's for sure.'

'I mean it. Anything you need, you let me know.'

They chatted easily after that, keen to move on to less intense topics, and Freya enjoyed the feeling of having less weight on her shoulders. It had felt good to share, although she hadn't expected to disclose so much, but there was no doubt she felt better for it.

Lucy closed up the café after the last customer had left with his takeaway coffee, and wished them goodnight. Jake and Freya walked back to her block in the darkness that had descended, and she let him walk her right to the entrance.

'Thank you for a lovely evening,' she said.

'You're very welcome. I had a good time. Thank you for trusting me with your story.'

She pondered for a moment. 'Was it Maya Angelou who famously said there is no greater agony than bearing an untold story inside you.'

'I don't know, but I like the quote,' Jake said. 'I also like the colour in your cheeks.'

A smile crept across her lips. 'I feel better for sharing, so thank you for listening.' She didn't know why she trusted him, but she did.

'My pleasure.'

She fought the urge and then could not resist standing on her tiptoes to lean in and plant a small kiss on his cheek.

He smiled, caught unaware, and she liked that she had made him smile in such a way. Something just for her.

'Night, Jake.'

'Goodnight, Freya. I'll see you soon.'

18

'Liam's been simply marvellous,' Freya's mother chimed as she chatted happily down the phone. 'I don't know what we would have done without him.'

'Really, Mum. That's great,' Freya replied through a tense jaw as she sat at her window, finishing the last drops of her cup of tea. She hadn't had any further contact with Liam since his drunken visit the other night, and she was glad of it.

'Of course he was too busy to be on hand every day, but he always checked in with us and made sure the best people were on the case.'

'Uh-huh.' Freya had to bite her tongue. If she heard any more about Saint Liam, she'd blow.

'And the small bits that were taken were found dumped in a car park bin not three miles from here. What are the chances of that?'

'I don't know,' Freya mumbled.

'Luckily for us, it was only a few bits of old jewellery and a couple of trinket boxes. I know it sounds contrary, but I didn't want them once they had been in someone else's hands. They were not of sentimental value, so I let them go to charity and on to a new home.'

'Well, that's really good news. And the house, is that all sorted now?'

'Yes, your father brought some decorators in to brighten the place up. He's been promising to do it for years, and this seems to be the push he needed. It feels like home again, I'm pleased to say. The nightmare is finally over.'

'That's wonderful.'

'And in the clear-up, we found some old schoolbooks and things in the loft from your school days. Probably best if you collect these when you're next over. You can decide what to do with it.'

Never one to beat around the bush, what Freya's mum was telling her was that she no longer wanted that kind of clutter in her home. That was fine. No problem. Freya would come and collect it, take it off their hands. 'Great, well, leave it out for me when I next visit, and I'll take it off your hands.'

Movement in the corner of her eye turned her attention to the figure walking up the path. Elliot. She hadn't seen him for a day or two and noticed the large bandage on his hand and wrist and the way he cradled it in his other hand. He looked tired, worn, and a black mood was etched over his face. Something stirred inside her, and she couldn't help but think of Liam and how he could be involved with it somehow.

'You'll have to come and visit soon,' her mum said. 'You, Rosie and Ben. And of course if you wanted to bring Liam, I just thought I'd let you know that he would be most welcome.'

'Thanks, Mum, but that's not going to happen,' she said as she watched Elliot disappear into the building.

'Ah, that's a shame.' She paused. 'And I can't say I know what's gone on between you two, as you won't tell me, but he genuinely seems to care about you. Whatever has happened, I feel he's very sorry.'

She raked her fingers through her hair, unprepared to discuss her relationship with Liam and the end of it, but could ignore it no longer. 'Look, there's something I need to tell you about Liam and why we're never getting back together.'

'And what's that?' her mum asked innocently.

'I can't discuss it over the phone, but why don't I come up on my next day off work and have lunch with you guys or something?'

'That sounds wonderful,' her mum said, preening on the other end of the line. 'And whatever you want to discuss, I'm sure it wouldn't be as bad as you think it is. We've been around the block a few times; there's not much you can shock us with.'

'We'll see, Mum. We'll see,' Freya said, wanting to shut the conversation down. 'And I can't chat much longer. I'm about to go out.'

'Really, somewhere nice, I hope.'

'Just some errands right now, but later, yes, I think so. Dinner at the Italian around the corner.'

'Oh, nice. Is that with Rosie and Ben?'

'No, just a friend.'

'Hmm, the male or female variety?'

'It really doesn't matter, does it. I need new friends; that's what's important.'

'So it's a man, then.'

'Mum,' she said, frustration laced in her voice.

'I just don't think you should rush into anything that you might regret later.'

'It's just a meal out.'

'But it can quickly become something more. I know how it is. I was young once too, you know.'

'Mum!' she said, wincing at the thought.

Her mum laughed. 'Well, I was. I lived a very fulfilling life before I met your father, you know.'

'Okay, Mum. I don't need details.'

'I'm just saying I know what it's like,' her mum replied. 'You're vulnerable. Open to persuasion.'

'Mum, I have to go. I appreciate that you care, but let's save this for another time.'

'All right, dear.'

'I'll speak to you again soon,' Freya said and hung up the phone.

FREYA PUT whatever thoughts she had about Liam getting to Elliot out of her mind for now. She grabbed her bag and keys and left the flat. Today was going to be a good day. She'd received her first payment since starting her new job – her wages paid every two weeks – and she needed to set up a bank account so that all future payments could be paid directly. The thought excited her. A mundane task for most, but for her it signified independence. A new life, without Liam watching over her shoulder. Of course the money wasn't much, but it was enough to be able to pay her way and, after the next couple of cheques, no longer be a financial burden to Rosie and Ben.

The process was easy enough. She could have done it online but chose to go into the branch on the high street. She completed the forms, showed her ID and was advised that she'd get account details and a card in the post in the next seven days. With a lightness in her step, she continued out into the high street, ready to tackle her next task: to buy the dress that she had been admiring since she'd arrived here.

She pushed open the door of the shop and smiled at the assistant behind the counter, who looked up at Freya as she arranged earrings on a chrome stand.

'Hi,' Freya said, recognising the woman from before when she and Ava had played dress-up here. 'I wondered if I could try that dress on again. You know, the striped button dress?'

'Ah, yes,' the woman said as she went to the rack where the summer dresses hung. 'I remember because it looked lovely on you.' She deftly pulled out the dress in her size and handed it to her. 'You remember where the changing rooms are?'

Freya took the dress and gave her thanks as she went to the cubicle at the back of the shop. The memories of her shopping trip with Ava made her realise how long it had been since she'd last seen her. Freya found she was missing her new friend and hoped that she was surviving and that their friendship was not over before it had begun because of her meddling.

The dress was perfect, and Freya did one last little three-sixty spin to make absolutely sure that she should buy it and then changed back into her jeans and T-shirt.

'Are we buying today?' the woman asked with a smile.

'We are indeed,' Freya said with a wide smile, laying the dress on the counter.

The woman rang up the sale, which was still at fifty per cent off, much to Freya's delight, and she paid with the cash in her purse. Money she'd earned, that was hers to spend as she chose. This would be the only thing she'd buy though, the rest would go on food and towards the next rent bill, but it made her happy that she'd managed to treat herself too.

She would wear it tonight at her meal with Jake, and although short-sleeved, she'd sling a denim jacket over it if the weather turned cold. A long silver multi-layered necklace borrowed from Rosie's collection would complete the look.

After popping in to see Lucy and check her rota and grab a coffee to take away, Freya made her way home. The sun was bright in the sky, and people milled about. It occurred to Freya that she hadn't felt watched or monitored while she'd been out. Perhaps it had been her imagination all along.

Perhaps her luck was changing.

'So you're happy with how you look?' Rosie asked through the speakerphone, her voice filling the room.

'Yes, I think I am,' Freya said as she checked herself in the mirror and then grabbed her mascara and lipstick to refresh her make-up. She ran her fingers through her hair and spritzed some perfume over her neck. Again, all stuff borrowed from Rosie. She hadn't taken so much care over her appearance since she'd gone for the job at the café, and it felt good. There was no denying the pleasurable sensation of butterflies dancing in her stomach at the thought of meeting Jake again either.

He'd offered her his number at the end of the evening when she last saw him, and with much encouragement from Rosie, closer to nagging, she'd messaged him. After messaging back and forth, he finally phoned her, and they continued chatting until late into the night. After that, they messaged frequently, and she found herself looking forward to receiving his texts.

Jake was everything Liam was not. He was strong, fit and masculine in a way that Liam would never achieve. Liam was handsome, yes, but he was cunning, assured and manipulative, all toxic traits hidden behind the charm that, once focused on a person, made them feel at the centre of his world. It was clever and effective, and most people fell for it. And from the earlier phone call with her mother, so had she.

The buzzer went, and Freya gathered up her keys, bag and denim jacket. 'Wish me luck.'

'You don't need it,' Rosie replied. 'I bet you look gorgeous, now go and have a lovely evening, and call me when you get back. I want all the details, okay?'

Freya laughed. 'Okay.'

Jake was waiting outside, dressed in jeans and a white short-sleeved shirt, which fell open at the neck. He smiled as she walked out to him, and she watched as his gaze fell over her.

'Hi, Jake.'

'Hey, Freya. You look lovely.'

'Thank you, so do you.'

'Shall we?' he asked as he held out his arm, an invitation for Freya to link hers through, which she did without hesitation. He'd gained a trust from her that she never thought she'd be able to give so soon, but it felt too right to ignore, and she was determined to enjoy the evening. Her first date.

They'd decided to stay local, and started at Berties, a cellar pub with outside seating that allowed them to enjoy the early evening sun. After a couple of glasses of wine for her, and beers for him, they moved on to a cute little Italian bistro, where they indulged in delicious food, good wine, and better company.

'Gonna need a few extra gym sessions if the rest of the food is as good as this,' she said as they both picked at their shared platter of breads arranged around a large bowl of olive oil and balsamic vinegar dipping sauce.

'We can sort that,' he said with a mischievous grin. 'It's nice to see a woman enjoy her food on a date.'

Suddenly aware of how she might look, she paused. 'Am I binging?'

'No, not in the least, but women I've taken out before just pick at a salad all night.'

'Let me guess,' she said through mouthfuls, 'and then gaze hungrily at whatever is on your plate.'

'Yup.'

She smiled and took a sip of her wine and wiped her fingers on her napkin. 'Look, it's difficult for women. We want to impress, and gorging on food is not delicate and not elegant. We're not supposed to behave like that, especially on a date, so we order a salad, knowing that we'll eat again when we get home.'

'But it's ridiculous; if you're hungry, eat.'

She laughed. 'I know, right? That's exactly what I'm doing!'

He laughed too. 'Then I'm happy!'

'And I'm going to order the largest, juiciest steak after

this, and if there's room, which I hope with all my heart there will be, order the sweetest, most indulgent dessert I can find.'

His eyes twinkled in the candlelight, clearly, and pleasingly, affected. 'I'm not sure if I should be impressed, which I kind of am right now, by the way, or worried.'

'Worried? About what?'

'That you're on a date with me and don't care about being all the things you said you have to be on dates.'

She gazed at him. 'Maybe it's because I'm comfortable with you. The first person in a long time.'

He nodded, the tilt of his lip telling her he was happy with that response. Very happy.

'But I can order a salad if you'd prefer...'

He laughed. 'No way.'

They'd managed to avoid speaking about Liam or what he'd done to her, and instead she discussed her neighbours – Elliot and Ava – to get Jake's take on it.

'I think that if you're concerned, you should keep an eye on them.'

'That's what I'm doing,' Freya said. 'Even though I know people think I'm projecting my trauma onto the situation somehow.'

'Who?'

'Rosie, Ben. But it's only coming from a place of love. I know that.'

'Then keep doing what you're doing, but just be safe.'

She'd been receiving texts from Rosie periodically, which she assured Freya were to ensure she felt okay, but Freya knew that it was for her to enjoy the moment too – to be caught up in the heady heights of first-date fever. Freya would reply and give just enough of a snippet to keep her sister happy, and she was always discreet so Jake would not feel like he was being ignored.

'Where to next?' he asked as he finished his coffee.

'It's still light out; maybe a walk would be nice. If you want. I don't mind.'

'Sounds perfect.' He gestured for the bill, and their waitress prepared it and brought it to their table.

'I don't know how you feel about this, but I'd love to pay for this evening,' he said, 'if you are okay with that?'

She smiled at his consideration. 'I would be very happy to split the bill, but if you'd like to pay, I will smile graciously and say: "thank you very much, that's very kind of you".'

'Great, and of course, it doesn't mean anything other than I'd like to pay.'

She laughed at him tying himself in knots. 'Again, thank you very much, that's very kind of you.'

Colour flushed his cheeks as he paid for the food.

They strolled along the pathway until it came out into a large open park still busy with families and other couples before the night would bring out the more unsavoury characters.

They found a bench and sat.

'Do you live near here?' she asked.

'Not so far away. About ten minutes. Morden. Do you know it?'

'Not really.'

'You're welcome to come over if you'd like. Anytime.'

'That sounds nice, thank you.'

The breeze was cooler now, and a small shiver crept down Freya's back, making her tug the denim jacket closer over her shoulders.

'Are you cold?' he asked as he removed his jacket. 'Here,

have this.' He gently wrapped it around her shoulders and kept his arm wrapped around her. She liked the warmth of him against her and couldn't help but lean into his side.

'I really like you,' she said quietly. Sincerely.

He looked at her, a warmth of sincerity in his eyes too.

'I don't know what we're getting into here, but please tread gently. Don't hurt me,' she continued. 'I couldn't bear it if you did.'

He laid his hand over hers. 'I will never do anything to hurt you. I promise you that. I really like you too. I have for a while now.'

She smiled and rested her head on his shoulder as they watched the sun go down on the horizon. The night crawled across the sky, darkening it to an indigo hue. The streetlights from the roads that edged the park cast an orange glow just beneath the treeline, and the crowds slowly began to dissipate.

'Perhaps we should go back now,' Freya said, ready to leave the park behind.

'Yes, of course.'

They stood, and she linked her arm through his as she kept his jacket around her shoulders, feeling happy and safe, even out in a park in London at night, all because she was with a man who felt strong and dependable, but kind and considerate too.

They walked up to her building, and she considered what she should now do. Should she invite him in, and all the connotations that would bring with it, or should she leave him at the door and risk seeming like she wasn't interested in him. She couldn't decide and tensed her body as her thoughts began to race the closer they got to the main entrance.

'It's okay,' he said calmly, as if reading her mind. 'There's no pressure. I wanted to make sure you're home safe and leave it there.'

They stopped outside the door, and he faced her, holding her hands in his. 'Although I think you know I'm really very attracted to you, and I would love to do this again. I've had a lovely evening.'

The way his fingers rubbed against the palms of her hands caused a tingle that ran through her body.

'I'd like that too,' she murmured as she looked into his eyes.

He paused for a moment and then leaned in to place a soft, warm kiss on her lips. She responded, her body rising to his. It was gentle and sweet and full of restraint from what she could feel of it. The power of what he could give in a kiss was there, but it was concealed, held back, for now. She enjoyed the thought of what might be to come when she was ready.

She went back to her flat, smiling at the memories of the evening until an unwelcome sense of being watched pervaded all corners of the room. She glanced out her window and caught Elliot standing at his window, staring straight at her, contempt in his eyes.

Was he blaming her for something? Had she tipped him over the edge with her meddling, or was there something else going on here?

She stepped back, uncomfortable under his watchful gaze, closed the curtains and rechecked her locked door.

Liam wouldn't leave her mind, and her suspicion that he had something to do with Elliot's injury wouldn't leave her be. It was just like him to act in this way, abuse his power this way. He probably thought this would be a fast-track into her good books again. Little did he know.

She needed answers and pulled out her phone, messaging Liam. *What have you done?* She hit send and waited.

The reply was immediate. Seconds later, he called.

She hit the green button. 'Liam.'

'Freya, what's going on?' The noise in the background could have been a pub or club or another social event. Music thumped in the far distance, and someone laughed loudly.

'Where are you?' she asked.

'Back down south. Have been for the last week, tying up some loose ends here. Why? What do you think I've done?'

Flustered, she struggled to reply. He couldn't have done any harm to Elliot; he hadn't even been here. And why would he? What would he gain from that? 'Oh, nothing, I just thought... it doesn't matter.' She bit her lip hard. Paranoia had got to her, and now she looked a fool. 'Crossed wires, that's all.'

'Are you all right?'

'I'm fine,' she snapped. 'I've got to go, bye.' She thumped the screen to end the call.

She tried to get back the ease she'd enjoyed earlier and peeped through her curtains for any sign of Elliot, but there was none. He'd gone, the lights turned out. She could relax, and should, but her senses remained on hyper alert, listening for every noise and creak that the building liked to throw out to her.

19

Freya ran up the stairs to her floor. She had a couple of hours to kill before a shift at the café, the last before a couple of days off. She looked forward to having some time to herself to make some plans. Jake had been in touch, and they had discussed the possibility of another date, which excited her. Liam had been in touch too, which excited her less so, but since his drunken escapade, he hadn't shown up here. Part of Freya wanted to believe that maybe he had changed and had kept to his word, but she knew to be cautious when it came to anything to do with Liam. She would also use this time to meet her parents as promised, and use the time to discuss the truth about who Liam really was.

Freya immediately spotted Ava standing at her door as she rounded the corner. Ava was waiting for an answer, clearly, and Freya was pleased to see her, hoping that this was not a hostile confrontation but something kinder – something that would allow them to restart their friendship. 'Hey,' Freya said as she approached Ava. 'How are you?'

Ava jumped, zoned out in her own little world, but she smiled when she saw Freya, and it told her that whatever interaction they were about to have was likely to be okay.

'Hey,' Ava said. 'I was knocking for you.'

'Can see that,' Freya said with a smile and pulled out her keys. 'Want to come in?'

Ava's eyes were wide, a little manic, and darted from Freya to down the hallway in quick bursts, convincing Freya that she might be on something – medication or something else – to keep her pepped. Perhaps her doctor had got involved and prescribed, but whatever it was put Freya on edge. It was also at this moment that she realised she hadn't seen Elliot for a while, and perhaps that was contributing to her erratic state of mind.

'Are you okay, Ava?'

She nodded quickly. 'I'm fine, really, just glad to be out of the flat, even if it is just down the hall.'

'Where's Elliot?'

'He's away at the moment.'

'Ah, I see. When is he back? Imminently?'

'Possibly.'

'Would you like to go? Are you wanting to get back?' Freya asked, understanding the rules that had probably been imposed.

'No, no, it's fine. I'm just a bit jittery. Listen, I wondered, would you like to come over for coffee? It's been a while since I've seen you, and I thought it would be nice to catch up.'

'That sounds lovely. I worried you wouldn't want to after the last time. Elliot was angry, and I thought you might be too. I was only looking out for you, you know that.'

Ava nodded again quickly, distracted. 'Yes, yes, I know

that. I'm not angry. I've just had a lot to sort through. You know how it is.'

Freya nodded. She did indeed know how it was.

'So you're up for it? Coffee at mine?'

Freya shrugged. 'Of course, sounds great.'

'Perfect,' Ava said as she grabbed onto Freya's arm and hurried them back to her apartment.

Ava opened the door and let Freya into the spacious apartment. Freya was keen to see it, having only caught glimpses from the door. From a quick glance around, Freya calculated that it was probably three times the size of her little studio, at least. 'Wow, this is gorgeous,' she murmured, looking up at the high ceilings with ornate architrave. The living space was open plan, and the kitchen area was to the right with dual-aspect windows. 'So spacious.'

Ava smiled as she strode past Freya towards the kitchen. She pulled two mugs from the cupboard and switched on the kettle. 'It's lovely. A bit of a find. There are not many units like this one. We're very lucky.'

'Indeed.' Freya cast her eyes over the large L-shaped sofa with huge slouchy and very comfortable-looking cushions.

'Please, sit,' Ava said, noticing Freya's gaze. 'I'll bring these over.'

The place was just like something out of a beautiful home magazine. Everything had its place, from the green velvet sofas to the copper and rose gold accessories, mirrors and lighting, and the lush, oversized palms carefully placed to fill a corner or punctuate the zonings of the room.

'I'm glad you like it here,' Ava said as she stood in front of the kitchen window that Freya had so often spied them in. A tingle of embarrassment fluttered in her stomach that she had behaved in that way, and it was not something she'd likely admit to, unless of course she had to.

'My sister would love it here,' Freya said. 'She's an interior designer.'

'Ah, you have a sister,' Ava said. 'How lucky. I had the misfortune of having three brothers. All boisterous. Growing up with them was a battle. I would have loved a sister.'

'I'm very lucky,' Freya said. 'We're close.'

'You should bring her over,' Ava said. 'Maybe I can show her around the place too.'

Ava was calmer now, safely nestled within her own surroundings again, and although the mass of copper and blonde spiral curls framed her facial features, Freya could see no bruises or marks that indicated a recent beating. Freya was relieved. They were probably back in their post-confrontation honeymoon phase. Freya remembered feeling upbeat whenever she was in that place, so she understood how it could be possible for Ava to feel the same. Medicated or not.

Ava brought the two mugs of tea over to Freya, who was happy that the sofa was as comfortable in reality as it looked from afar, and balanced a box of expensive-looking chocolates over her mug.

'Those look dangerous,' Freya said, eyeing the chocolates as she took the mug from Ava.

'A present from Elliot,' Ava replied as she sat and pulled off the lid. 'He wanted to treat me.'

I bet he did, Freya thought.

Ava held out the box to Freya.

With no little card to indicate which chocolate to choose, the assumption that any choice from such an expensive brand would be divine, Freya picked the nearest one to her and popped it into her mouth. 'Thank you.' It was indeed divine, the flavours of chocolate and black cherry bursting on her tongue.

Ava did not eat, however, and placed the box on the table, next to a carefully positioned stack of expensive-looking magazines, a round tray with a large candle, and a cute succulent in a marble pot, all matching in silver and white tones. Exactly like Freya had seen when she'd scrolled through Instagram. She felt as if she'd stepped into an actual Instagram reel, the place was so aesthetic. She sipped her tea to wash away the sweet treat, so as not to crave another.

'So where is Elliot?' Freya asked.

Ava shrugged. 'He's at work, I think, but I'm not sure. He should be home soon though.'

Freya frowned. Her frantic need to be tucked safely back here now made sense.

'It's no lie that we're struggling a little at the moment,' Ava admitted without any encouragement. 'He has a lot on his mind. Work is very demanding, and that spills into our home life.'

Freya placed her mug down on a coaster and looked at Ava. 'I'm sorry to hear that. It must be very hard for you.'

Ava nodded. 'It is.'

'Well, please know that you can count on me, you know, if you ever need a friend. I mean, if you want some respite if things get a bit hard, I'm just down the hallway, and you're always welcome.'

'That's sweet of you,' Ava said, 'but just not possible at the moment. Elliot won't be happy if he knows what I've shared with you. He's a very private man.'

'I understand, but it's not like you've told me your life history. I'm the one joining the dots here.' She held Ava's gaze. 'I know what you're going through. I've been where you are.'

'Oh, really? I wouldn't have put you down as a relationship kind of person,' Ava said bluntly. 'You're quite the introvert.'

Ava's words stung, but Freya understood why she might have that impression. 'I am now, but there are many reasons for that. I was married, but it was an abusive relationship. I'm here to make a fresh start.'

Ava wrinkled her nose a little, apparently not liking this information. Perhaps abusive relationships didn't fit into her perfect aesthetic, or perhaps she was in denial. 'I wouldn't call what Elliot and I have abusive. Perhaps volatile.'

Freya needed to tread carefully. One push too far and Ava would shut her out completely. 'Okay, volatile, but I just want you to know that I understand, and I'm here if you ever need it.'

'That's sweet,' Ava replied dismissively.

There is nothing sweet about it, Freya thought. *I'm just doing what I desperately needed myself.*

Freya felt the mood change – Ava's sudden indifference – but she was glad she'd managed to get her point across. She was doing the right thing by paying it forward now that she was free, although Ava did not look like she appreciated the offer or this conversation.

'How's that café,' Ava asked, changing the subject, 'you know the one where you wanted the job?'

'Well, I got it. Lucy took me on, and I have worked several shifts since. It suits me for now. Gets me back into the working world.'

'How quaint,' Ava said, her tone slightly aloof. The person sitting in front of Freya was not the same woman she'd had fun with, trying on dresses and drinking coffee. Even persuading Lucy to take Freya seriously.

'And do you work?' Freya asked, running through her mind how she could make her excuses and leave.

'No, Elliot and I agreed that I'd be a homemaker.' She gestured outwards. 'So I've designed this place right down to the tiniest detail.'

'You've done well. It is beautiful.'

'Everyone says that when they come here,' Ava said aimlessly. 'The place was also included in a local magazine. We had a lot of attention, which Elliot loved, and I hated. I think it's too much, myself.'

'Could you change it?'

'Gosh, no. Elliot wouldn't allow that.' Ava sighed. 'No, I just float around here doing very little, but I'm happy.'

Freya frowned, unsure how to respond. The silence and general air of awkwardness filled the room. Ava was obviously trying to make the effort, why else would she have knocked on Freya's door, but something wasn't quite right, and Freya felt too uncomfortable to stay.

She stood, placed her mug down, ready to leave. 'I really should go,' Freya said. 'I have a shift in a little while, so I should get ready for that.'

'Of course,' Ava said as she jumped from her seat in agreement.

Ava leant against the front door as she held it open for Freya, fixing her gaze on her. 'This stuff you've been seeing between Elliot and me, I'd appreciate it if you just forgot all about it.'

The sentiment of Ava's words hit Freya, and she immediately understood. This catch-up had one objective – to inform Freya how things would be from now on.

'We won't be involving the police again, and I wouldn't want anyone to make any assumptions or take matters into their own hands. Am I making myself understood?'

Freya nodded. 'Of course. I apologise if I did the wrong thing. I just wanted to make sure you were okay.'

'I'm absolutely fine. Elliot is my husband. He's not perfect, but neither am I. He understands me, and he loves me for who I am.'

'I get it,' Freya said.

'And I love him,' Ava continued. 'We just need our own privacy to live our lives.'

Freya stepped outside into the hallway. 'Well, I'll see you around, Ava. Thanks for the tea and chocolates.'

Ava said something indecipherable as she shut the door. The fact that she was smiling as she said it spurred Freya into thinking that it was pleasant.

Freya strode back to her flat. Irritation surging through her body. Elliot had worked wonders on his wife. She was as keen to keep whatever they had going on pushed as deeply under the rug as he was. He obviously had a firm grip on her behaviour. If he'd have known they'd spoken, even had tea together, he would have been furious and would likely dish out a suitable punishment, when in fact, he should be impressed by her fierce loyalty.

She tutted as she made her way down the hallway and back to her tiny flat, her black mood descending to darken her day.

Some things never change, she thought to herself angrily, *and they never will.*

She knew the anger would hang around for the rest of the day, and although she didn't want to think about medicating herself, the pack of sedatives in her cupboard were calling to her, telling her that they could help.

SHE WALKED out of the building, ready to make her way to the café, but stopped the moment she stood on the boundary line between the grounds of the flat and the pavement beyond. Something prevented her from stepping out. A sense of danger that would not budge despite her checking her surroundings and finding nothing of note and telling herself that there was nothing to fear. Her legs would not move. Irritated and spooked, she paused and tried again. The sense of being watched was as intense as the sense of fear that had temporarily incapacitated her.

Feeling dizzy, she had to calm her breathing, which had become erratic and shallow. She held on to the small, brick gateway and calmed her body and mind.

'Come on, move,' she told herself sternly when the light-headedness had passed, putting one foot in front of the other until she was walking again.

20

'Here you go,' Rosie said, placing the cardboard four-cup holder of tea she'd bought for herself, Freya and Ben carefully onto the table on the train.

They all murmured their appreciation as they grabbed a cup each and held it close, a caffeine comfort blanket. It was late in the afternoon, and all were a little jaded from a large meal at Freya and Rosie's parents' and the Sunday blues of the approaching week. But because it was Sunday, they'd managed to get an earlier train, and that meant they'd all be home earlier than anticipated.

'Come in, come in,' her father had chirped happily when he'd opened the door.

The mouth-watering smells that had drifted through the house had spoken directly to Freya's stomach, which grumbled in anticipation.

Her mum had been busy, apron on – as if people still wore those these days – and working in amongst the steaming saucepans.

They'd all chipped in, helping out with getting the food to the table and then sat and filled their plates, everyone chatting and catching up over a feast of food.

Freya still felt the knot of anxiety that had been with her since she woke, even after the dreaded conversation she'd had about her and Liam's relationship. But they'd needed to be told. They needed to know that their blue-eyed son-in-law was not the perfect man they'd thought he was. And she had managed to get the truth out after the abundant lunch, while Rosie and Ben took a stroll to walk off the food.

Her parents had taken it well. The shock on their faces proved to Freya how little they'd actually seen, or had chosen to ignore; Freya wasn't quite sure yet which it was. They had been supportive in all the ways Freya had hoped her parents would be – hand holding and hugs, voicing concerns and appropriately supportive statements when necessary. All the stuff parents are supposed to say, and Freya certainly was grateful for that, if she thought that they believed her as much as they indicated.

A couple of comments hinted to Freya that perhaps they weren't as on board as she had hoped – for example, her mum's assertion that 'perhaps this has changed him', or 'the break might have been something you both needed to be able to get clarity', or Freya's favourite, 'absence makes the heart grow fonder'. Whatever their thoughts, the only way they would have fully understood was if they'd seen her injuries in real time. And there was no one but Freya to blame for that.

They had tried their best to understand, however, and certainly had been supportive. That would be enough for Freya, for now. Whatever Liam had up his sleeve right now, he would eventually show his true colours again, and when he did, she wouldn't hold back with the truth.

Although tired, Freya was grateful to travel with Rosie and Ben, and grateful for the table seat they shared. The box of possessions Freya had collected from her parents sat on the empty seat next to her. Freya would enjoy sifting through the memories contained within it later. The carriage was busy with day trippers – families and couples, to people travelling alone, head in a book or headphones on. She enjoyed the bustle of it, no longer liking to be alone. Every day felt like she was being watched, monitored, by an unseen person, and the insidious feeling had intensified until she found it harder to leave the flat. The only time she managed it was for her shifts at the café and when Rosie came and joined her for their sessions with Jake.

The one shining beacon of hope that kept her going was not only her time spent with Rosie, but with Jake too. He was considerate, kind, and she had begun to look forward to seeing him at his classes. They had even managed to arrange another date at the last session, but feeling as she did, Freya was unsure if she'd make it.

Rosie and Ben had promised to walk Freya home, but at the last minute, Ben had to leave. Something about his father needing help. He'd been quite dependant since his stroke last year and relied on carers since his mum passed away, so Ben felt duty-bound to be at his side whenever he needed it. Rosie had suggested that Freya wait at hers so she could go with Ben to help out. When Freya saw her sister struggling with the conflict of knowing what to do for the best, she did what any normal person would do and said she'd be fine walking the short distance home on her own. She didn't really want to do it, her soul screaming at how much she didn't want to, but she'd been a burden on them long enough to not want to be any more of a hindrance when Ben's father was in need.

Rosie hugged her tightly and gave detailed instructions that she was to call whenever she wanted, or text during the journey home, and to let her know when she had safely made it back to her flat. Liam hadn't done anything to make her feel insecure, and Freya hadn't really shared how she felt she was being watched with Rosie and Ben for them to be aware.

No, she should do this. She should walk home. It was still light, and people were milling around. She'd be fine. She just needed to keep telling herself that as she walked down the road, and further and further away from Rosie and Ben's flat.

She decided to count each minute it took to walk to her flat, and when she was on the high street and moments away from home, she began to relax, proud of herself that she'd managed it.

Someone shouted from behind. The sudden sound caused a small squeal to escape from Freya's lips, which only captured the attention of whoever was behind.

The man mimicked her squeal, and from the sound of it, another man laughed. There could be more; she couldn't know and didn't want to look. She hurried, walking faster, willing her flat to come into view. A girl admonished the men, but when she giggled too, Freya felt no comfort from her being there. They were probably youngsters out for a laugh, and something like this was probably fun for them. A laugh. But to Freya and her racing heart, this was terrifying.

She almost broke into a run when she saw the opening

to the grounds of her building and turned into it quickly, darting down the pathway towards the entrance.

One of the boys behind shouted something incoherent, and although Freya didn't catch what he said, she felt it was for her.

When she caught movement in the corner of her eye, she shrieked again and desperately fumbled the entry code to let herself in.

21

'Freya, it's Liam.'

She turned and saw Liam walking towards her. 'I've been waiting for you,' he said with a look of concern she hadn't seen in years. 'What happened? Are you okay?'

She turned to him and froze. All the tension and the stress erupted inside her, too much to bear, and she opened her mouth to say something but instead burst into tears, her body trembling, her fists balled by her sides.

'Hey,' he said as he pulled her into a hug. 'Don't cry. It's all right.'

He held her close and rubbed her back as she cried into his chest. She couldn't think, couldn't process all that had happened, she had been too scared, and for now she didn't care that it was her soon-to-be ex-husband comforting her on the doorstep of her home.

She breathed a little easier as the emotion passed, and she became more in control. She sniffed and looked up at him. 'Why are you here?'

'To talk, that's all,' he said, looking over his shoulder. 'Just a few things about the house down in Hampshire.' He pointed to the bench that sat under a tree not a hundred yards from where they stood, a place for residents to enjoy the outside space. 'But that's not important right now. Let's sit there, and you can tell me what happened.'

He guided her to the bench, and she sat, wiping her eyes and nose. 'Thank you, I suppose. I thought I was being followed; it frightened me for a minute. Stupid, I know.'

He sat with her. 'No, not stupid. Do you feel better now?'

'A little.' She took a deep breath, composed herself. 'What is that you want to tell me about the house?'

'We need to discuss if we're selling.'

'I know, my solicitor said the same, but as I said, I don't want anything except my stuff.'

'I know, but my solicitor is pushing for an answer, and I'm sure yours will too.'

Freya thought of the last couple of phone calls she'd dismissed and failed to return.

'Despite being left to me by my grandmother, it was still our marital home, so it'll figure in the divorce. We need to agree if we sell it or if I buy you out. Either way, you're entitled to a proportion of the proceeds.'

She struggled to read him, if he was resentful of this fact. But he kept a good poker face. 'Oh, well, I don't know,' she said. 'What would you prefer to do? Do you want to sell it? After all, it has a family attachment.'

He shrugged. 'There's nothing there for me now, and I'm not sure I have the funds to buy you out right now. Maybe a fresh start is what I need too.'

She considered the options. She wanted nothing from this man, and the discussion of money felt crass, but perhaps she'd been too hasty in wanting to walk away without anything at all. She did need the money, that was true. She'd earned it from every punch thrown at her, every kick too, but she also needed to pay back the money Rosie and Ben had paid towards her keep. Any money she'd get from the house would help her do that, and if she had a little left over to put down on a larger flat in the future, all the better.

'If you're happy to sell, I'm happy too.'

'I'm not happy to do any of this, but I get it. I'll speak to someone to get it on the market, then.'

'Okay. Thank you.'

He was very different to how he was before, in his drunken state, or when she'd lived in constant fear of him. This person she did not recognise. He was calm, considerate, patient. But still, she didn't want to spend too much time with him and made a move to leave.

'Great, well, if that's it, I'll get back to my flat. You look like you need a good meal and evening to relax yourself.' She noticed he looked tired, probably a long day, a nasty case, perhaps. Something that had taken its toll.

'Is that you caring about me?' he asked coyly.

'Just saying what I see,' she said, wanting to shut this down as quickly as possible.

He chuckled. 'I thought you couldn't wait to see the back of me.'

'That's only true because of what you did. I loved you once.'

'Loved. Past tense.'

She nodded.

'Well, I guess that's to be expected. Given that we're divorcing.'

'Let's not do this,' she said. 'You need to move on. We're not good for each other. Toxic is an understatement.'

'We can work it out. I know we can.'

'No, Liam, we can't.' She stood to leave.

He stood too. 'Listen, just think about it. I was good for you once, and I can be good for you again. Say the word, and I'll have you out of here faster than you can say tiny studio flat. Tell me, and I'll make it happen.'

'That's not a good idea.' She turned to go.

He held her arm and edged closer. 'There's no escaping what we had was fantastic before the fights. Just remember, I know you. I know how you work and what you like. Can you say that about anyone else? Even in the bad times I managed that.'

It was true that the sex had been a great bandage over the wound of their fractured relationship, and he always had known how to make her feel oddly cherished. It was the only way she could feel loved by him in those intimate moments, but now, the thought of contemplating going back to that world turned her stomach.

She snapped her arm out of his hold. 'Liam, go home. Get some food in you and get some sleep.'

'You know I'm right,' he said from behind her. 'You still care. You wouldn't get so angry if you didn't. Think about it. We belong together. There's no one else but you.'

She walked the small distance to the entrance, let herself in and waited for the door to close firmly behind her. Now glass and metal separated them, and her body finally began to relax.

When he was out of sight, she returned to her flat, kicked off her shoes and sat on the sofa. She ruminated over what he'd said. She needed to be more careful. Yes, he'd said all the right things – house sale, divorce, new start – but he wasn't going to give up easily, and she needed to bear that in mind.

Unable to sit still, she went to the kitchen, poured herself a large glass of water and popped a tablet out of the packet from the cupboard. If ever she needed something to help her relax enough to sleep later, it was now. Before the pill worked its wonders, she messaged Rosie to let her know she had made it home safely.

———

THE DATE that Freya had arranged with Jake had arrived, and Rosie agreed to walk Freya to his place to help with the nerves. Rosie spent the entire journey convincing Freya that it was the right thing to do. Freya needed to live her life, no longer under the spell or dictatorship of Liam. She was free to do as she pleased.

She checked that she had the correct address, noting the modern block of flats matched Jake's instructions, then buzzed for his flat.

He buzzed them both in, and they walked the length of the building to his flat. When she saw him, the nervous anticipation disappeared, and she knew that this was the right thing to do. Relaxed, barefoot, and dressed in casual shorts and a T-shirt, he greeted her at the door. He invited them both in, and once Rosie had said her 'hellos', she set to work arranging a taxi to collect her, not wanting to be a third wheel of the evening. She waited with them, enjoying a glass of wine in his modern kitchen, full of white gloss cabinets and minimal décor, until the Uber arrived, and she made her exit.

'You look lovely,' Jake said once they were alone, taking her by the hand into his living room. 'That a new dress?'

The long narrow room was as modern as his kitchen, white walls and a limewashed wooden floor. A black velvet sofa sat against the wall with an armchair either side of it, which faced the TV fixed to the opposite wall. In one corner of the room, next to the window, a large plant reached for the ceiling and in another a desk that housed a gaming console, headphones and a laptop.

'Thank you,' Freya said, nervously looking down at the black linen shift dress, smoothing it in her hands. 'No, it's one of Rosie's. I've still got to add my wardrobe. Sorry, add *to* my wardrobe.'

Jake frowned at the way she stumbled over her words. 'Would you prefer to go out rather than be here? I can see you're nervous.'

'Is it that obvious?'

He smiled. 'A little.'

'I'm sorry, but I am. I want to be here, but it's all so new. I can't lie, I'm a little overwhelmed.'

He walked closer, his eyes kind. 'I completely understand. I'm not going to do anything that makes you uncomfortable. I hope you know that. Whatever you want to do.'

She looked up at him, gazed in his eyes, tempted and terrified to take this to the next level. 'I'm not sure.'

He gently ran his hand up her arm. 'Why don't we pop out for a drink at the pub around the corner and then take it from there. I am in no rush with this, us. I want you to feel comfortable with me.'

'I do, and that sounds great, just until I get my head around this.'

'There is one thing I'd like to do, though.'

'What's that?'

'To kiss you. I've wanted to do it since the other night.'

'Oh,' she murmured as a smile crept over her lips. 'That would be nice.'

He smiled and leaned in, gently placing his lips on hers as he pulled her closer, both hands on her back. The soft warmth of his lips on hers drew a moan from her throat, the vibration buzzing against her lips. It was everything she'd hoped it would be and the beginning of something she thought she'd never have. She tasted him as their kiss deepened, the fresh hint of toothpaste, and the scent of his aftershave that drifted into her nose. His body was firm against hers, and she felt so small but so safe in his arms as he held her.

THEY FOUND a corner of the pub garden and sat at a wooden picnic table that had a large blue umbrella above. The shade was unnecessary, as there was little heat left in the sun, but it gave her a sense of privacy, and it was a nice place to sit and enjoy the evening. She sipped on her drink, no alcohol for her tonight, just a soda and lime.

'So tell me about your day,' she said.

'Got a call from my mum, had a chat, filled out the paperwork to attend an upcoming conference, had a session in the gym, and now I'm here with you.'

'Do you have a good relationship with your mum?'

'Yeah, I'm close with both my parents.'

'Are they together?'

'Yes, they are. They bicker a little, but overall, I think they're happy.'

She smiled. 'Sounds like mine.'

'I think if I can get what they have, I'll consider myself very lucky.'

She had been keen to have this date and was happy to be there, but her nerves wouldn't behave, and the jittery sensation of being out and visible made her more uncomfortable as the minutes passed.

He noticed and smiled. 'Are you all right?' he asked.

'Of course,' she said, masking it – trying to ignore the uneasy feeling. 'I've got a lot on my mind, that's all.'

'Do you want to share?'

'No, it's just Liam and the neighbours. You know, the usual. I don't want it to spoil tonight.'

'Is Liam bothering you?'

She couldn't hold back. 'Yes. Well, no, not really. He's just persistent. He says he misses me. Everyone thinks he might really have changed.'

'Would you want him back?'

'No, I don't, but he seems so genuine. I'm confused.' She sighed. This was not how she wanted the evening to go. 'And Elliot worries me. I've made an enemy out of him, but again, no proof of anything. Ava is stuck there with no one to help her.'

'Freya, she's not your problem.'

'I know that, but what if I'm all she's got. I can't walk away knowing what she might be going through. I know how it feels to be alone. Everything is so overwhelming.'

He rested his hand on her leg. 'I think I need to take you home.'

'No, please, I'm fine,' she said. 'I'm sorry, it's been a stressful time. I guess I just need to relax. Maybe we could go back to yours.'

He smiled reluctantly. 'I would love to take you back to mine, but that's not what you need right now.'

'Can't I decide what I need?'

'Of course you can, if you're going to be honest with yourself.'

'I am.'

'I don't think you are. It's very sweet, but you're thinking of what I want. Not what you want.'

'No.'

'I'm guessing a night at home with whatever drink you'd prefer in your hand while listening to a favourite podcast is what you need. Not all this stuff going on here,' he said as he tapped his temple.

She glanced down, sad that he'd hit the jackpot with his assumption.

He leaned in and reached out to tip her face to his. 'Look, it doesn't mean anything except there will be a next time. You have to take care of yourself, and I know you have a lot going on. You need space to unpack it all.' He pecked a small kiss on her nose. 'Come on, let's get you home.' He stood and held his hand out for hers.

She took his and held it tight. 'You're right. Thank you,' she said. 'I'm sorry.'

'You have absolutely nothing to be sorry for. Believe me, there are a few people out there who have big apologies to make to you.'

'Can I see you again soon?' she asked.

'Yes, of course you can. Whenever you're ready.'

They walked the ten-minute journey back to her place mostly in silence, but not the uncomfortable kind, the peaceful, easy kind of two people content in the moment.

When they reached the entrance, he pulled her in for a

hug, and when she looked up at him, inviting him to kiss her, he did just that. Another warm, tempting kiss that she wished could become more.

'I'll see you soon,' he murmured as he released her from his hold. 'Go on. I'll wait until you're safely inside.'

She nodded and smiled, inputting the code to push open the door. 'See you soon, Jake.'

By the time she'd reached her flat and had looked out her window, he'd gone into the night. She didn't expect him to remain, but she was sad that she didn't get to see him one last time.

Glancing to her left, and in the direction of Ava and Elliot's kitchen, she saw them once again locked in a heated debate. She sighed and turned away. That was none of her business and really never had been.

She turned away, deciding that she needed to protect her own peace and well-being by choosing to ignore it. Whether or not she'd regret that decision was something she'd have to live with, but she had neither the energy nor the will to get involved, and she knew that they would not want that either. It was pointless to worry; she just needed to move away from the window.

Just as she was about to, a shadow in the trees caught her eye, and she froze, staring out the window at the spot where she saw movement, trying to make out who, or what, was there. She squinted to see more, but as quickly as it'd moved, it was gone.

She tutted and pulled the curtains closed. It might only have been a bird or an animal shuffling around out there, but still, she wanted to block out all the bad things in the world and do just as Jake had said, put on a favourite TV show and drink endless cups of tea.

THE THUMPING against her front door snapped Freya awake. She rolled off the bed and stumbled to the door, trying to focus and gain some sort of equilibrium. She'd taken another pill and fought to wake up her body, which was still in the throes of medicated sleep.

'Help me, please!'

The voice was familiar and moved Freya to hurriedly unlock her door and open it. 'Ava.'

Ava looked at Freya, a terrified expression etched into every part of her face and tear-filled eyes. 'Please help me; he's going to kill me.'

22

Ava checked over her shoulder and cried out at what she saw.

Freya took Ava by the arm and pulled her into her flat but not before looking out into the hallway to see Elliot striding towards them.

'Ava,' he called, 'please stop this.'

Freya slammed the door shut and swiped the chain across as Ava began to cry hysterically behind her. 'It's okay; he can't get in. I won't let him get to you.' She was glad that she sounded more confident than she felt because there was no way she'd be able to stop him if he really wanted to get in or get to Ava. Both petite women, they certainly fitted a certain type. But she was stronger now; she'd had the lessons from Jake and the knowledge that she'd managed to pull herself out from the hell that was her life with Liam. She was someone who had fire inside her.

'Ava,' Elliot shouted from the other side of the door, 'let's not do this again.'

Ava stood in Freya's little hallway, pressed against the

wall, both hands up at her mouth as she trembled and panted her breaths.

'What do you want me to do?' Freya whispered to her. 'Call the police?'

Ava shook her head vigorously. 'No, no, no. That'll make it worse. So much worse.'

'I understand,' Freya soothed as she stood between Ava and the door, blocking her from harm.

Elliot banged hard against the door, eliciting cries from both women.

'Go away!' Ava bellowed as she ran into the living room and onto Freya's bed.

'Please stop this charade,' he moaned. 'Jesus, just come out here, and we can talk about it.'

'You heard her,' Freya shouted. 'Get the hell away from my door, or I'll call the police myself.'

'No!' Ava cried. 'No police.'

Freya held out a hand to reassure Ava. 'I know,' she whispered. 'Let me handle this.'

'I just want to talk,' Elliot said, calmer now.

'I don't want to talk to you,' Ava cried.

'I think you ought to leave,' Freya shouted through the door as she leant against it.

Elliot was silent for a moment, and Freya placed her ear on the wood, listening for the sound of movement.

A few minutes of waiting and the faint sound of a door closing moved Freya into action. She slowly unlocked the door, careful to keep the chain in place. Trembling, and with the sound of Ava's sobs mingling with the whooshing sound of blood pumping in her ears, she looked through the crack in the door and listened. There was no sound, just the faint buzz of the lights in the ceiling above. She pushed the door closed and released the chain, pulling open the door to step out into the hallway. She jumped and cried out when she came face to face with Elliot standing in the hallway, waiting.

'Fuck,' she gasped as she rushed to move inside.

He grabbed her arm, pulling her back. 'Freya, wait.'

'Don't touch me,' she barked as she pulled his hand away.

'Just listen to me.'

'What, so you can string me along with your lies?'

'This isn't what it looks like.'

'Funny that, it never is, is it? So it doesn't look like you wanted to beat the living crap out of Ava, then?'

'No, I haven't.'

'I don't believe you.'

He looked stern. 'Our relationship is complicated.'

'Yes, they always are when men like you want to silence a woman.'

'That's not what I'm doing.'

'Then why did she come running to my home in the middle of the night?'

'Ava knows what she did,' he said, looking over Freya's shoulder. 'Don't you, Ava? You know the truth.'

'Leave her alone.'

'Come on, Ava,' Elliot said, ignoring Freya. 'Don't make this more difficult than it needs to be. Come home, and we can sort this mess out.'

Ava did nothing.

Freya turned to face Elliot and folded her arms, a small act of defiance. 'Ava can stay with me tonight,' she said, hoping Ava would stay hidden.

But Ava stunned them both when she appeared out from

the flat, joining them in the hallway, her face pink and blotchy from crying. She walked towards Elliot.

Freya's mind whirred. Instinctively, she reached for Ava's arm and pulled at her. 'No, Ava. You don't have to do this.'

'It's okay, Freya,' she said sadly. 'I'll be fine. I'll go home.'

Elliot looked at Freya, happy he'd got his way, but she refused to release her grip. She couldn't let Ava return to the danger. 'No, you absolutely don't have to go with that man. You can stay here with me.'

Ava placed her hand over Freya's and gently removed it from her arm. 'It's fine. I have to go. We should work this out on our own. I was wrong to come here and involve you. I'm sorry.'

'You don't have to apologise to me. I am happy to help.'

'Honestly, I'll be fine.'

Ava walked towards Elliot, and they both walked away in silence, confusing and infuriating Freya even more. She tutted at the absurdity of the situation and her own frustration that she was helpless in actually doing something good here.

She went back into her flat and locked and chained the door. She flopped down on her sofa and quietly seethed. Another one to the slaughter. She just hoped Ava would be okay. She could never live with herself if she allowed her to go back to him only to be hurt, or worse.

LIFE FOR FREYA had been uneventful since her last confrontation with Ava and Elliot. She hadn't seen or heard from them since, and it worried her despite knowing that it was also none of her business. She carried on with her life, walking to work and returning home. She'd continued her sessions with Jake, and he was still pleasant and keen to see her. Something that warmed her, that she hadn't pushed him away too.

It pained her, but she had to stay out of Ava's business. Of course if she ever saw anything going on, she'd have to step in, but there was no need for her to go looking for trouble by knocking on their door. It was a hard pill to swallow, but with each day that went by, she found it easier to deal with.

Another pill she'd managed to control was her diazepam. Since the fateful night with Ava and Elliot, she'd managed to leave them untouched and safely tucked away in her cupboard. She felt better for it, disliking the groggy mornings that followed the medicated nights and the effort it took to get energised for work when all she wanted to do was sleep.

She hurriedly readied herself for Rosie's arrival, happy to leave. When she made her way down the corridor, she noticed Elliot before he saw her. She shrank out of view, wanting to avoid another of his bitter stares. He strode down the hallway and out of view. She didn't want to consider what he was up to. People like him aren't for figuring out, they're for avoiding like the plague.

The gym was full when Rosie and Freya arrived, but there was no Jake. Another man replaced him, and Freya felt in her gut that something was wrong. She walked across the room to the man. 'Hi, where's Jake tonight?' she asked.

'He's not able to make it.'

'Oh really, nothing wrong, I hope.'

'No, just nursing a few bruises and a bit of hurt pride.'

'What?'

He continued with his set-up. 'Why don't you speak to

him about it later; we've got to crack on.' He moved away and clapped his hands, shouting at everyone to find their places so that they could begin the session.

Freya went through the session in a robotic fashion, her mind rushing with possible scenarios. Bruises? Hurt pride? What the hell had happened? A botched mugging perhaps? A fight in a pub after a few drinks? She didn't really know him that well, but he certainly didn't seem the type. He was a big man, however, and that probably brought its own problems with men wanting to start trouble with him due to his stature.

She willed the session to be over, and when they'd finished, Rosie knew exactly what Freya would want to do. 'Come on, then,' she said. 'Let's go and see him.'

They hurried outside and walked briskly to his flat, guided by Rosie and Freya's hazy knowledge of the area. It took a couple of attempts, but when his purpose-built building loomed into view, Freya was pleased she'd found him.

She buzzed and waited. There was a long pause before he spoke over the intercom, and that filled her with more dread. 'Hello?'

'Jake,' Freya said, attempting to keep her voice level, 'it's Freya. Rosie, too. I hope you don't mind us dropping by.'

The door buzzed, releasing the catch. Freya pulled it open and walked inside.

When his door eventually opened, both Freya and Rosie gasped at the sight of him. Bruises covered half his face, his left eye particularly, and there was a deep cut above his lip.

'Jake.' Freya sighed. 'What happened?'

'You'd better come in.' He stepped back to let them both in. 'I take it you've come straight from the session?'

'Yes, of course,' Freya said. 'I couldn't wait any longer.'

He smiled, winced at the pain it caused, and held his finger to the cut on his lip to stop it bleeding.

'Jake,' she murmured, unable to stop herself from reaching out to him, 'how did this happen?'

'Rather embarrassing, really. I was jumped on the other night. Four lads. Not a lot I could do, but it could have been much worse. They'll be nursing a few bruises of their own.'

When she saw the marks to his knuckles and hands, she believed him. She knew his ability to fight back would have caused plenty of injuries to his attackers. 'Jesus, but why? Did you know them or recognise them at all?'

'I've no idea. Went to the pub with some mates, and they were there. They were acting pretty strange, watching us all evening. We didn't think anything of it, but when I split from the others to make my way home, I noticed them following me.'

'Oh God.'

'It's okay. I'm not that badly hurt. It's all superficial.'

'Yes, but *why* did it happen?' Freya asked, fear growing inside her. Something wasn't right.

'It could have happened to anyone. There are some nutcases out there, and I was unlucky. They took a disliking to me for some reason, and that's enough.'

'Have you been to the police?' Rosie asked.

'No point. What can they do? I can't really remember them. Could be anyone. Best just to let it pass. One of those things.'

'Where else are you hurt?' Freya asked, scanning over him.

'Got a couple of bruises on my stomach, a few on my back, and a lot of damaged pride, let me tell you.'

'Damaged pride? But there were four of them against you. The odds weren't good.'

'No, I should have been able to take them easily, but they weren't just a bunch of weedy kids out looking for a fight. They knew what they were doing. They had training.'

'I don't get it. You don't have anyone out there who's an enemy enough to do this to you, do you?'

'No,' he said, noticing her distress. 'But sometimes, that's just the way it goes,' he said gently. 'Honestly, I'm fine. This will all heal in a couple of days.'

Freya began to pace, her nerves shredded, putting her on edge. 'I don't like it. Have you iced your bruises?'

'Yes, boss. All of the above. Ice and heat intermittently, painkillers for the pain, and keeping the cut clean.'

'Good, good,' she said as she paced. 'And you definitely don't have anyone who would want to do this? No old scores to settle?'

'No, Freya, but you need to chill out.' He looked over to Rosie.

'Rosie, would you wait outside, please,' Freya said.

'Yes, all right.' She glanced at them both and left.

Freya turned to Jake. 'Look, I really don't want to do this. I really like you.'

'And I like you.'

'But I can't help think that this had something to do with me.'

'Of course it hadn't.'

'But you don't understand. I have so much going on. What if someone got to you because of me?'

'Freya, that's not what happened.'

'Isn't it?' she snapped. 'Well, I'd rather not test the theory and keep you safe than brush all this under the carpet and have you hurt even worse next time.'

'Come on, Freya. It was just one of those things.'

'What if Liam was behind this?'

'Freya, why would it be him?'

'Because it's a warning. If he knows we're friends.' She held her hands in her hair as she realised the significance. 'What if one of them has a knife next time, or a gun. Jesus, what then?'

'There might not be a next time.' He sighed. 'Look, if you're right, and you know Liam well enough, I'll just be more aware, keep an eye on my surroundings.'

'It's not as simple as that.'

He moved towards her, but she took a step back. Tears stung her eyes. 'No, I'm sorry, Jake, I can't do this. You don't deserve to be caught in the crossfire. I'd never forgive myself.'

She turned and went to the door.

'Freya, wait.' Jake reached out a grabbed her hand. 'Please. Look, I know you've been through something terrible, and Jesus, maybe Liam did have something to do with it, but we can't let him tell us what to do. We can figure this out, together.'

He pulled her close, and for a moment she wanted to believe it was a simple as that, that they could work it out together. But something told her Liam was just too dangerous to risk it.

She pulled away. 'I can't. I'm sorry.'

She opened the door and rushed outside to where Rosie was waiting for her.

'What's going on?' she asked when she saw the state Freya was in.

'Let's go,' Freya said, 'now, before I change my mind.' She grabbed Rosie's arm and walked her quickly away, hoping that Jake hadn't followed her out to persuade her to stay.

When they reached the high street and were on their route home, Rosie pulled at Freya's arm, stopping her in her stride. 'Right, you need to talk to me. What is going on? Why are you pushing Jake away, the best thing that's going on in your life at the moment?'

Freya turned. 'Because he *is* the best thing in my life at the moment. Don't you see? What Jake has been through is because of me, I'm sure of it.'

'Freya,' Rosie snapped, 'just stop it.'

'Stop what?'

'You're being paranoid. All this stuff with Elliot and Ava, and Liam. Christ, what happened to Jake is nothing to do with you.'

'Paranoid? Really. You remember what he did to me a couple of months ago?' she asked as heat filled her cheeks.

'Of course I do, and he is truly evil, but it just seems like a connection that isn't there.'

'Fine, have it your way,' Freya burst out, angry at her dismissal. 'It's nothing to do with me. I couldn't possibly know what my abusive husband is capable of. I'm going home.'

She turned and marched away.

Rosie caught up with her. 'Freya, stop!'

'I am done with being dismissed,' Freya puffed as she walked. 'And I felt you both did that to me tonight.'

'Are you overreacting a little?'

'No, I don't think so.' Freya sighed. 'Why don't you go home.'

'Freya,' Rosie said.

'I mean it. Why don't you go back to your perfect life with Ben and let me get on with repairing mine.'

Rosie stopped where she was and watched as Freya strode away.

When Freya turned around, Rosie was gone. Freya immediately felt both hurt and regret at what she'd said. Rosie had only ever wanted to help and was the one person who believed in her more than anyone else. Her sister had supported her in ways she could never repay. Maybe she had got it wrong, perhaps Liam was nothing to do with what happened to Jake, but she just wanted to be heard, listened to. With each stride, her anger calmed, and Freya felt that perhaps Rosie was right; maybe she had overreacted. It could have been anyone who'd decided to jump Jake, and they could have just been thugs who were proficient fighters, nothing more. If she had stayed calm, she could have talked it through with both of them, discussed all the options, but she let anger get in the way.

Freya groaned and ran her hand through her hair. She'd mucked up. Acted out like a child and stormed off. Why were her moods still so unpredictable?

———

FREYA SHUT herself in her flat and pulled out her phone, dialling Rosie's number. No reply. She sent her an apologetic message instead and waited. No response, but the message had been read. Well, she deserved that. Freya put the phone on her table and went to the bathroom. A shower would help clear her mind.

When she returned, dressed in her pyjamas and leaving her hair to dry naturally, she found that she did not feel better. She checked her phone. Nothing. Needing something to soothe the knot of anxiety in her stomach, she went to the cupboard. Her supply of tablets was dwindling, but she had enough, for now. She popped a pill and grabbed a soft drink from her fridge.

She waited, but the anxiety that swirled in her system would not be dulled by the sedating drug. Frustrated, she scrolled through her phone, wanting to numb her mind and check for any sign from Rosie. After an hour of no contact, the bleakness within Freya had taken up space around her too. She lay on her sofa, wanting sleep to take her away.

Loud music from her TV agitated her, and she stumbled to her kitchen. The tablets weren't working, so in frustration and determined to sleep, she popped a handful from the packet and downed them without liquid.

The room quickly began to sway, and she enjoyed the feeling of disconnect it gave her. There, but not there. Alive, but not living. Everything blurred. She stumbled to her bed, ready to get the escape that sleep would allow.

Dreams filled her consciousness. Elliot, Ava, and her family all collided, tension and fear filled her at their presence, and she walked away, looking for something but not sure what it was she was seeking. She opened one door, then another, and another until frustration at not knowing where she was or what she was looking for filled her. Now, she was falling, and the cry that escaped her mouth in her dream quickly changed to a scream, shrill and high.

The screaming continued; she couldn't control or stop it. It changed in tone, became buzzing, intermittent, and then continuous.

She snapped open her eyes. The door buzzer was going, pulling her back into the world.

'All right, all right,' she snapped as she threw her legs over the side of the bed to stand. 'I'm coming.'

The room seemed to move, causing her to stumble into furniture that sat in her way as she ambled to her door. She grabbed the intercom phone. 'What?'

'Freya, it's me,' Liam said. 'I've been trying to contact you.'

'Go away,' she mumbled, her mouth dry.

'Freya, are you okay? You sound weird.'

'I said go away.'

'Let me in.'

'No.'

'Freya, let me in.'

Without much fight, and too woozy to care, she hit the button to let him in, opened her door and waited as she heard him climb the stairs.

He strode in, his eyes wide when he saw her.

She could gauge what he was thinking. Anger, no doubt. Probably another punishment too. At least feeling this way, it wouldn't hurt. But then what did she know? She was probably being paranoid.

'What do you want, Liam?' She swayed.

'Freya, what's going on?' he asked, scanning his gaze over her, focusing on her eyes. 'What have you taken?'

'What are you talking about?' she said, struggling with the words, her slurring getting in the way. 'I've been asleep. So what? Nothing you haven't seen before.'

He held her shoulders. 'This is different, and you know it.'

Her legs wobbled, and she struggled to stand.

He grabbed her and carried her to the sofa. 'Tell me what you've taken, Freya. Now.'

She curled up, wanting to rest. 'Nothing.'

He held her shoulders and gently shook her. 'Freya, wake up.'

'Leave me alone.'

He did, but only to go to her bathroom. She heard him rummaging through her things. *He shouldn't be doing that,* she thought. *He has no business being here anymore.*

She was aware of him brushing past her to go to the kitchen, and again began opening and closing doors.

He returned, a foil packet in his hand. 'Have you taken these?'

She glanced at him and nodded, closing her eyes, which were too heavy to stay open.

'Jesus Christ. How many?'

'I can't remember, a few. They're not working.'

He went to the kitchen, and she heard him fill the kettle with water before she slipped into sleep.

'Freya. Freya,' Liam said, breaking her dream.

She opened her eyes.

He sat with her on the sofa and held a large mug in his hand. 'It's coffee. Come on, I want you to drink it.'

'I don't want to.'

'Freya, come on. You need to drink it.'

She raised her head to do as she was told, and he supported her, gently guiding the mug to her lips, tipping it carefully to pour the coffee into her mouth. She took a few gulps but had to stop. Nausea filled her, and she could take no more.

'Here, now have this,' he ordered, holding a glass of water to her lips.

He kept interrupting her sleep and kept waking her,

ordering her to drink. She did as she was told, frustrated. She just wanted to sleep.

———

THE NOISE FROM THE TV, people speaking, music playing grew louder and louder until Freya was awake and aware.

Lying on her sofa, she rested against something warm. Something comfortable. She opened her eyes and looked up at Liam, watching the TV, smiling at whatever was going on. His shirt was undone at the neck, and he looked tired, faint shadows curling under his eyes.

Aware of being watched, he looked down at her in his lap, his smile growing when he saw she was awake. 'Hello again,' he said.

'Hi,' she murmured, reaching for her head. 'What's going on?'

'You decided to take too many of your tablets. I've been giving you drinks since I've been here. You look a lot better now, let me tell you.'

She moved to sit, her head pounding. 'Ah.'

He helped her up. 'Take it easy. No sudden movements.'

She sat, using the cushions of the sofa to support herself. 'How long have you been here?'

'Most of the night.'

'But what about work?'

'They'll cope for a while. This was more pressing.'

She rubbed her forehead and sighed.

'Yeah, you're going to have one hell of a hangover.'

'What was I thinking?'

'You weren't. Clearly. I'm glad I came over when I did.'

'Thank you,' she murmured.

He glanced at his watch. 'Well, as you're now back with us, I'll have to go, but I'll call in later.'

'No,' she said quickly. 'You don't have to do that. I'll call you when I feel more awake.'

He shrugged. 'Okay, whatever you want.'

He went to the kitchen and poured another glass of water and placed it down on the table in front of her. 'You need to find something to eat too.'

'Ugh, I can't. Not yet.'

He smiled. 'Okay, well, don't leave it too long,' he said as he went to the door. 'I'll see you soon.'

She nodded, lay back down on the sofa, closed her eyes and listened to him leaving.

23

More knocking on Freya's door pulled her from her slumber. She was on the sofa still, propped up, just as Liam had left her. Feeling more alert now, she stood and went to the door. 'Who is it?'

'It's me,' Rosie said.

Freya opened the door. 'Rosie, I'm so sorry.'

'No, I'm sorry,' Rosie replied. 'I was angry last night. I should have been more understanding.' The expression of horror that crept over Rosie's face at the sight of her sister saddened Freya. 'What the fuck happened to you?'

Freya let Rosie in. 'Nothing, I'm fine. Had some sleeping tablets. Took too many apparently.'

'That's not fine,' Rosie said, checking her over. 'We need to get you to a hospital.'

'No, you know how I hate those places. Anyway, Liam gave me coffee and water, and really I'm—'

'Liam?'

'Yes, Liam. He came round, although I'm still not sure

why. But anyway, he sorted me out. Just feel a bit drowsy now, but I'm okay.'

'At least see a doctor.'

'No, there's no need for that. I'm fine. I just need to wait for it to leave my system.'

Freya downed the glass of water that Liam had left for her.

'Do you want more?' Rosie asked.

Freya nodded.

Rosie took the glass to the kitchen and refilled it. 'Here,' she said, placing it down.

'I'm sorry,' Freya said, catching the concern in Rosie's eyes. 'I didn't mean to worry you. I just wanted everything to stop.'

'What if Liam hadn't come around, Freya? What if we'd lost you?'

Freya shook her head. 'It wouldn't have come to that.'

'You don't know that for sure.'

'You're right, I don't.' She held her head in her hands and felt them moisten with tears. 'I just wanted to sleep.'

Rosie went to her and sat, wrapping her arms around her, and sniffed back her own tears. 'Shh, it's okay. I'm sorry. I didn't think about how much you're still going through, how much this has affected you.'

'I shouldn't have reacted the way I did. I shouldn't have shut you out.'

'You've been through enough. I'm truly sorry for ignoring your texts and calls.' She hugged Freya tightly. 'Do you want to talk?'

Freya nodded. 'I feel like I'm being watched all the time, Rosie. Elliot is beating his wife, and there's nothing I can do about it, and I'm sure he'll be coming for me when the moment allows.'

'We should go to the police, then.'

'What will that achieve? Nothing. He's already warned me off, and the only police I have is Liam. What good is that?'

'Hmm,' Rosie said. 'Not sure. Although if he came around and cared for you, that's something, isn't it? Maybe he has changed?'

Freya shrugged. 'I don't know. I really don't know anything anymore.'

'Well,' Rosie said, giving Freya another hug, 'we're going to figure this out together, you and me.'

FREYA DRIED her hair and pulled on a green summer dress. After a long chat, Rosie had left her in peace, and after another sleep, she showered and dressed. She moisturised her face and the freckles the sun had recently dotted over her nose and put balm on her lips. Not only had the sun given her freckles, but it had also lightened the tips of her hair. She shook it out, letting it fall into its natural curls. She kept it down to settle on her shoulders rather than pulling it up into a high bun as she had done yesterday. She realised how much it had grown, her normal style a short, curly bob. She'd have to find somewhere new for a hairdresser, but right now that was her lowest priority.

Her intercom buzzed, and she groaned, wanting to be left in peace.

'Freya?'

'What do you want, Liam?' she asked, clutching the

intercom phone to her ear, wishing it were Jake who had called instead.

'Hello to you too,' he said quickly. 'I see you're feeling better.'

She sighed. 'Okay, that was rude. I'm sorry.'

'No problem. Look, I just wanted to let you know that we have an offer on the house.'

'That's good news.'

'I thought so too. Well, can I come up?'

'I don't know, I'm still quite tired. What about tomorrow?'

'Can't. I'm working tomorrow, a double shift. I'll be five minutes, that's all.'

She rolled her eyes and sighed. 'Okay, I suppose so.' She buzzed to let him in and tidied the place, putting the mugs and plates into the sink.

She opened her door and waited for him to come up. A strange feeling to let the man who had caused so much damage into her life again, even if it was only to tie up what was left of their old life together. But part of him had changed too, in this process. He seemed more at ease, calmer. Maybe the destructiveness of his character had waned in the process of them separating. She shook her head. She wouldn't make excuses for him. What he did was out of control and so terrible that there was no forgiving the violence.

'Hi, babe,' Liam said as he approached, a bottle of wine in one hand and a large bouquet in the other.

She didn't know what he thought this meeting was, but she shuddered as he drew near. 'Hi, you really didn't need to do that,' she said as he handed her the flowers.

'I thought it was the least I could do for you. I should do

so much more to make it up to you, but this will have to do right now.'

She hesitated to take them, and that hesitation gave him enough time to reach down and place a tender kiss on her cheek. She didn't flinch this time and struggled to move out of his way, her body enjoying the familiar feel and scent of him so close. He smiled when she finally did pull away to invite him in, flustered at what she'd just allowed.

'I can't be too long,' she said quickly. 'I've got things to do.'

'Of course, whatever you want,' he replied assuredly. 'I just need you to see what I'm accepting on the house. It's seven grand under the asking price, but I think we can let it go in the circumstances. There's still a healthy profit to be made. We'll both do well enough.' He pulled out some papers from his inside suit pocket, tri-folded, and handed them to her. 'Here's the information. Have a read through.'

She placed the flowers on the table and took the paperwork to check over the details, feeling strange to be looking at photos of the house that used to be her home, if she could ever call it that. The place that she resided was more accurate. It was never a home where she could fully relax or unwind. Always on edge. With a sigh, she looked over the document, happy that it was just as he'd said it was. 'Are you sure about this? Our marriage might be over, but this was your house. Your grandmother left it to you.'

'Yes. I mean, you're right, it was my house, but it was your home too. You're entitled to benefit from it, so I won't stand in the way of you getting what you are owed.'

His use of words made her uncomfortable. Guilty. Was he being genuine, or was he subtly blaming her for having to sell the house? She only agreed to it because he had suggested it, but now it was as if it were all her idea, as some sort of money-grabbing bitch when all she wanted was to be out of the marriage and free.

She handed the paperwork back to him. 'Thank you.' She needed to stay strong. This was the right thing to do. The house was just bricks and mortar. There was nothing there for them now.

'Shall we open this?' he asked, pointing to the wine in his hand.

'I suppose we can, if you want?' Wine was not what she wanted, feeling muzzy and hungover from the tablets still, but anything to keep Liam happy would be fine with her.

'I think it would be a nice way to toast the end of us, I guess.'

She smiled. 'That sounds sad.'

He shrugged. 'It is sad, but it's the right thing for both of us.'

She stared at him, surprised that he was conceding in every way. 'Really?'

'Yes, really,' he said as he moved closer. 'I made the biggest mistake in my life mistreating you and letting you run away from me.'

'You're just saying that. They're just words.'

Close enough to kiss her again, he looked down at her with sadness in his eyes. 'No, I mean them. I have thought about nothing else recently. My actions were horrible, and I'll have to live with that every day of my life. I've finally accepted it. I'll get your stuff packed up and sent to Rosie's in the next week or so, and when the house sells, you can decide if there's anything else you'd like to take with you.'

She looked up at him, wanting to believe what he was telling her. 'I don't know what to say.'

'There's nothing to say,' he murmured, too close now. 'Well, maybe one thing?'

'What's that?'

'Where's the wine glasses so I can have a drink?'

She laughed with him and moved to grab two from the kitchen cupboard.

He unscrewed the lid and waited for Freya to hold the glasses so he could pour. He took a glass and placed the bottle on the countertop. 'To us,' he said, holding it up.

She clinked her glass to his but said nothing. She couldn't toast what they had been; it was too terrible.

They both drank, and the wine would have been lovely if she didn't feel as nauseous as she did, a perfect Shiraz. But it stuck in her throat and turned her stomach. She placed her glass down. There would be no more of that.

'Have you eaten?' he asked.

'No.'

'What do you say to a takeaway, something to be washed down by the wine.'

'I don't know.'

'One last "date",' he said.

She sighed. 'Okay, one last date.' She pulled up an app on her phone. 'Pizza, pasta or Chinese?'

'You know me well enough to know my favourite.'

She clicked the Chinese options and selected Malaysian-style satay beef with crispy noodles for him and a chicken noodle soup for herself. She was not hungry and unsure why she was agreeing to this in the first place. 'There, ordered. Will be about thirty minutes.'

'Great,' he said as he made himself comfortable on her sofa and switched on the TV.

She didn't know what to do, so she sat on the chair by the window.

He patted the seat next to him and moved along the cushions to allow more space between them. 'Come here. I'm not going to bite.'

Hesitantly, she sat and stared at the TV, not wanting to do anything that would invite him over. He scrolled the channels until he found an old comedy show that they both liked, and it wasn't long before they were both giggling and laughing.

She was aware of what he was doing, the charm, the familiarity, but she couldn't stop herself either. Somewhere deep inside, she wanted this too. Her life had been tumultuous in recent months, and this somehow offered a little bit of the stability she craved. It was the honeymoon period, the time between the beatings when he was on his best behaviour, and she could tell herself it would be just tonight, a parting shot, even if she was weakening for him again.

He'd gently moved closer at certain intervals until he was close enough that she felt his warmth and the soft touch of his arm on hers. She looked at him. 'What are you doing?'

'Nothing. I'm sorry, I don't want to freak you out. I just want to be close to you, is that okay?'

She shrugged. 'I guess so.'

The programme's slapstick comedy had them laughing hard again, and Liam felt it necessary to point out why it was so funny. They stared at each other as the laughter drifted away, and she only became aware of him.

He reached up and cupped her cheek. 'Whatever happens, you'll always be my Freya,' he murmured sadly. 'You're the light to my darkness. Your mood so calm, so patient. So kind. I could never quite manage that, could I? I have too much rage in me. But you? You levelled me out.'

'I tried,' she whispered. 'I wanted you to change so desperately.'

The buzzer sounded, and she sat back away from his hold and moved to stand. 'That'll be the food. I'll go down and get it.'

'No, don't worry, I'll go,' Liam said as he went to the door. 'It's the least I can do.'

She let him and paced the room while he was gone. What the hell was she doing? This was not going to end well. They'd fall into bed together if she wasn't careful. Food, wine, and nostalgia would be the undoing of her and all she'd accomplished these last few months. But she wasn't going to ask him to leave either, despite knowing that fact.

They ate in comfortable silence, with him murmuring at the good food he enjoyed. Afterwards, she cleared away the tubs and leftovers, placing them in the bin. When she walked back into the living room, he was topping up their glasses.

'Do you like it here?' he asked, sitting back on the sofa with his glass in hand.

'Yes, I think so. Are you happy being back in London and at the Met again?'

'Yeah, nothing changes there. Still the old politics and backbiting, but at least I know the score. It's fine.'

She wanted to ask where he was living but worried that that would show too much interest.

He flicked her shoulder with his finger. 'Nice being here with you.'

She nodded. 'As long as you haven't got anywhere else to be.'

'No. Well, nowhere else I *want* to be.' He checked his watch. 'But I do have to call in to the station in a bit.'

'Oh,' she said, surprised. 'You're working tonight and doing a double shift tomorrow.'

He smiled. 'Yes, that's right. Well remembered.'

'I see.'

His finger trailed down her arm. 'Would you miss me?'

'No,' she said quickly.

He smiled, amused, and she remembered the early days of their relationship when his smile would cause butterflies in her stomach, he was so handsome. 'Okay, then.'

He grabbed the remote control and scrolled until another show they both liked popped up.

As he hit play on the show he'd decided on, the last until he had to leave, she wondered if he had changed, if he had managed to put his demons to rest, finally. She stared at the screen, appearing to watch and enjoy while her mind raced.

24

W alking home from work, Freya felt the distinct sensation of being followed again. She'd checked over her shoulder a couple of times but never spotted anything. Still, the sense remained. She glanced across the road and immediately caught the culprit. Elliot was a few strides behind and on the other side of the road. There was no mistaking him. He wore sunglasses, which could be explained away by the beautiful sunny day, but at 3 p.m. on a Wednesday, he surely should be somewhere else other than following her home. She kept a swift pace as she walked towards her flat and checked over her shoulder. Now, Elliot had disappeared again.

Frustrated and a little frightened, she wanted to be home, safely locked away again. Her evening with Liam had been a mistake, and now she was paying for it by having to avoid his calls.

She made her way into the entrance, and when she expected him to follow, there was only silence. She listened out all the way up the stairs and along her hallway – still nothing. Now she doubted herself. Maybe she'd been wrong. Maybe it wasn't Elliot at all, and she had just mistaken a passer-by for him.

She let herself into her flat and dumped her bag down and kicked off her shoes. She washed her hands and switched the kettle on for tea. She'd been serving it all day, but now she wanted her own. Lucy had offered one to take away with her, but Freya just wanted to be home, drinking from her own mug.

Realising she hadn't checked her post box, and while she waited for the kettle to boil, she wandered back downstairs. On her way back up, Ava was standing at the top of the stairs, staring into space, dressed in a lightweight cotton dress, no make-up, and summer slippers.

'Ava,' Freya said, 'everything okay?'

'Hmm,' Ava murmured, looking but not seeing.

'It's me, Freya. Are you okay?'

Ava laughed. 'No. I'm really not okay.'

Freya gently took hold of Ava's arm, her pulse increasing. 'Ava, where's Elliot?'

Ava's gaze moved to Freya. 'Who?'

'Elliot, your husband.'

'He's not my husband,' she whispered.

'Where is he?' Freya's mind was racing ahead at what to do next. Call the police? Take Ava to her flat or go to Ava's?

Ava made the decision for her by turning and wandering slowly back to her place. 'Come, Freya. Come with me.'

Freya felt the unease, the strange mood she found Ava in. Was it drugs or drink? Had she finally snapped? Was this the result of an injury? Freya hurried alongside Ava.

'Do you need me to call someone?' Freya asked. 'I can call the police.'

Ava shook her head. 'No, no one can help me now.'

Worried for her friend, Freya followed her into their flat and gasped at the sight in front of her. It was a mess, not the usual pristine condition she'd seen in it before. The sofa had been upturned, and the cushions that had been so comfy when she'd sat in them before were strewn about the floor. The palms were out of their pots, the earth scattered, their leaves ripped apart. Glass littered the place from broken frames that lay smashed on the floor.

'Ava, what the hell happened?'

Ava smiled, but said nothing, only staring at the state of the room.

Freya looked more closely at Ava and noticed small specks of reddish-brown marks littered across her dress. *Dried blood.* She was hurt, and probably the reason she was not coherent.

'Ava,' Freya said, trying to get her attention, 'I need you to come with me.' She gently took hold of Ava's arm and led her to the kitchen. She picked up one of the counter stools and guided Ava to sit down. 'I need to call the police. I think you might need an ambulance too.'

Ava grabbed her arm, her thin fingers biting into her skin. 'No, you can't do that. They'll find out the truth.'

Freya pulled up another stool and sat next to her. 'Sweetie, everyone already knows what's been going on. There's no shame in it. You were just hoping and waiting for things to change, that's all. I understand. I've been there.'

Ava smiled – one of the saddest Freya had seen. 'You don't know the truth. You think you do, but you don't. How can you?'

'Then tell me,' Freya said gently.

'I asked him to change. I begged him. I wanted to leave;

we're too volatile together. Dangerous. We rub each other up the wrong way. Toxic.'

'But he wouldn't listen?'

'No,' Ava said thoughtfully. 'I told him to leave me, but he wouldn't go.' She turned and looked Freya in the eye, unnerving her. 'I didn't want to do it, but I had no choice.'

Unease dropped in her stomach. Self-defence is self-defence, and Freya knew that Ava would have done whatever she needed in order to survive, but that didn't mean Freya could ignore the well-being of Elliot. 'Ava,' she said as calmly as she could, 'where is Elliot now?'

Ava shrugged, staring into space. 'He's in there. The bedroom.'

'Okay, you stay here,' Freya gently ordered as she clutched a glass in her trembling fingers, poured Ava a glass of water from the kitchen tap and placed it in front of her. 'And I'm going to go and check on Elliot.'

Freya strode across the bomb site of a living room and noted the ominous silence that came from the bedroom. She wandered down the hall and pushed open the first door she came to. The bathroom. Smears of blood covered the sink and the mirror above it, and a bloodied towel lay crumpled on the floor. 'Oh, Jesus.'

She went to the next door and tentatively pushed it open, terrified of what she'd find.

The horror before her took a moment to comprehend. Elliot's feet poked out between the bed and the wall, one shoe on and one shoe missing.

She hurried to him and looked down to see him lying in a bloodied mess on the floor, his face turned to the side, bruised and bloody. Blood had sprayed on the walls and bedding, and large droplets covered the carpet. Freya's first thoughts were just how a woman of Ava's size could manage to cause so much harm.

Freya pushed the bed out of the way as hard as she could, allowing her the space to get to him. 'Elliot, Elliot,' she ordered. 'Can you hear me?' She sat back on her heels and pulled her phone out from her pocket. The sound of shuffling footsteps caught Freya's attention, and she turned to see Ava behind her. 'I need to call an ambulance,' she said, looking up at Ava.

A maddening smile covered Ava's face as she raised the heavy metal ornament gripped in her hand and swiped it down.

A strange whelp escaped from Freya's lips before everything went black.

25

The ringing in Freya's ears wouldn't stop, loud and piercing enough to pull her from the dark. She opened her eyes and tried to move as her head pounded, and red-hot splinters of pain burst above her right ear. She had been propped up against the bed, her hands crudely tied together, and her head lolled to one side.

Elliot was conscious now too and sat next to her, against the bed. They were alone, the door closed, and Ava apparently gone.

'What happened?' Freya whispered with a wince. It hurt to talk. It hurt to think.

'You finally met the real Ava,' Elliot said, his voice cracking.

'What?'

'My wife, the psychopath.'

'But I thought—'

He snuffled a laugh, clearly causing pain in his head too, judging by the wince that followed. 'You thought wrong. You saw our arguments, and you assumed it would be me who was hurting her, when really, it was the other way round.'

'Oh,' Freya whispered. 'I just assumed. I'm... I'm so sorry.'

'She lost it this time,' he said, ignoring her apologies. 'Went completely crazy.'

'Why? What happened?'

'There never needs to be a reason, but her moods have become increasingly more volatile recently. And she's been refusing to take her medication. Until today, that is. She took more than enough after she beat the shit out of me.'

'Why did she refuse to take her medication?'

He looked straight at her. 'Because someone has been filling her head with the idea that she's the victim here. She convinced herself her doctor was trying to poison her, so she refused to take the tablets.'

Heat filled Freya's face. 'I can only apologise. I thought I was helping.'

'No, you thought I was the bad guy, and you interfered.'

'My God,' Freya whispered, stunned she had got it so wrong. 'I'm so sorry.'

And she *had* got it wrong. This was just another blunder in a long line of misunderstandings. Elliot hadn't assaulted Ava, and Liam hadn't assaulted Elliot. So maybe he had nothing to do with Jake's assault after all. Nothing more than a nasty coincidence. She frowned.

He sighed and relented a little. 'It's not your fault. From what Ava has shared in her lucid moments, you've been through something traumatic. I guess you were only looking out for someone.'

'I have, and I was. I only wanted to help, but I missed the mark completely.'

He shrugged. 'I could have shared rather than try to

scare you off. That was stupid of me. I handled it badly. I'm so lost in my relationship I fucked up.'

'Has she always beat you?'

'Pretty much, yeah. I may have fought back once or twice, and I tried to defend myself today, but I could never land a punch on her. I could never do that.'

'Even when she's pounding her fists into you?'

'No, even then.'

'But she's hurt you, badly.'

He shrugged. 'Still a no.'

'I don't understand. Why would you stay?'

'Because I loved her and thought she could change. I thought my love and patience would help her to do that. I warned you off in the hope that you'd back off and leave us alone so I could convince Ava that fists were not the answer.' He glanced down at his wound. 'But I was wrong. I realise now that I can't help her at all.'

'I know how easy that is. I've been where you are. Liam, my ex, was abusive. He beat me badly. My experiences with him made me judge you.'

Elliot rolled his eyes. 'I didn't know that. I guessed you and Liam were going through some stuff, but I never realised it was that. I would not have said what I said to you, warned you off like that.'

'We both could have handled it differently, I suppose.'

'Sometimes it's hard to trust, isn't it,' he said.

She nodded. 'So where is she now? From the look of you, we need to get you checked over at a hospital.'

'Gone to cool off, I would imagine. It's what she normally does. I think this one sent her a little crazy. I've not seen her with so little behind the eyes before.'

Freya moved to stand and managed to wriggle off the tie around her wrist. 'Where are you hurt?'

He moved his hand that covered his stomach to reveal a puncture wound that had bled out onto his clothes. 'She's stabbed me.'

'Oh, Jesus,' Freya groaned.

'It's not deep, but it hurts like a bitch, and I'm not going to be much help if she gets physical again.'

'We need to get out of here and call for an ambulance.' She reached for her phone.

'I wouldn't bother. She would have taken that too.'

Freya began to panic. 'We need to get you to a hospital immediately. Do you think she'll be back soon?'

'Oh, she'll be back,' he warned. 'Question is what we're going to do about it.'

'What can we do? I assume that door is locked.'

'You'd assume correctly.'

'Is there another key?' she asked desperately as she rushed to the door and turned the handle anyway, just to be sure. She didn't trust anyone in this relationship.

'There is,' Elliot said, wincing as he tried to move. A rush of fresh blood spilled over his hands and stained his clothing.

'Stay there; don't move,' she ordered as she stripped a couple of pillowcases from the pillows on the bed. She put them together and folded them multiple times and placed the makeshift pad firmly on the wound. 'Here, hold down on this. Keep the pressure if you can. Tell me where there's another key, and I'll get it.'

'I'm not sure,' he said, weakening. 'There might be a bunch of keys in the safe that's in the wardrobe. At the top, behind my sweaters.'

'Right,' Freya said as she threw open the doors to check, ignoring the shards of pain in her head, and began pulling out all the clothes. 'Where?' she ordered, the desperation to get out building. For herself but for Elliot too, whose skin was now pale and grey.

'At the back,' he whispered.

At that moment the door opened, and Ava walked in, dressed in fresh clothes, her rational, normal self again. 'What the hell are you doing?' she asked as she stared at Freya.

'What am I doing?' Freya asked in astonishment. 'Trying to get us out of here after you stabbed him and knocked me out.' She pointed at Elliot. 'He needs to go to hospital, right now.'

Ava went to him and crouched down, gently wiping his face. 'Are you angry with me?' she asked him in a strange baby voice. 'Did I go too far this time?'

'I don't blame you, Ava. I just need to get someone to look at this,' Elliot replied with a weak smile. 'You want me to get better, don't you?'

Ava nodded.

'We can go back to how we were, can't we,' he said, a fixed expression of happiness on his features.

She nodded again. 'It's all I want.' She began to cry. 'I'm so sorry, I didn't mean to hurt you, I really didn't. I love you. I love you so much. I don't know why I get a little crazy.'

'I know, and I love you too,' he soothed. 'But right now, I need to get to a hospital. Can you help me with that?'

Ava stood up and clutched her head. 'I don't know. They'll ask questions. I don't know what to do.'

Freya edged towards her and ever closer to the door, her heart hammering in her chest. 'Ava, why don't I go and get some water for Elliot. He looks thirsty, and I can find some painkillers to give him. Maybe you and I can bandage him up for now. What do you say? No one has to know what's happened right now, but we need to stop the bleeding if we can.'

'Yes, that sounds good. Thank you, you're a good friend, Freya.'

'So you'll let me just go to the kitchen,' Freya asked, pointing in that direction.

'I suppose so.' Ava went back to sit with Elliot, resting her head against his. She whispered her apologies to him.

Freya ran out towards the kitchen. She plunged her hand into her pocket to check her keys weren't there, but nothing. Ava had taken those too. 'Damn it,' she cried.

For a moment she paused and realised where she stood. She was alone, in their living room and only a few strides from their front door. Ava had remained in the bedroom with Elliot. She had a chance to leave, and one to stay. Her heart raced, and she felt as if she'd stopped breathing. She desperately wanted to get out of this place, call for an ambulance, but could she do that to Elliot? How safe was he with Ava? What would Ava do to him if she escaped now. No, she had to help him.

Reluctantly, Freya turned her back on the front door and rushed to the kitchen. She hurriedly looked in each drawer, for any first aid kit or to find her phone, whichever came first. No phone, wherever she looked. Frustration gnawed at her insides. She found some clean tea towels, a packet of paracetamol and grabbed the untouched glass of water she'd left for Ava earlier and went back to them.

'I've found these,' she said. She moved quickly towards Elliot and knelt beside him as she bundled a couple of the towels together to form a pad for his wound. The pillowcase was soaked through with dark red blood. 'This might hurt,' she warned as she placed it on his stomach and applied pressure.

He cried out with pain as his head fell backwards.

'I'm sorry, I'm sorry,' Freya repeated hopelessly, noticing her phone poking out from Ava's back pocket.

'I should do that,' Ava murmured as Freya did what she could.

'Get your hands off him,' Ava bellowed, furious when Freya didn't move quickly enough. She slapped Freya's hands away, fury in her voice. 'He's *my* husband, not yours!'

Freya stood back immediately. She did not want to anger this woman any more than she already had. Standing behind them both also gave her a better chance to swipe her phone from Ava's pocket, who was too preoccupied to notice. Freya hoped so, anyway.

But each time Freya reached to retrieve her phone, Ava moved or turned her body away from Freya, thwarting each attempt.

Elliot noticed what Freya was doing and began engaging with Ava, holding her hand while he reminisced about good times in their past. Thrilled, Ava eagerly participated, giggling at the stories Elliot told. She became animated, happy, unnaturally so, but also enough for Freya to take her chance and pluck the phone from her pocket.

Gripping the phone tightly in her fingers, Freya turned and raced out of the room. Her head pounded with each stride, and Ava's screams filled the silence in the flat, growing louder as she followed in pursuit. Freya ignored the pain, the throbbing in her head, and continued out of the flat.

She bolted down the hallway and somehow managed to

dial for the emergency services. Holding the phone close to her ear, the moment she heard the operator's voice, she barked out the address and a brief description of what had happened as she ran out of the building and into the street. Without thinking, she turned and rushed to her place of work, desperate to get herself to safety even though it might cause enough of a scene to get her fired.

She just wanted to get somewhere safe.

Lucy's face dropped at the sight of Freya as she rushed into the café, customers looking up too.

'What the hell happened?' Lucy gasped as she rushed for Freya.

'My neighbour,' Freya panted. 'She's hurt her husband. She's stabbed him.'

'She's hurt you too,' Lucy said with concern.

A couple of customers shuffled out of the café at the commotion, and Lucy announced to the others that they were to leave, the café was closed. She took Freya by the shoulders and sat her down. 'Turn the sign over and lock the door,' she instructed the student who worked there a couple of afternoons a week.

He quickly did as he was told, the café empty except for the three of them.

Lucy sat opposite Freya. 'Grab her a drink too. Something sugary. Hurry.'

The poor boy grabbed a can from the fridge behind the counter, taking it to Lucy.

Lucy pulled the ring pull and handed it to Freya. 'Thanks, and get me the first aid kit, some paper towels and some water, please.'

He did as he was told and laid everything down on the table.

'You can go and take your break now if you want. It may be the end of the day too. I'm not sure yet,' Lucy instructed.

He disappeared out the back. Freya hadn't met him yet, nor even knew his name, but as introductions went, this was pretty extreme.

Lucy ripped several squares of paper towel from the roll and plunged them into the water. She squeezed the excess water out and moulded it into a pad to place gently against her head. 'What the hell happened to you?' she asked. 'You're covered in blood.'

Freya looked down at herself. She indeed looked like she'd come straight from the set of a horror movie, only there was no faking this blood. It was as real as it could get. 'Oh God, sorry. I hadn't even noticed. It's not mine. It's his, Elliot's.'

'Good. I thought I was going to have to plug a multitude of holes,' Lucy said with a sly smile.

'I'm sorry, this can't be good for business, but I didn't know where else to go. She's got my keys. I only managed to grab my phone and get out of there because Elliot distracted her.'

'Don't worry about that,' Lucy replied. 'A few will have a story to tell over dinner tonight. Who cares; they'll be back.'

'I've made the biggest mistake,' she said as Lucy tended to the nasty wound on her head. 'I assumed he was beating her, when all along it was the other way round.'

'Who was beating who?'

'My neighbours. Elliot and Ava. I assumed it was him hurting her, because of my trauma. Because of what happened to me.'

'Okay, slow down,' Lucy soothed. 'Take a drink; you'll

feel better with some sugar inside you. It'll help with the shock.'

Freya took a large gulp of the soft drink. It was sweet and necessary, and she took three more gulps before she even attempted to speak again.

Lucy continued to nurse her wounds. 'Does it hurt?'

'What?'

'This wound.'

Freya frowned. 'A little, I guess.'

'It's just that I expected you to flinch more while I cleaned it up. There is an open wound here, but to you it's like it's just a scratch.'

'Oh,' Freya said. 'I guess I've had worse.'

'Wow,' Lucy murmured under her breath. 'Now, tell me again, who was hurting who?'

Sirens sounded in the distance.

When Lucy stopped to pull clean sheets of towel off the roll, Freya called up the camera app on her phone and checked herself. A long line of dried blood covered her cheek, dipping underneath her chin and then continuing down her neck. Her cheek was bruised, and blood had smeared across her top. 'Oh my God,' she whispered.

'It's okay; don't worry about it. That'll soon clean up,' Lucy said as she dipped the towel in the water that had tinged pink and wiped the bloodstains away. 'I can't do much about your top, but at least your face looks better. You have a pretty significant cut on your scalp. She got you good and proper there. You should get it looked at.'

Freya knew she wouldn't. She'd survived so much worse on her own, she wasn't going to hop to the hospital now. Thankfully, with a careful prod of her fingers she found that her eye socket bore no brunt of the blows to her head. She thanked the universe for that. 'It's fine. I need to go back. I need to check how Elliot is doing. Who knows what she would have done once I left, but I had to get out.'

'Of course you did, and calling the police probably saved his life. And yours.'

Freya drank again, more as a distraction than anything else. 'I want to go.'

Lucy nodded as she gathered up the used bits of towel and her first aid kit. 'Of course, I'll come with you.'

Lucy shouted out instructions to the poor student who was trying to do anything to keep out of their way, and then they walked the short distance over to her building to the sight of a police car and ambulance outside. They walked quickly towards the ambulance and looked through the open doors at the back. Elliot was inside, conscious and talking to the paramedic as he received treatment. He glanced Freya's way and mouthed a 'thank you' before lying back against the bed.

They continued on and saw Ava being put into the back of the police car, her features devoid of any expression, her eyes blank, lost in her own world, wherever that might be. Freya resolved to give that an allotted amount of time to consider later, but no more. She'd wasted too much time on that woman already, and it stopped now.

The paramedic called after her just as she was disappearing through the doors of the building. She hurried over, concerned that Elliot had taken a turn for the worse. She still had so much she wanted to say to him, if she could ever convey how sorry she was.

'He wants to speak with you, just for a second,' the paramedic said.

'Is he getting worse?' Freya asked.

'No, he's stable, but we have to get going soon. I can spare a minute, max.'

Freya nodded and climbed into the back of the ambulance.

'Freya,' Elliot said, 'I just wanted to thank you for what you did.'

'It was nothing. I'm so sorry that I misjudged you,' she said. 'I assumed, and that was wrong of me.'

'You helped me when I really thought I was going to die. She's lost it, I'm afraid.'

'She'll get the help she needs now, and that's important for everyone.'

'Are you okay?' he asked. 'She whacked you pretty hard.'

Freya smiled. 'Yeah, gonna have a headache for a day or two, but I'm fine, really.'

He smiled and winced, his body twitching as if in pain. She panicked.

'This can wait. You need to get to hospital,' she said. 'Let them take care of you. I'll see you when you get out, okay?'

He nodded.

She turned to leave, but he grabbed her hand. 'And watch out. That ex of yours hasn't changed. He's trying to win you back, but he'll never change, not really. I've seen it all before, as have you. Ava and Liam are the same. Our love for them is not enough to change the issues they have deep inside. You have the chance to start again. Take it. Learn from my mistakes and move on. Find happiness.'

Before she had a chance to reply, the paramedic appeared. 'I'm afraid we have to go.'

'Of course,' Freya said as she stepped out of the back of the ambulance.

'Think about it,' Elliot said.

'I will, I promise. I'll see you soon,' she called out to Elliot as the paramedic closed the door.

After the paramedics had left, Freya and Lucy spoke to the police. Lucy had little to share except the condition in which she'd found Freya, and spent most of the time wide eyed and confused. Freya gave her account of what had happened and her contact details but declined the offer of a hospital check when it was offered. She did, however, let the first responder at the scene look over her wound. He cleaned it up some more and confirmed what she had hoped – that she didn't need stitches. He gave her some tips on how to keep it clean and dry and then let her go. She was also required to go down to the station later to give her statement, but given the circumstances, they'd allowed her time to go back to her flat and change and gather herself. One of the police officers handed her keys over, and she was grateful for the chance to get out of there and back home.

After releasing Lucy from her commitment to stay, she walked up the stairs to her flat. Every muscle ached, her body sore. She would shower, change and give Rosie a call, update her on everything that'd happened, but after that, she was keen to put this nightmare behind her. And somehow, she had to figure out a way to get Jake back into her life.

26

She spent the next morning at the police station, giving her statement of events. When she returned, she waited for the police to finish up at Elliot and Ava's taped-up flat, gathering their evidence before releasing it. She offered to tidy the place and focused on getting as much done as she could in a couple of hours, righting the overturned furniture and repotting the plants that could be saved. Ava was the least of her problems, but she felt for Elliot. A man who had been silently suffering for goodness knows how long. This was her way of supporting him, and knowing how Ava had probably manipulated everyone into believing he was the abuser, he was very likely to be alone when he was discharged from hospital. This way, he would come home to a place that looked reasonably normal, a place for him to heal and begin to move forward. She scrubbed the walls and floors of the bedroom and bathroom and even found clean bedsheets to replace the bloodied, which she'd run through their washing machine, dried, and put away.

HER PHONE BUZZED in her pocket. She pulled it out and sighed. 'Jake,' she said.

'Hi, Freya,' he replied. 'Look, I know how you're feeling at the moment, but Rosie filled me in about Elliot and Ava. I just wanted to check you're okay.'

She smiled, he was so kind, and it was so unfamiliar to her. 'No, I'm so glad you called, really. I'm fine, a little bump to the head but nothing I can't recover from. Elliot took the full brunt of Ava's rage.' She heard him sigh. 'Listen, I wanted to apologise. I was too hasty before. I've... I've missed you.'

'I've missed you too.'

'And although I'm still worried about the circumstances of your assault, if you still want to see me, I'd love to meet up, to talk.'

'Yes, I'd love that too,' he said quickly.

She hesitated. 'You would?'

'Yeah. Can't tell you how difficult it was not to come over to you last night after I'd spoken to Rosie.'

Relief warmed her body. He cared. She didn't need to shut him out. 'Where are you now?'

'At home.'

'Would you like to come over?' she asked. 'I'm just finishing up at Elliot's flat. Tidying up for when he leaves hospital. We can talk. Properly.'

'Give me thirty minutes.'

She did one final check of Elliot's flat and then closed the door, ensuring it was locked tight and safe.

She went home and waited for Jake to arrive, having a quick tidy of her flat too, noticing that it had been neglected in the events of recent days. She washed and put away the dishes left in the sink, folded the clean clothes hanging on the airer, made her bed and fluffed the cushions on her sofa. She felt tired, it had been an emotionally draining time, but she was excited to see Jake, telling herself not to get too carried away with what it meant, but still checking the window to watch for his arrival.

When she saw Jake stroll up the pathway, her heart danced in her chest.

She ran out of her flat and down the stairs so she could greet him immediately.

His smile, and the way he said her name, gave her the confirmation that this was right; he was meant to be in her life. Letting go of her inhibitions, she threw herself in his arms and hugged him tight in the lobby as he buried his face in her hair and breathed her in.

She pulled away and smiled. 'Come up.'

They held hands as they climbed the stairs, and she let him into her flat.

'Can I get you a drink?'

He turned and clasped her face in his hands and placed his lips on hers. A hungry kiss that demanded to be felt. And feel it she did as she responded, her lips speaking to his, sharing the hunger. He wrapped her up in his arms, and she reacted, jumping up to wrap herself around him, her hands in his hair, her legs around his waist. They had so much to share, so much to say, but for now it was left to their bodies to speak, and she melted into his long, divine kiss, not wanting to break the bond they were building.

He placed her down, his smile wide, and he swept his hand through her hair. 'Hello.'

She smiled too. 'Hello.'

'What happened?' he asked.

'What do you mean?'

'While that was probably the best greeting I've had in a long while, I was expecting us to talk it through. Something has changed.'

She nodded. 'Let's just say that I've realised what's important over the last couple of days. I've been cautious for too long.' She held his hands. 'I'm sorry to admit that I let my relationship with Liam affect the decisions I made. I was letting him control my life again – who I saw and what I did – but I was also being drawn into his charm, and for that I feel terrible.'

He tipped her face up to his. 'No, no, there's no need for that. He is very manipulative, and you're bound to question everything when he's been such a controlling force in your life. I don't blame you for being confused, but I'm glad you've woken up. Not for me, but for you. You know that going back to him would be a mistake.'

'I do, and that's not what I want anyway. If I had scrutinised how I was feeling, I would have seen that it was loneliness and wanting familiarity back in my life that was pulling me to him. Not love.'

'And that tells you everything you need to know.'

'Absolutely.'

Another of his smiles had her stomach fluttering again. 'I'm so glad.'

'But I don't want to rush into this, either.'

He held his hands up. 'There'll be no pressure from me. I can take things at your pace. It would be my pleasure just to spend time with you.'

'Really?'

He chucked her under the chin. 'Really. Now, do you need anything to finish up at Elliot's?'

'No, that's all done. I just have a couple of bags of rubbish to get rid of. If you wanted to help with that...?'

'I will help you with that, and then I'll take you out for something to eat if you'd like. Your choice.'

'Now you're talking, thank you.'

WHEN THEY WERE DONE DUMPING the bags of rubbish into the communal bins at the back of the building, and she'd smothered sanitiser over her and Jake's hands, they walked down the path.

'Where to next?'

'Hmm,' she said, considering her options. 'I'd like to go back to the pub we visited last time, and perhaps a trip back to that nice Italian restaurant. But it's on me this time. You paid last.'

He raised a brow. 'You're telling me I get a free dinner out of this.'

She checked her phone for the time. 'Well, I guess once we've wasted an afternoon in the pub garden, it will be evening, so yes, you do get a dinner on me.'

'Wow, that's an offer I'm not going to refuse.'

'Good, then take me to the pub. I feel like a cocktail.'

He held out his hand. 'Shall we?'

So much weighed in that question. Was she ready for Jake, ready to trust? Ready to live again?

Looking at him, she saw her future, and she found she was ready for it.

AFTER THEIR DELICIOUS DINNER, he took her hand and entwined his fingers with hers. They took a stroll in the late evening light, both enjoying the unusually quiet environment. Perhaps something was going on somewhere, a sport or event that she was unaware of, taking everyone away from the high street.

'You really didn't have to pay,' he said, gently swinging her hand in his. 'I would have been happy to.'

'It was my pleasure,' she said as they ambled up the pathway to her building.

'But what am I to do?' he asked playfully. 'Now you'll expect all sorts from me, and I'm really not that kind of boy.'

She laughed and turned to face him. 'Are you not?' she teased. 'Well, that's disappointing. I thought I was onto a winner there.'

He shook his head, playing along. 'I'm sorry, my mother didn't raise me that way.'

She smiled and pulled him closer as they reached the entrance. 'Really, not even a kiss at the end of a date?'

He looked up, thought about it. 'Well, I suppose a kiss wouldn't hurt.'

She reached up to kiss his lips and let out a little moan when they touched. She wanted more, so much more, and hoped he'd read her mind.

His mouth parted, his tongue exploring, and she encouraged him, gave him permission, telling him that it was his, and more, if he wanted.

He pulled away, looking deep into her eyes, the playfulness gone, replaced with desire. 'You're serious, aren't you?'

She nodded. 'I mean, I know I said I didn't want to rush

into anything, and I wasn't sure how this evening was going to end, but all I know is that I want to be with you tonight. So, yes, would you like to stay?'

'Are you sure?'

'Yes, I am.'

He pulled her closer and pressed his lips to hers, another kiss that carried her away from all that had happened and the danger she'd constantly felt since she'd left Liam.

When he ended the kiss, she let them in, and he took her hand as they made their way up the stairs to her flat.

He gently nuzzled her neck as she unlocked her door, leaving her breathless and fumbling with her keys. She felt herself tremble now that she was alone with him in her flat, the outside world shut out, but this was what she wanted. She felt safe.

He moved closer, his warm smile reassuring her. 'We can do whatever you want,' he murmured. 'I'm here for you.' He tipped her face up to his. 'All night, if you wish.'

She opened her mouth to speak and then closed it when nothing emerged. He decided to use the silence as an opportunity to kiss her again and held her gently, his lips on hers until she relaxed into it.

She led him to her bed and sat, pulling him towards her.

'You're trembling,' he said, his gaze on her body.

'I'm sorry, I...' she whispered, suddenly overwhelmed.

'Shh, it's okay,' he soothed as he grabbed the folded blanket at the end of the bed and wrapped it around her shoulders. He scooted back against the headboard and pulled her close to his side, wrapping his arm around her. 'I say we stay here and just be together. That's all.'

She nodded as the warmth from his body and the blanket soothed her, easing her trembling body.

THEY TALKED, easy conversation, discussing everything and nothing, laughing at silly anecdotes and memories of their past. She relaxed in his arms, the warmth turning into desire. He picked up her unspoken command and stopped talking too, and instead caressed her skin, his fingers trailing wherever they chose as his gaze flicked between her eyes and her body. He continued slowly, seeking her permission to peel off a chosen item of clothing when the time was right. And she gave that permission; she let him take the lead, having no idea of what intimacy was supposed to be like with a man other than Liam. All she knew was that she wanted Jake as much as his whispered desire for her.

He was careful with her, gentle, always reassuring as their hands explored each other's bodies in the warm light of her room. She held him, her hands touching his skin, her fingers entwined in his hair, encouraging him on. She wanted him, wanted to be close to him, and gazed into his eyes when he whispered tender words to her. They would consummate whatever their relationship was, here, in her tiny flat, and she was ready to do it, willing to take the next step.

27

'I'll see you later, then?' Jake said through kisses as they stood in the lobby, arms slung around each other.

'You will,' she replied. 'When?'

'Well,' he said as his hands roamed over her back, 'the conference for fitness instructors that I mentioned before. I need to attend today, but I'll give you a call when it's done. Maybe we could get together again this evening? Dinner on me this time, and then perhaps go back to mine?'

'Sounds lovely,' she said, kissing him again. 'Please take care though. Keep safe.'

He smiled. 'I will, don't worry.'

She held onto his hand until the very last moment, watched him leave and then jogged up the stairs to her flat.

The buzzer on her intercom was going when she walked in. She laughed, he'd forgotten something, so rather than answer, she ran back to him.

The vision of Liam standing outside, waiting for her, startled Freya. She moved cautiously towards him.

'Hey, Freya,' Liam said. 'Let me in.'

'Liam, what are you doing here?' she asked as she opened the door.

'That's a nasty wound on your head,' he said as he stepped into the lobby. 'What have you been up to?'

'It'll heal,' she said dismissively just as the door clicked again, and the elderly man who lived above Ava and Elliot walked into the lobby, clutching another potted plant in his hands. He greeted them both but kept walking towards the lift. He pressed the button and waited.

'I heard about what happened through the guys at work,' Liam continued after he'd glanced at the man waiting for the lift. 'Thought I'd check on you.'

'I'm fine,' she said.

'The information only just filtered through to me, which is why I've come over. See how you are.'

The lift clunked to a stop, and the man pulled open the door and closed it behind him. Another clunk and the lift travelled upwards and away from them.

Liam eyed her and her pyjamas. 'Not up yet?' Everything changed. His tone wasn't warm, and the hairs on the back of her neck immediately prickled in response. It was clear that the concern he'd showed before was not for her benefit but rather the elderly resident.

'No.'

He nodded thoughtfully. 'Busy night?'

His tone was accusatory, knowing, and she was suddenly aware that she hadn't had the chance to shower yet. He'd know. Somehow, he'd smell Jake on her, smell the sex they'd had last night. 'Liam, please don't do this now. I have to get ready. I have to go to work.'

She wasn't due at work until later in the day, but Liam didn't know that, so she'd use the excuse to try to rid herself of him. Something about him wasn't right. The old Liam had returned, and she was alone with him.

'Of course,' Liam said.

'Yes,' she said as she began to tremble, 'I think it's best you go.'

'But I don't want to, Freya. I want to talk about what you've been up to. Can't you understand that you owe me that at least.' He went to hug her, scooping her up into a tight embrace that was neither loving or kind.

'Now,' he murmured. 'Let's go upstairs and discuss this further.'

'Liam,' she pleaded, struggling to free herself, 'I don't want to go up there with you.'

He moved his mouth to her ear as he held her tightly, crushing her to him. 'Yes, you do. I'm your husband still. We're not divorced yet, so you'll tell me all about your dalliance last night. Do you understand? And then I'll figure out if I forgive you or not.'

He knows, she thought, her worst fears confirmed. *The bastard knows about Jake.*

'Liam,' she said, trying to pacify, 'don't do this.'

'I'm not doing anything,' he said bluntly. 'I just want to talk.'

Trapped, she knew punishment would be coming her way. Her mind raced. Rosie and Ben would be working, Jake was at his conference, and Lucy was not expecting her until hours from now. Her phone was in her flat, but with Liam there, she would struggle to get a message out unnoticed.

He walked with her up the stairs, his hand clutching her waist, and marched her to the door of her flat. With trembling fingers, she opened her door, filled with dread at what was to come.

'Now, I ask you again,' he said to her as he slammed the door shut. 'What were you doing last night? Or should I say, *who* were you doing?'

'Liam, please.'

'Did you see your fitness instructor, huh? Did he give you a special lesson? The one he reserves for his little sluts. Did you let him fuck you as payment? Did you let him run his dirty little hands over your body, eh? Pound you again and again and again.'

'Stop it,' she cried.

'Ah, you did,' he murmured. 'Just as I thought. You're full of him right now, aren't you? Standing there in front of your husband, pumped full of another man's juices, and you have the nerve to tell me to stop it.'

'Get out,' she blurted desperately. 'Now. I want you to leave.'

'I can't do that,' he said, his tone a low growl. 'I can't have my wife fucking other men and not have an opinion on it.'

Tears welled in her eyes. 'Liam, please stop this.'

'Oh, come on, Freya,' he said. 'Not the waterworks.'

'How did you know?' she whispered.

'How do you think I know about that?'

She stared at him, understanding. 'Your massive abuse of power in the police.'

'And what a power it is,' he murmured.

'But that's not all you do, is it?' she whispered, her voice shaking as she tried to fight back. 'You even arrange for people to be attacked, don't you?'

'I don't know what you're talking about, but if I were to talk hypothetically, I would say that some people need a little more persuasion to stay away from other men's wives.

It's a tricky one, but usually gets the message across easily enough.'

'Oh my God.' She hadn't expected him to rush to an admission so quickly. His apparent pride knocked the wind out of her.

'Like I said, only hypothetically, of course.'

She glared at him. 'You bastard.'

Quickly, he swooped to her and backed her up against the wall. Using the weight of his body, he rammed himself against her and breathed her in. 'Yes, I smell him,' Liam said with disgust. 'I know exactly where he's been.'

She felt the hardness in between his legs and prayed that he wouldn't go any further. He'd assaulted her before; of course he had. Nothing was off the table where he was concerned. He'd forced himself on her when she'd had the audacity to refuse him one night, still bruised and sore from one of his previous punishments. He'd enjoyed it too, his eyes wide and filled with a dark pleasure – his dominance and her inability to stop him from doing whatever he wanted.

'Liam, stop it,' she snapped. 'Get off me. Now.'

He ignored her pleas and pushed himself harder against her. 'Now listen, I've been well behaved. I have given you space, I've even let you go out on a couple of dates with that fuckwit of a trainer, but this is too far.' He reached for her face and gripped it in his hand. 'You're my wife. Mine. And whatever time out you've needed from our marriage is over. Do you understand? Now, that's enough talking. It's time you came with me. Where you belong.'

'But the house is sold?'

'Don't be so ridiculous.' He laughed. 'Do you think I'd really go ahead with that? No, I think I'm gonna pull out of the sale just before the contracts are signed. Change my mind. Then we're going to tell our solicitors that we've reconciled. We are going to try again.'

She struggled to free herself from his hold, but his grasp on her was firm. 'Let me go.'

'No, you see, that's what you're not understanding, is it, you stupid little bitch. I'm never going to let you go. You're my wife and will always be my wife. Forever. Until death do us part. So you're gonna get dressed, and I'm gonna take you home.'

'No.'

'Oh yes, you are. It will be hard to forgive you, and I can't promise I won't have a problem with your betrayal in the coming weeks and months, but I know you'll make it right and work to repair the damage you've cause in our marriage. It will be difficult, but I will love you again one day.'

She cried out and struggled again, and with her desperation came anger and strength. All the lessons with Jake rushed into her mind, her newly exercised body fit and strong. She threw him off, using every muscle to free herself and unbalance him.

'No,' she yelled. 'You're not capable of love. You're only capable of imposing fear and violence to get what you want. I'm going nowhere with you.'

He stepped back, stared, genuinely shocked that she'd managed it. He swiped the back of his hand over his lip and approached her for round two.

She raised her hand, a warning. 'Liam, I said no.'

He grabbed her by the arms, holding them hard against her sides.

Trapped, she lashed out, used the one thing he'd least expect. She threw her head back and slammed it against his face. She made contact with his nose, dizzy from the collision and the sound of cracking bone. His bone. Regaining her balance, she saw the red gush of blood flooding from his nostrils and thought she heard him cry out.

With his face contorted with pain and fury, he launched himself at her again, clutching her to him until they bumped into the table, where a thick, glass bowl that housed all the paraphernalia that never found homes – receipts, coins and paperwork she had yet to deal with – toppled to the floor. Smashing, it launched its contents across her living room, and pieces of glass crunched underfoot as she tussled with him, desperate to be free.

Reverting back to his old ways, he swung his arm back and landed a hard blow to the side of her face, knocking her to the floor.

She cried out, the pain blurring her vision and pounding her head. But undeterred, she moved and began to crawl towards the door, her hands grasping whatever she could find to move her along.

He laughed and slammed his hand on her head, wrapping his fingers around her hair to pull her to her feet.

With survival now her only thought, she pushed him away, hard, and with enough strength to free herself.

He stumbled backwards and lost his footing, falling onto the floor. She watched him fall, his mouth agape that she'd actually broken free. His free fall seemed to slow, everything seemed to slow, and the next sound she heard was the crunch of glass and thump of bone as he hit the floor. He let out a stifled cry and breathed heavily, clutching his leg.

'What happened?' she cried as they both looked at his leg and the blood that oozed through his clothing and covered his hands, little red rivers of blood. From the intensity of colour and the way it quickly flowed, it was clear to Freya that he'd likely done extensive damage.

He laughed as he stared at it, watching the blood drip from his leg and pool underneath him.

She gasped and glanced at the door, her body ready to run, to leave the danger behind, but something in her hesitated. She couldn't leave him; he'd die if she did. Instead, she grabbed her phone and called 999, asking for an ambulance, just as she had done the other day with Elliot.

He looked at her, a smug realisation plastered over his pale, clammy face. 'Oh my God. You hesitated.'

'I did not,' she lied as she held the phone to her ear. 'You don't know what you're talking about.'

'You did. Saint Freya considered leaving me here to rot.'

'Shut up, Liam.'

Next, as instructed by the operator, she rushed to the bathroom to grab fresh towels from the shelf above the sink and yanked the belt free from her dressing gown. She returned to him and tied the belt tightly around his leg, above his wound, to act as a tourniquet to slow the flow of blood. Then she grabbed a couple of cushions from the sofa and laid them underneath his foot to raise his leg and placed another towel on top of the wound, leaning against it to apply firm pressure.

'You think you're an angel,' he whispered, his head lolling, weak now from blood loss, 'but you're not. We're the same, you and me.'

'We're nothing alike,' she hissed, her phone jammed between her ear and her shoulder as she listened out for further instructions.

'You wanted to leave me here,' he continued. 'Even

though I'm injured,' he said with a nod. 'For a moment you considered it.'

'Would you blame me,' she gasped. 'You attacked me.'

'No, I wouldn't. Maybe now you see that life is not quite as simple as you'd like it to be, eh? We all have flaws. Things we regret.'

'Just be quiet,' she snapped as she used the full force of her body to lean down hard on his leg. The blood still seeped through, but at a slower pace. 'Save your energy. They'll be here in a minute, and then they can take care of you.'

'You need me just as I need you.'

'I don't need you, and you never needed me. You just needed a punchbag. It's different.' She stood up to look out her window for the emergency services.

'Still, there's no denying it,' he continued. 'The devil on your shoulder almost won.'

She ignored him. She had bigger things to worry about. Where the hell were they? The blood began to flow again, reddening the towel, so she went back to it and applied firm pressure.

He laughed a bitter, weak laugh. 'Look at you.'

She ignored him and focused on what she was doing.

'Desperately trying to keep me alive because of what you did.'

'I may hate you right now,' she said, 'but I don't want you to die.'

'Because you couldn't even get that right, could you? You couldn't even leave me here to bleed out. So pathetic,' he murmured. 'You are weak and so pathetic.'

'No, Liam, that's where you're wrong. I'm not doing this because I'm weak. I'm doing this so I won't have your death looming over me for the rest of my life. Simple as that. I only need you to survive so that you can be held accountable for your actions.' She grabbed another towel and placed it on top of the bloodied one, pressing down until the sound of sirens grew louder. 'Oh, thank God.' She looked at him. 'Press down on this,' she instructed angrily.

He did what he was told, mute now.

28

S he rushed for the door and down the stairs to the waiting paramedics. She let them in and hurriedly explained what had happened as they climbed the stairs.

Once inside the flat, she stood back and let the paramedics attend to Liam.

'What's his name?' one of the paramedics asked as he knelt next to Liam and unzipped the huge backpack he'd brought with him.

'Liam,' she replied. 'Liam Walker.'

'And you say he fell on glass.'

'That's right.'

Both paramedics worked together and with expert skill; they tended to his wound, stabilised the bleeding, and wrapped an oxygen mask over his mouth, all while explaining every aspect of the care to Liam even though he looked as if he had checked out. In a blur they lifted him onto the evac chair one of the paramedics had brought with them after a quick discussion dismissing the suitability of the lift, instead opting for the stairs. She hurried after them, leaving behind the bloodied mess on her living room floor. They had got him down to the lobby when, without warning, Liam's head lolled, and his eyes fluttered shut.

'Liam,' one of the paramedics shouted as they removed him from the chair and laid him out onto the waiting stretcher. He checked his pulse. 'Okay, we've got a cardiac arrest.'

He began immediate chest compressions. Again, they worked together, communicating efficiently a well-practiced procedure to bring Liam back from the brink.

She watched, horror filling her as she willed him to live. She didn't love him or want him back in her life ever again, but he didn't get to die and leave her with all that baggage. He didn't get the easy way out, without having to face the consequences of his actions. In no world would that be fair.

One of the paramedics mentioned a weak pulse after the last round of compressions, and once the next course of action was quickly agreed, they wheeled him out of the lobby and into the waiting ambulance.

They asked if she wanted to be with Liam, but she refused, choosing to stay. One of the paramedics asked if she was okay, if she needed any assistance. She wasn't sure what she needed, but she kindly declined. She'd be fine, and the hospital was the last place she wanted to be. When she had convinced them both that she was feeling okay but promised to seek assistance if she deteriorated, she let them go. Working quickly, they shut the doors, fired up the engine and drove away, the sirens wailing and blue lights flashing.

Standing in the lobby, her body began to tremble, which she recognised as the onset of shock. Then came the guilt, like a shroud of shame, that her motivations for wanting him to live were not based on simple humanity, but in the fact he needed to pay for his crimes.

She would wait. Wait and hope. She would call the hospital for updates. That was as far as she could go, because that was as far as her emotions would allow.

Slowly, and still dazed, she walked up the stairs. Glancing down at herself, she saw that she, too, was covered in blood. So much blood that she couldn't work out the colour of the pyjamas she was wearing. She took each stair tread one at a time, caring little that she might be seen. She'd been through so much, it didn't matter what anyone thought about her. She was the neighbourhood crazy anyway, so who cared? Not her.

She just needed to get to the sanctuary of her flat.

SHE PUSHED the door shut and listened to the sound of her phone ringing somewhere in the room. She wandered around to find it, avoiding the mess by the table, until the ringing seemed to get louder as she searched.

Finally, it was in her grasp, but her movements were slow, and she had to concentrate hard to form the words she needed once she'd answered the phone. 'Hello?'

'Freya,' Rosie said, 'what's wrong?'

The lump in her throat stopped any more words from forming. Her legs gave way, and she collapsed to the floor as tears flooded out of her, and she blurted out a stream of incoherent sobs. Rosie wasted no time and told Freya to hang on, she'd be there in a minute.

Rosie knew the code to her flat, so Freya only had to open her front door when she arrived.

Rosie's face of horror at the sight of her sister covered in blood would forever be etched on Freya's mind. 'It's okay,' Freya said quickly. 'It's not my blood. I'm fine.'

Rosie grabbed Freya and tried to embrace her, but Freya held her back.

'Don't touch me; it's gross.'

'Freya, what the hell happened?'

More tears flowed as Freya sobbed out what Liam had done, what had happened with the glass bowl and where he was now. She tried to remain calm but quickly became hysterical.

Rosie intervened and held Freya by the shoulders, calming her. 'It's okay,' she soothed. 'Breathe.'

All Freya could do was focus on Rosie's eyes, breathe when she was instructed, and try to compose herself. Rosie guided her through it, speaking calmly, ensuring that Freya only focused on the present moment and didn't become distracted by the enormity of what had happened.

Finally, when Freya had steadied her breathing and calmed her mind, Rosie smiled.

'You're okay,' she soothed. 'It's over now.'

***

'What do I do now, Rosie?' Freya whispered.

'Firstly,' Rosie said, casting her eyes over Freya's wounds, 'do you need to go to the hospital?'

Freya began to panic. 'No, don't send me there. I really don't want to go.'

'Okay, okay. That's fine. I'm not going to make you do something you don't want to do.' She grabbed her phone. 'But please allow me to take a couple of pictures of your injuries. Just a little insurance in case this business gets nasty.'

'What, do you think I'll be arrested?'

'No, no,' Rosie soothed. 'Of course not, but it can't hurt to capture the evidence of what has happened to you.'

Tears welled in Freya's eyes. 'You're sure,' she sobbed. 'I don't want to go to prison.'

'You won't. Believe me, that monster will not get away with all that he's done to you.'

Freya nodded and let Rosie take pictures of her face and head injuries.

'Now, I need you to go into the bathroom, okay,' Rosie said, 'and I need you to take off these clothes and have a shower to clean off. Can you do that for me?'

Freya nodded as she tried to control her breathing.

'Good, and then we'll have a cup of tea and sort all this out.' Rosie went to the kitchen and found a bag under the sink and handed it to Freya. 'Put everything in here, and we'll figure out what to do with it later.'

Freya went to the bathroom, removed all her clothes and placed them in the bag, as instructed. She stepped into the shower and turned on the tap, watching as blood-pink water flowed down her body and into the plughole. She waited until the water ran clear before she smothered herself in soap and rinsed, turning off the shower. Pulling back the curtain, she saw a neat pile of clothes placed on the edge of the sink, ready for her. Her movements were slow, dazed, and the strong sense that she was in another world to everyone else wouldn't leave her. How had she missed what Liam was up to? How had she been so fooled? At one point she really did believe he had changed. Or had wanted to. Her heart ached for all the unnecessary damage done both physically and emotionally. She even mourned for him. Of what he'd become. His soul so damaged, so full of hate. She hoped his wounds would heal. She hoped he would survive what had happened, but she also hoped he would realise who he had become before it was too late. With a sigh, she dried herself and dressed, then left the bathroom.

In the time it had taken to take her shower, the police had shown up and were talking with Rosie. Everyone looked at Freya as she walked into the room.

'Freya?' one of the officers asked, approaching her.

He was an older man, experienced, and she felt reassured by him and let him ask her as many questions as he needed. She answered truthfully and thoroughly, wanting to leave nothing out. Liam would not have the final say on this one. Rosie shared the photos that she had taken too.

'How is he? Liam?' she asked when they'd finished.

'He's okay,' the officer said with a smile. 'He'll have surgery to repair the laceration to his leg and the nick in his artery, but he's stabilised and no longer critical.'

She sank into the sofa. 'Thank God for that.'

'Freya, there will be another team out to see you, I'm afraid,' the officer said, sitting beside her. 'There's been an internal investigation on him, and they may want to speak to you about it.'

'An internal investigation?'

'Yes, for his part in the assault on Jake Evans. One of his colleagues got wind of what was going on. That he'd arranged for it to happen.'

She nodded. 'I figured it out. He confessed to it too. Not that he would admit to it now, probably.' She sighed. 'Poor Jake. He did nothing but be a friend to me.'

Rosie joined her and laid a comforting hand on Freya's arm.

'Anything I can help with, I will,' Freya replied. 'He needs to be behind bars. He can't be allowed to abuse his position like that.'

'And would you be prepared to make a statement about the domestic assaults you've suffered at his hands? To press charges?'

She shook her head. 'I don't know. That's a lot to ask. He'll take that personally. Very personally. I'm his wife. What if he gets off? Look what he was prepared to do today. If he finds out I've exposed the real him and all of his demons, he'll kill me.'

'That's what we want to prevent. We want to put him away for a long, long time, Freya. We can only do that with your help.'

'I need to think about it.'

'Of course, take as long as you need.' He pulled out his notebook. 'We'd also like to speak to you about the burglary at your parents' house.'

'Yes, what about it?'

'We have reason to believe that Liam set that up. He got a little drunk one night and overshared with a colleague, who recently reported it to us. Apparently, Liam made threats to his colleague, but when the chap realised what had happened to Jake, he decided to come forward with what he knew. It would be good to get your version of events too.'

She stared, unable to process what she was being told. 'You mean my parents went through all that for nothing. Liam ransacked their home to make himself look good for me?' she asked.

'It certainly looks that way.'

Rosie gasped. 'I can't believe it. The bastard.'

The policeman continued, 'If you could let us know what happened and when...'

Freya stared, trying to calm her rushing thoughts, the policeman's voice fading into the distance.

Next, she heard Rosie's voice.

'I think you need to leave that one with us,' she said, intervening. 'She's been through enough today.'

The officer nodded. 'Of course. We'll leave you in peace, but please give us a call on this number.' He handed her a card, which Rosie reached out to take.

The officers wished her well and left.

Freya glanced over to where Liam had fallen and noticed it had been cleared of debris, and the floor was clean and wet, recently mopped. All that remained was the coppery twang of blood that hung in the air, which Rosie had sought to remove by opening a window.

'Thank you so much,' Freya said gratefully.

'One of the officers helped,' Rosie said. 'He had special gloves to prevent any cuts from the glass and helped me get it all into bags.' She looked down at herself. Not a spot of blood on her clothing. 'Remarkable, but I'm completely clean.'

Tears stung Freya's eyes. 'Oh, Rosie, what am I going to do?'

Rosie went to her and wrapped her arms around her sister.

'I SHOULD CALL THE HOSPITAL,' Freya said, sipping at the tea Rosie had made for her. 'It's been three hours; he should be out of theatre now.'

'That can fucking wait,' Rosie said as she inspected the area around the window, a wet cloth in hand to wipe away any errant spots of blood. 'Gosh, there's so much of the stuff.'

The buzzer went, and Freya jerked so violently at the sound that some of the tea spilled out of the mug and over her hands. She flicked it away as she cursed under her breath.

'It's okay; it'll just be Ben,' Rosie said as she went to let him in. 'He's been so worried.'

Rosie pulled open the door and waited for him by the door, out of Freya's view.

Freya tried not to stare at the floor where Liam had lain, but she was compelled to do so, a morbid desire to remember what had happened.

Ben walked in and went straight to Freya, pulling her into a warm hug. 'Freya,' he said, 'how are you doing?'

'I'm okay,' Freya said, hugging him. 'A little shocked, but okay.'

'I'm so glad to hear it. I can't believe the nerve of that man. I hope they throw the book at him.'

'Me too.'

'If he survives,' Rosie chimed in.

'Oh, he'll survive,' Ben said. 'People like that always do.'

Rosie went to Freya with a fresh dressing to replace the one that had cleaned and drawn out a few spots of blood from the wound in Freya's hair. She gently tended to it and then left it to dry out.

Ben knelt by Freya. 'There's someone downstairs to see you,' he said gently.

'Who?'

'Jake. Can he come up?'

'Jake?' she said. 'But wasn't he away at a conference?'

'He came back the minute he heard what had happened. Rosie contacted him.'

The rush of emotion that flowed in her body startled her. 'Of course,' Freya said, realising how much she wanted to see him. To be held by him.

Rosie and Ben went down in unison to get Jake and told her they would wait in the gardens so that Freya could have some alone time with him.

Her heart pounded as she waited for him to come up. When he walked into her flat, she realised everything she wanted in life included him.

'Jake,' she sobbed as he rushed to her and gathered her up in his arms.

'I'm so sorry for what Liam did to you,' Freya began as he sat with her. 'When I found out what he'd done—'

He wrapped his arms around her. 'You have nothing to be sorry for. You are not responsible for that maniac's actions.'

She hugged him close, wanting the warmth from him to chase away the misery inside her.

'I'm glad you're okay,' he said.

'I was so frightened. Liam knew everything. What we'd done. Everything. He was furious and wanted to take me away from everyone, back to Southampton. I was terrified.'

'I bet you were, but from what I've been told, you fought him off this time. Pretty successfully too, by the sound of it.'

'I did, thanks to your lessons. Didn't expect him to nearly die though.'

He smiled. 'Listen, all you did was defend yourself, and that was your right.'

'I know,' she murmured. 'He would have done terrible things to me given half the chance. I'm glad I got away, but it was so awful. He was so spiteful even injured.'

'It seemed like he always showed his true colours when backed against a wall, and being injured didn't change that for him.'

'You're right. There was no redeeming side to his character. He would have died spewing hate until his very last breath.'

'I'm glad you're finally free of him.'

'If the police do their job correctly.'

'Oh, I'll make sure they do that. For this assault alone, I'll do everything I can to make sure he goes down for it.'

She hugged him close. 'I'm so glad you're here.'

'It's my pleasure, believe me. Although I'm going to step over the line here and say that I'll struggle to leave you alone for a while. I hope you don't mind that.'

She smiled. 'No, I don't mind. Not at all.'

WHEN FREYA SAID HER GOODBYES, albeit reluctant ones, to Rosie and Ben, she hugged them close, not able to fully say how much she loved them and needed them. Jake remained with her even when her parents were on their way, hurrying to be with her. He would leave once they had arrived, but wanted to stay with her so that she wasn't alone. She appreciated his care. She was tired, and she knew she needed to find the energy to share what Liam had done, and their sham of a burglary, while soothing them that she was okay, Liam too.

How they reacted was irrelevant now, almost, because this last act of violence had proved to Freya that she was the one who mattered, not Liam, and not the opinions of anyone else. She had lived through the nightmare of being married to a dangerous man, and they could accept it or not.

She was a survivor and would not hide any longer.

EPILOGUE

The train to Freya's parents' was on time. Rosie, Ben, Freya and Jake had all managed to bag a four-seater table.

Jake's hand rested gently on Freya's leg under the table as they chatted with Rosie and Ben. Something that had become routine whenever he was with her. But this was different to Liam. It wasn't about control or abuse. This was thoughtfulness, an unspoken gesture of affection that told Freya he was there for her; he cared and would take care of her.

In the six months that had passed since Liam's attack, they had become close, and while he referred to them as being in a relationship, something Freya was happy for him to do, she was also content to inwardly leave it undefined and just enjoy the time she spent with him. No labels. No expectations. She divided her time between her and Jake's flats, in no hurry to rush into something that could get too serious too quickly, and something that would be harder to leave. Jake understood, and his patience for her warmed her heart and deepened her ever-growing feelings for him. Feelings she had tucked away within a secret place in her soul, which she would share with him when she was ready.

She had initially struggled living in the place where Liam had been so terribly hurt. Jake had offered to help her find somewhere else to live, but as time passed and newer, more pleasant memories replaced those of Liam's near death, she became more comfortable in her surroundings again. It was her home, and she felt a strong tie to it. Too much to leave.

This visit to her parents' was the first to include Jake, at her request rather than theirs. Her parents were keen to meet him, but Freya wanted to be cautious, uncomfortable to introduce someone into their lives until she felt she knew him well to trust that she wasn't being manipulated again. Something she hadn't done with Liam, heady with the high that comes with new relationships, and the excitement that comes with them too. In the months that had passed, she'd got to know Jake, really know him, and believed that the kind and generous personality was not a façade, but genuine. The true version of himself, not just what he wanted her to see.

The shock and aftermath of Liam's attack was fading but would forever remain in Freya's memory as a painful reminder of the evil that men are capable of.

She had been regularly updated by the hospital, as his next of kin, and advised that Liam's surgery, although long, had been a success, and he was comfortable. He would recover, and apart from sporting a large scar on his leg, he would be fine.

Relieved, Freya could finally let go. His injuries wouldn't have to play on her mind, even though she'd only ever acted in self-defence and understood that guilt had no place in her conscience. The incident had indeed sparked an internal investigation at his work, and they had found evidence that firmly implicated him in Jake's attack and her parents' burglary. He'd been suspended while the investigation continued, and the last update she'd been given was that he was likely to serve time once the court case was done, although how long she didn't yet know. She might have to give evidence, share all the things he'd done to her, but she had enough support to get through it. She was strong enough. He would get what he deserved. She felt nothing for him, not even hatred; she was just glad he was out of her life. Her divorce was finalised soon after the attack, and the weight that had seemed to endlessly push down on her had lifted immediately.

However, the incident wasn't without its consequences. It had left her wary and careful of whom she would trust and allow into her life. He'd given her the gift of suspicion and the need to always assume the worst until she was proven otherwise. But she was working on that and had sought the necessary therapy to help her through it. That, and the love and care of her family. Her parents had surprised her. They'd stepped up and wrapped a parental blanket of love and protection around her. The family closed ranks, leaving Liam out in the cold. He was dirt in their eyes, and if they ever did speak of him, it was always with anger.

She had also ditched the pills. The day after Liam's attack, she'd tossed them away, deciding that the medicated blur they provided only helped her hide from her problems rather than deal with them head-on. She'd shared what she could with Jake, whenever he asked, but that was very much still a work in progress. She would let him in gradually, learn to trust him and reveal more about herself and her past when the time was right.

What she felt strongly was that she had been given another chance. She could move on, free, and no longer have to look over her shoulder. Liam was out of her life, and she had the gift of starting again. This time it would be on her terms. She'd grown so much despite the pain and had clear boundaries of what she would and would not accept. She knew exactly who she was and the value of her worth and knew who deserved her love.

And that, in her eyes, was a win.

THANK YOU FOR READING

Did you enjoy reading *If I Can't Have You*? Please consider leaving a review on Amazon. Your review will help other readers to discover the novel.

ACKNOWLEDGMENTS

My thanks, as ever, go to everyone at Inkubator Books, whose support and encouragement kept me motivated throughout the journey of writing this book. Their insights and feedback were invaluable in shaping the ideas within these pages.

To my family and friends, thank you for your patience, understanding and continuous belief in my passion for writing.

And to all my readers – thank you, thank you, thank you! Your support means the world, and I hope you enjoyed reading this book as much as I did writing it.

ABOUT THE AUTHOR

G.M. Lawrence writes fast-paced, standalone psychological suspense novels that can be read in any order.

Originally from Kent, Gemma's family moved to the New Forest in the south of England when she was a child. She's been lucky to have had the opportunity to travel and has spent time in New Zealand, America and Spain. She lives in Hampshire with her husband, daughter and two chaotic cats.

Compelled to write and get her imaginary worlds out of her head and onto paper, Gemma completed a creative writing course, which kick-started her writing career. She believes in capturing the many issues women face today, often in silence.

Previously self-published under Gemma M. Lawrence, she now publishes under G.M. Lawrence.

Visit G.M. online at:

gm-lawrence.com

ALSO BY G.M. LAWRENCE

You're Not Alone

When I Know Your Name

If I Can't Have You

Printed in Great Britain
by Amazon